ICON'S REQUEST

BY THE SAME AUTHOR

I Am Dead

ICON'S REQUEST

GARETH WILES

Matador
9 Priory Business Park
Kibworth Beauchamp
Leicestershire LE8 0RX, UK
Tel: (+44) 116 279 2299
Fax: (+44) 116 279 2277
Email: books@troubador.co.uk
Web: www.troubador.co.uk/matador

ISBN 978 1780881 799

British Library Cataloguing in Publication Data.
A catalogue record for this book is available from the British Library.

Typeset in 11pt Book Antiqua by Troubador Publishing Ltd, Leicester, UK

Matador is an imprint of Troubador Publishing Ltd

Printed and bound in the UK by TJ International, Padstow, Cornwall

MIX
Paper from
responsible sources
FSC
www.fsc.org   FSC® C013056

For Victoria

PROLOGUE

War? Strange, meaningless. Alien to us. It no longer applies to us!
Wars raged on. When It came. But then. Oh then, my children!
No longer do wars rage on.

Societies were built on the teachings passed down from generation
to generation. Love. Friendship. Respect. On these three was
such importance placed. Just like the others our own society
valued, above all else, what we were taught. Generation after
generation endlessly self-replenishing, trundling, trundling
along, repeating what had gone before. But remember, though
we were part of the Great Collective, we were still apart. No
boundaries. No battles.

All was well. We all had space, and we all had The Space.
There was the anchor, the purpose we clung to. The purpose of
life itself. But then. Then It came. From not so far, but close to
home. From within our own selves. The Space ebbed away. The
societies grew together. Physically. Mentally, they grew further
apart. Love. Friendship. Respect. All lost. Then, we had to protect
our teachings. We must protect! War came. Societies crumbled.

Wars raged on. Internal wars. The mind became the
battleground of every living being. Every living thing torn
apart. Torn, broken, divided between oppositions, slipping into
mental vagary. We were desperate to cling to one set, to escape
the torment. But, colliding, colliding, there was too much to
cope with. And then…

Peter Smith. Our last chance. The final link between the
Great Collective and The Space. But he too was in torment.
Ravaged by madness.

Elder Icon

PART ONE

ICON'S COLLECTION

Bow down before the tight space between us

TONY IS MY BEST MATE

Tony is great because every time I see Tony he looks at me with that funny face of his and doesn't grin. That's what's great. We don't need to smile and shake hands and all that crap. We just nod and then sit down. What's great about Tony is he knows what I'm thinking and what I'm about to say next so I know I don't have to say anything. But he's got this other mate which makes me feel left out a lot. Sometimes I see this other mate, but mostly I don't. I don't want to see this other mate. He's not my mate. He's *Tony's* mate. Not mine. When I saw Tony, his other mate was there and didn't make me feel welcome at all.

I live with my mum. Dad's dead, but Mum is still alive and she lets me know it. There was this time Tony came round and she calls him Nobhead, that's her nickname for him. This time he came round and asked if I was in and Mum said I wasn't, but I was sitting at the top of the stairs. I didn't want to go out with Tony, but Mum didn't want me to go out either. I do want to go out with Tony sometimes, just not today. Today, something else was happening. Today, something really bad was going to happen.

I put my coat on even though it was really hot outside. Mum told me I'd get a chill. 'Your father caught a chill. Next thing he was dead,' she went on at me as I struggled to do the zip up. But Dad blew his brains out. 'If you want to kill an animal, stick it in a draft.'

I like drafts. Did that mean I wasn't an animal? What was I, then? I felt like an animal. I had fears. I feared Tony. Tony is great but he can be scary. He likes to get angry and if he does get angry and I'm the only one there, he'll take it out on me. Mum says he's a bit simple, but he couldn't be a *bit* simple. He was either a lot simple or not simple at all. Being a bit simple made me think he was more of something else, but not actually pointing out what that lot of something else was was confusing. Why not say he's a lot clever instead of 'he's a bit simple'? What was the rest of him, if he was only made up of a bit of simple?

As Mum opens the door, Kelly steps in. She looks at me just as Mum tells me to go upstairs. Somehow I can't go upstairs. Something strange comes over me, stopping me from moving. Next thing I'm upstairs.

'Tony?' Kelly calls from downstairs.

'Yes?' I reply.

'You must come down quickly, Tony, you must come down and see this!'

I run down the stairs just as Kelly stands up off the floor. On the floor lies Mum and she doesn't look at all well. Tony must have come round. Tony has been really bad this time. Yet, I am Tony and I wouldn't do this to Mum. Or would I? Sometimes I get very confused about who I am and I am not my friend any more. Kelly is holding a knife and passes it to me. I take hold of it tightly, just like she asks.

SOME TIME LATER

Kelly was driving. I didn't feel at all well. We had just left The Dealer and my bum was really aching for some reason and things felt very wet down there. She placed her hand on my leg and squeezed it a bit, smiling as I looked over at her legs. Suddenly she slammed the brakes on. Somebody was stood in the middle of the road. It was dark. What were they doing stood in the middle of the road? I know not to stand in the middle of the road because you can get knocked over. Kelly honked the horn but still he stood there. He looked through the window right at me. Not at Kelly. I don't think he saw Kelly at all. She wasn't going to have this and she jumped out of the van and marched over to him, but something awful happened and she flopped onto the ground right in front of him, just straight down onto her knees. She seemed to be begging or praying. All the time he kept looking at me, starting to move slowly towards me. I felt drawn to him, like I was being called by him. He wasn't Tony. I was Tony. And I am Tony. He called out in silence, telling me who he was and that he had come to collect me for his plan. Kelly wasn't part of the plan. She was to be left on the ground. She could stay there. I knew what she had done to Mum.

FIXING JIM

(JIM)

I walked past the shops as I do every morning. I bin what milk and bread I don't use in one day. I get fresh every day. There's probably a number of reasons I do this. Not that you need to know. I came to the last shop, the convenience store on the corner where I always went every morning. That girl worked there. She was probably a bit young for me, but that wasn't really too much of a concern. Nothing would ever come of it. I wasn't really old, but I had a bald patch and a bit of a hunch and I didn't really wash all that much. I never made enough of an effort to get her attention. I'd rather just look at her from afar really, which is what I do.

I went straight to the milk, picking up a pint. Next I went to the small loaves. I had to survey them, make sure I got a well-dated one, even though I'd chuck most of it away tomorrow morning. There was one with no crusts. This was pretty convenient because I didn't like crusts at all. I didn't want curly hair. Now my eye and cheek spasmed. This was a bit awkward. I looked up. Chloe was watching me. That was her name, behind the till. She had it printed on her little badge on her left breast. It wasn't much of a breast, though her top was always quite baggy, so underneath it may have been more ample. At least her trousers were tight. I rubbed my eye, looking down again.

I took my milk and crustless loaf to the counter. Chloe wasn't really very nice to me. She would only look at me when I was far away. When I got up close, she'd keep herself turned sideways and look outside as though she didn't want to serve me.

'You want your whisky today?' she asked me. I nodded, having to rub hard at my eye to stop it jerking about. She turned and bent down, those tight nylon trousers pulling hard at her crack as it waved about, mere feet from my face. She picked up a bottle of whisky and slammed it in front of me, calculating the amount on the till.

I placed the milk and loaf next to the whisky on the counter, taking my money bag from my pocket. I handed it to Chloe, passing her a further coin from another pocket.

'This loaf is a bit more. I'll have to recalculate my order for next time.'

Chloe frowned, looking down at my loaf. 'No crusts. Don't want curly hair, huh?'

I picked my goods up and promptly left. I looked back as I hurried away, Chloe watching through the shop window as I left.

'I'm home,' I called out, opening my flat door as the sound of laughter hit my ears. It must be a show I didn't like. I dropped my shopping on the table and reached for the remote control, silencing the TV. I liked my flat. I could see everything no matter where I stood in it. It was all confined to one space and I could keep a watch on things unless they were laughing. I poured a glass of whisky and put my bread and milk in the empty cupboard, sitting down in front of the TV. I changed the channel and put the sound back on. 'Chloe served me again today... Oh... Well, her name badge of course. Only says her first name. She's very attractive.' The TV seemed to taunt me, so I argued back: 'No she's not, she's at least seventeen.' My face twitched. I had to try and conceal it. It was showing me up. 'What do you mean?' I felt a bit agitated, rubbing my eye. 'Don't be rude... I'm getting bored of you.' I changed the channel. 'Yes, fine thanks,' I replied to the next channel. No, this wasn't finished. I changed back to the previous channel. 'She knows who I am, anyway. She kept my drink aside for me.' I took another sip. There was a knock at the door. I turned the sound down. Another knock.

'Hi Jim,' a voice called from the other side of the door. I'd heard it before.

'Hello.' I did not open the door.

'Fancy some work?'

'Yes.'

'You know where to come.'

'Yes.'

'Come tomorrow morning, Jim.'

My twitch had gone. I stood up, looking for something to reflect my face back to me. Perhaps the window would? I caught a half-image of the face in the window. My face? 'Jim?'

This was a nice, quiet residential area. I walked on the pavement, passing a row of detached houses, stopping outside number thirteen. There were no cars up the drive and the garden was a little overgrown. There *was* a garden spade propped against the garage, though, and I walked up the driveway and picked it up as I approached and opened the gate at the side of the house.

I looked around the back garden. It was big, but still untidy. I shook my head at the sight. A lot could be done to make this a very tidy space. There was a noise from behind me; the back door opening. I turned to look at the door. The voice spoke to me.

'Ah, you've arrived. Good work, Jim. Now, you know what to do, don't you?'

'Yes.' I turned back to the garden, resting the spade against my leg before turning back to look at the door. I turned back to the spade, lifting it to my eyes. 'I need the toilet.' I opened the door and stepped inside, slipping my shoes off.

The large living room was neatly furnished. Lovely things

everywhere. Too many things. A large flat screen TV drew my attention. Spade in hand, I approached it carefully. 'What do you think?' It was also displeased. 'No, me neither.' We moved on upstairs.

I walked into the bedroom and placed the spade down, leaning against the big bed. There was a small TV in this room, just like my TV. I turned it on, opening the drawer of the dressing table beneath it. I picked out a bra and knickers, placing them on the bed. Closing that drawer, I opened the next one down. That one contained tights. I put a pair on the bed and closed the drawer. I turned to face the bed and took my clothes off, replacing them with the bra, knickers and tights. They were lovely and soft so I decided to keep them on, folding my clothes up and putting them in the drawers. There was a full-length mirror on the other side of the room. I approached it, confused. 'Jim?' There came a noise from outside. I looked out of the window to see a car pulling into the driveway. 'Shush,' I told the TV, turning it off. I walked up to the wardrobe and opened it, climbing in and pulling the doors shut on myself. In here, my bra didn't feel quite right. It wasn't on properly and I needed to adjust it.

Somebody entered the room. I paused, holding my breath. The footsteps stopped so I cautiously opened a wardrobe door, speaking out. Nothing. I opened the other door and stepped out. Lying on the bed, soaked in blood, was a naked woman. I got closer to her face to see if I recognised her. 'Do I know you?'

'I am dead,' she replied. 'Don't question me further.'

I looked in the full-length mirror again. The bra, knickers and tights were covered in blood too. Strange. I turned and picked the spade up to have a look at it. That too was covered in blood. Where had it all come from? I lay down on the bed next to the woman and leant over to study the blood on her body. Rubbing my hands in it, I began to paint it onto my own body in the same patterns it appeared on hers. Ultimately I was dissatisfied.

Another car pulled up outside and I could hear laughter. Not long afterwards, two policemen entered the room. By now I had one leg in my trousers and was about to put the other one in. There was no struggle and they led me back down the stairs, through the living room and back out the way I had come in.

(OFFICER HELYN)
Jim sat motionless at the table. The room was grey and bare - no windows for him to look out of. I stood the other side of the one-way mirror with Daniels looking in at him. What he'd just done was horrific. Well, words simply couldn't describe what vile perverted crime he'd just committed. Yet, there he was, sat a couple of metres away from us as if butter wouldn't melt. I didn't know about Daniels, but I certainly felt this would be one of those career-defining moments for me. Yes, I'd seen horrible sights before - decapitated heads in bins looking up at me, even bodies left hanging for a couple of days - but this felt different because of Jim. He seemed... I'm not sure how he seemed, to be honest.

Kennedy entered. I was a little surprised.

'Inspector Kennedy?' I blurted out.

'Officer Helyn?' he replied, flapping a clipboard around. Daniels and I looked at each other.

'We thought you were off for another week,' Daniels elaborated.

Kennedy flicked through some papers on the clipboard. 'Well I'm back now.'

'But.'

He slowly lowered the clipboard from his sight and looked up at Daniels and myself. 'You thought what?'

'Officer Daniels thought that...' I cut in, stalling, scratching my ear.

Kennedy smiled. 'Officer Daniels doesn't think. Officer

Daniels takes orders,' he snapped. I turned to Daniels, who was biting his lip. Kennedy turned to look at Jim through the one-way mirror. 'Fit for questioning? He murdered someone, of course he's fit.' Suddenly Jim turned to look at the mirror, right at Kennedy. Daniels and I stood back as Jim stood up and stepped up to the mirror. Now Kennedy stepped closer, right up against the glass, as Jim did the same the other side. He stared intently at the mirror, almost as if he could see Kennedy. He couldn't possibly see him. Either way, he couldn't see me or Daniels as his eyes never left Kennedy. Unnerved, Kennedy squinted. Jim did the same. Kennedy turned away and scratched the side of his head. Jim did the same. Perturbed at my reaction to Jim, Kennedy slowly turned back to face him. Jim too looked back and lowered his hand in tandem with Kennedy. But Jim could see only his own reflection the other side; it was Kennedy who was looking in here. Yet Jim seemed to be the one looking in. Kennedy leant back in towards Jim, who did the same to Kennedy. 'Jim,' he whispered.

'Kennedy,' Jim whispered, smiling. Kennedy pulled away in fright as Jim returned to his chair. Jim started talking. All three of us listened in, but it made little sense, as though he was narrating some hallucination he was having. 'Chloe has entered the room and just sat across from Jim. From me. I am Jim. She is dressed exactly how she dresses in the shop. She's folded her arms and is leaning back in her chair. "That facial tick again. Why, Jim?" she says. "Tell me about yourself, Chloe," I reply. "I'd much rather know about you." She's just bent down and picked up a small wooden box from under the table and placed it on the table in front of me.' He leant back in his chair. 'The lid of the box has four shaped holes cut out of it: a triangle, square, circle and rectangle. Chloe is removing the lid and lifting out five small shaped blocks: a triangle, square, circle, rectangle and pentagon. Each piece is a different colour. "How old are you?" I ask her. "Seventeen", she replies.' He smiled. 'She's just replaced the lid of the box and pushed it towards me with the five pieces.' He proceeded to pretend to pick up these imaginary pieces he could apparently see and slot them in to the lid of the invisible box. '"Do you like me, Chloe?" I ask her. "No" she replies.' Kennedy stormed out of the room. 'I've fitted the four shapes in the box now, but I've still got the fifth piece. The pentagon.' Suddenly Kennedy appeared in the room.

(INSPECTOR KENNEDY)
'You gave your name as Jim to my colleagues Daniels and Helyn. What is your full name?' I asked. Jim seemed to ponder this for a while.

'Just Jim.'

'James something, obviously…'

'No. Jim.'

'Okay, Jim. You carry no identification.'

'Ah.'

'Where do you live?'

'Flat number 13. Harnlan North.'

That sent a shiver down my spine. '13, Harnlan North. That's my daughter's flat.'

'The daughter you murdered.'

I stared intently into Jim's eyes. 'What?'

'That's where I live.'

'What do you know about my daughter?'

'You are a murderer.'

'What makes you say that?'

'I know who you are, Inspector Kennedy. ' He looked down.

'Why have you broken eye contact with me?'

'I'm nervous.'

'Why?'

'Because you're violent.'

'You are the violent one, Jim.' He looked down again.

All of a sudden, I was beaten to a pulp. I did not see Jim move, and I felt nothing until the realisation that I had been badly beaten. Blood poured from me as Helyn and Daniels rushed in and seemed to hold me down rather than hold Jim back. Jim was unmoving, sitting across from me. He held his hands up; they were clean. He stood up and walked casually up to me, dipping a finger in the blood on my forehead, approaching the mirror and smearing it on his own as he studied himself.

Miss Grainger turned up in her suit and with her scalpy haircut. I didn't like her and she didn't like me. She slammed her briefcase down on the table as I stumbled in.

'Kennedy? Why the hell are you back?'

'My leave was up,' I replied, sitting down to rest after the beating I had just had.

'Yes, but under the circumstances…'

'Well, you're the psychologist. You tell me.'

Doctor Johnson walked in through the opposite door to me, the same door as Miss Grainger. He smiled nervously at me, turning to speak to her. She kept her eyes on me as he spoke.

'There were no marks on Jim. Officers Helyn and Daniels say Kennedy beat himself.' Johnson now turned to me, briefly, before looking back at Miss Grainger. He seemed to be searching for her gaze, but she kept it fixed on me.

'Thank you, Doctor Johnson.'

He dawdled for a moment, looking for more from her. She would not give it to him and so he left.

'It appears you attacked yourself earlier today,' she addressed me, more formally than earlier.

'I cannot remember. All I remember is Helyn and Daniels holding me down. That Jim - he seemed to know things about me. He said he lived in my daughter's flat.'

'And so you smashed your own face in?'

'I don't know what I did.' I stood up, holding my hands out in front of me. They were bruised. 'I must have done, mustn't I? There isn't a mark on this Jim.'

'Fascinating.'

'Is it?'

(MISS GRAINGER)

The cell is small and grey, with padded walls. Jim is sat on a mattress in a straitjacket. I think this is a little odd, considering he has not been violent. Yes, there is the brutal murder at the house, but he has only found himself in the straitjacket since Kennedy pounded his own face in. Kennedy thinks Jim made him do it somehow.

Jim is staring right through the cell door window at me as I look back at him. The very large police officer who is accompanying me is just about to open the door, and the first thing I really notice about Jim is his all-encompassing vacancy. He's looking at me, yes, not through me, but I don't think he's seeing me physically here. Perhaps he's not vacant at all. Maybe he can only see the mental - if that makes sense. Regardless, we both enter.

The police officer steps in first, directing his hand towards a very large baton as though to warn Jim. As I enter, Jim suddenly smiles.

'Look, this is madness. I mean, a straightjacket?'

'Jim, isn't it?'

'That's right. And who are you?'

'I'm Melanie Grainger.'

'Hello, Melanie Grainger.'

'Look Jim, I've, err…' I try to lean in towards him, but all I feel is the police officer's domineering presence. I turn to him. 'Do you have to stand in? Please, could you give me and my patient some space?' I've always seemed to have the knack with getting people to do what I want if I will it enough and, as if by magic, the frowning police officer reluctantly steps outside the cell.

'Patient?' Jim asks.

'I'm a psychologist, but I'm not a magician. I've seen the CCTV footage, Jim. Kennedy beat himself up.'

'We all need some space.'

'Yes. And what about Kennedy?'

'That's what I'm on about, Mrs Grainger.'

'No, Miss Grainger.'

'Lesbian?'

'No. And I'm not obsessively dedicated to my work, either. I just don't believe in marriage.'

'I'm unmarried too. I've never even had sex.'

'Ah. Then who are you, Jim? What's your full name and where do you come from?'

'Well you see, Miss Grainger, that's where the problem lies.'

'It does?' I lean in closer to him, I feel drawn to him.

'You see, I haven't always been like this. There was a time when I was quite normal.'

'What made you change?' I encourage him.

'Not a time during this current lifetime. Sometimes I can remember the time I lived this life before. The same life as Jim, only I did different things. Made different decisions. I was normal. Actually, I was a policeman.'

'I don't understand.' I am confused, though fascinated at his delusion. But suddenly he just collapses onto the floor. I call out for the police officer outside, who quickly rushes in with baton in hand. 'He just collapsed. He needs a doctor.' The police officer stands over Jim to get a better look, but he suddenly recoils, blood streaming from his ears. He stumbles back and collapses against the wall, sliding down onto the floor. I step back out of the cell, unsure of what to do. Suddenly

Jim opens his eyes and smiles at me through the open cell door.

'You must help me, Miss Grainger. You have to fix me. Fix Jim.'

I call down the corridor for help, turning back to Jim. 'Fix you? I'm not sure I *can* fix you. I don't know what is wrong.'

'Fix me.'

They now have Jim in a sealed perspex tank. He is lying flat on the floor, still wearing that useless straitjacket. I am outside the tank, looking in. They won't let me in. Even Helyn, Daniels and a few others are stood in the shadows. They think Jim cannot see them. They think he can only see me. I'm not so sure. His eyes are shut but he speaks to me.

'Life is like a box of chocolates. You wait patiently for your turn, then when your time comes to pick, all the best ones have gone.' He laughs. 'You're usually just left with the nutty ones.'

'How do you do it, Jim?' I ask him.

He opens his eyes and lifts himself up. 'Kennedy.'

'What about Kennedy?'

'You are superfluous. Kennedy is key.'

I turn to Helyn. 'Is Inspector Kennedy fit to talk?'

'He left an hour ago.'

'What? Why was this allowed to happen?'

'What's the problem?'

'For goodness sake, you saw what he did to himself. He could be dangerous.'

Helyn looks rather confused. 'What Jim did to him. This douche has some kind of power. He can make people do stuff.'

'We *must* get Kennedy back.'

'Put the wig on me, Miss Grainger,' Jim cackles in a very odd voice. It is almost as though he is trying to mimic my voice. 'No, you're Kennedy again. I'm Miss Grainger.' As I turn to leave, Doctor Johnson enters carrying a book, but he is obscuring the cover. Not that I am interested.

I opened the door to my daughter's flat. I didn't want to go in. There were such bad memories here, of what happened to her here. This Jim wasn't her killer, I knew that, but he also knew something about it. I stepped in and looked around. Somebody had certainly been living here, if only a very basic existence. An old TV was set up in front of that old armchair she had had from Gran when she moved in here. I knew it was a mistake to come and live here on her own, but what can you do? You can't keep them locked up forever, can you? You can try, but they just fight against it - unless you really beat them into submission. Then they have no life anyway. It was very hard.

Suddenly I didn't know why I *had* come here. What did I hope to achieve? Upsetting myself seemed the logical answer. The only real conclusion I could arrive at was that Jim certainly had been living here without my knowledge. And the only person who could explain why was Jim.

I entered the room where Jim was being kept in a perspex tank and bumped into Miss Grainger on her way out. However, after seeing me, she turned and walked back to Jim alongside me.

'Why have you been squatting at my daughter's flat?' I shouted at him.

'The policeman in you,' he responded, 'morally judging a situation you know so little about.'

'At least I have achieved something with my life,' I shot back.

'Oh, you little hero. Think you'll get immortality?'

I turned to Miss Grainger, who refused to take her eyes off Jim. For the first time since I first clapped eyes on her, many years before, I thought how defined her face really was. It came to a point at the end and didn't repel me. I turned back to Jim.

'I know I won't live forever.'

'And doesn't it crush you inside?' Jim exclaimed. I kept my temper at bay.

'I can die happy. I've given something back. You have yet to prove yourself. You contribute nothing.'

'You don't know who I am. Your understanding is flawed.'

'Explain.'

'I need not explain myself to you, *Inspector* Kennedy.'

'Silence. The last defence.'

'Perhaps one day you will discover that your own ivory tower is also constructed of meringue. Maybe I do contribute nothing. Maybe I don't wish to contribute anything.' Jim stood up, pressing his forehead against the box. 'Maybe I wish to take away.'

I heard a thud and turned around to see Helyn lying on the floor, blood dripping from his ears. Miss Grainger and I rushed over, checking for a pulse but it was no good; he was dead. I turned back to Jim, who was now curled up in a corner, crying.

'Fix me. Please,' he wept, shuddering in fear and unable to look up as I ran up to the box and thrashed at it to get his attention.

(JIM)

I eventually looked up, but my vision was all blurry from the tears, and I was unable to wipe them away because of the straitjacket. Kennedy was still banging and yelling at me, but he no longer interested me. There was somebody else, who had just come through the door, somebody I had not seen before. He stood still for some time, looking at me. Miss Grainger stood up and said something to him, but suddenly dropped to her knees in front of him as though she was begging or praying. He held out his hand towards me as Kennedy turned to look at him, beckoning me to approach him. But I couldn't because I was in this box. Kennedy ran over to Miss Grainger and pulled her away from this man. When she was far enough away she seemed to snap out of whatever had befallen her. Shaken, she embraced Kennedy with a gripping hug and weepy kiss. This angered me, for I knew what Kennedy had done to his daughter and he might do it to Miss Grainger. The man by the door kept beckoning me forth and I needed to go with him, but I physically couldn't get out of this box. When he knew I couldn't, he dropped his arm and stepped back through the door. I called after him, begging him to stay. I knew what I needed to do. I thought of somebody releasing me from this box, setting me free so I could go where I had been called to go. A police officer approached the box and released the door. Kennedy and Miss Grainger tried to stop him, but he was too strong for he had both his own force and mine holding them back as I stepped out. I walked through the door in pursuit of the man, but he was nowhere in sight. Ahead I saw Doctor Johnson drop to his knees, clutching a book in the air, weeping. Again I called for the man to return. I turned back and he was stood behind me and we went.

INTENT TO MURDER - PART ONE

He sat motionless, staring blankly at the psychiatrist. Doctor Johnson's patient hadn't uttered a single word in ten years - not since the disastrous night of his capture. As Johnson reeled off his usual batch of questions at the lifeless prisoner, vivid memories still lingered in the minds of the police officers in the room who remembered the night they lost four of their best colleagues. Peter Smith had certainly spoken that night. Nobody could ever forget what he had said.

The room was as grey as the ageing Johnson's facial features. Lifeless and motionless, the room oozed death and decay in its soulless shell. That was all that was now sat in front of Johnson. Peter Smith was a shell; a husk of a raging lunatic who had been near unstoppable in his rage. He was stopped eventually - well, he had stopped, of his own accord, as though his work had been done. The damage had been done.

Peter showed no signs of the man he had once shown himself to be: callous, psychotic and evil. His sad blue eyes gave no indication of the callous beast that had once occupied this now seemingly dormant body. Many of the newer prison guards saw him as a rather pathetic, weak figure who had never shown any sign of anger - no sign of anything. Many guards didn't even see the necessity to have constant watch over him, which was so demanded by Inspector Noose. In fact, several guards assigned to watch the prisoner often slept through most of their shift.

The prisoner seemed unaware of his surroundings as Johnson eyed the notes on his clipboard. He sat almost still, rocking ever so slightly to and fro, his eyes fixed on Johnson's shiny black tie. Slowly they moved up to his neck and face, but movement was about all they seemed to achieve. Little thought seemed behind them.

'You're thirty-six today, Peter,' Johnson observed, 'Did you know that?'

There was no reply from the questioned prisoner. Only a hum, a mumble, of vacancy filled his lips. Johnson looked uneasy and turned to Noose for a sign of support. He got nothing. Noose raised an eyebrow in exasperation. The inspector, drained of all reason, stared back at Johnson in very much the same way as Peter. Noose had been assigned to Peter's case for the last ten years, and couldn't see why so much time and effort had been given to discovering why Peter had done what he had done. In his eyes, Peter should have been hanged for the misery he had caused so many people in just one night.

Johnson turned back to Peter, pondering what to do next. He had been summoned to review Peter's case following his patient's remarkable behaviour in prison. In Noose's eyes, however, the fact that Peter was in a cell on his own and had constant supervision meant he couldn't exactly behave in any other way. Johnson didn't see it this way and really believed, despite his troubles with Peter, that he could be rehabilitated and moved to a lower security prison. If not released altogether.

'You know me, Peter,' Johnson continued, 'I've been reviewing your case.'

Peter appeared to have absorbed none of Johnson's words. He looked away from the psychiatrist and fixed his sight on a rather hefty police officer standing guard at the door. Before long, his sight became fixed once more on Johnson. Strangely, however, never on Noose.

'Now, Peter, I've been coming to see you on and off for the past ten years now - ever since your court case. You were deemed sane to stand trial. That means you knew what you were doing was wrong. Could you give me some sort of indication that you understand what I am saying to you, Peter?' Johnson asked.

A smile came upon Peter's face for a fleeting moment before, once again, his face fell still again.

'Can you hear me, Peter? Is it your hearing that's gone?' Johnson pressed further.

'Of course it's not his bloody hearing, man,' Noose broke in. 'He's a damn psychopath.'

'Thank you, Henry,' Johnson fired back angrily. 'Would you please allow me to talk to Peter?'

Noose looked at Peter with contempt, knowing all too well that he was in the same room as the man who had killed his own sergeant.

Johnson continued looking over the notes on his clipboard for some time before turning to Noose. 'Can we speak outside for a moment please, Inspector,' Johnson mumbled.

'Inspector Noose and Doctor Johnson leaving at ten fifteen,' one of the officers stated for the benefit of the tape recording the proceedings.

They entered a secondary room attached to the interview room, allowing them full view of Peter from behind a perspex panel designed to appear as a mirror from Peter's point of view.

'Why must you persist in trying to help this man? He is beyond help,' Noose shot out.

'This man has shown no signs of anger for ten years, Inspector,' he pointed out.

'He's shown no signs of anything, Doctor,' Noose responded. He continued, 'This man has wrecked all our lives. He killed some of the best officers this station ever had, not to mention a young woman.'

'I know that, Inspector, but-'

'You know what?' Noose interrupted, 'You know that this man caused the break-up of your marriage because of your obsession with him?'

'Don't bring my private life into this,' Johnson snapped back.

'You should take some of your own advice for once.' With this, Noose headed towards the door. Johnson pushed his way in front to stop Noose in his tracks. 'What are you doing?'

'Consider this: how much has it taken to look after Peter Smith in the past year alone?' Johnson remarked.

'Always about money, isn't it?'

'If he was moved to a normal prison, imagine how much would be saved. Imagine what could be done with that money.'

'Imagine if he was hanged in the first place, like I wanted. There would have been none of this.'

'Listen to me,' Johnson growled under his breath, his face dropping as he took hold of Noose's arm. 'This isn't just about money. We need to know why he said what he did that night.'

'And the only way to do that is to butter him up by moving him to a cosier prison?' With this, Noose pulled away from Johnson and stormed back into the interview room. 'Take him back, we're having no more of this rubbish today, thank you,' Noose ordered the guards.

Johnson watched as the placid Peter was escorted out of the room.

'You won't get away with this, Inspector. I was in charge of this interview, not you. You'll be hearing from your superiors.' Johnson calmly left the room in pursuit of Peter and his escorts. Noose dropped angrily into Peter's recently vacated seat. He stared blankly, as Peter had done, intently concentrating his anger to remain docile; to repress it. It was a double-edged anger, for he hadn't just lost his friends that day. He had been friends with Peter Smith, and it was this that angered him the most. That which disturbed him.

'Why does he want to help this man, this utter bastard?' the inspector asked himself aloud, knowing full well he would not receive a reply. Johnson clearly attributed Peter's now docile nature to the fact that he must be repentant for what he had done. That he may even be reintegrated into society. That would never do, surely.

Peter continued his silence, almost like he was waiting for something. He sat, strapped-up, in his room, his waiting room, waiting patiently for something or someone nobody could ever possibly imagine. Johnson walked in, carrying a book which he kept obscured from Peter's sight. Not that Peter was interested in looking at it. He stepped slowly up to Peter and stared intently at him.

'You were intent on murdering those people,' Johnson whispered to the bound man. 'But that doesn't concern me. That isn't really what I'm interested in. You see, I know why you murdered those people, Peter.' Peter remained motionless as ever. 'I know why you suddenly snapped in a manic frenzy and bludgeoned whomever you could get at. Your bizarre, random spree. You wanted to break that which would otherwise have happened. And I know why you said what you did.' At this, Peter suddenly made eye contact with Johnson. 'But I won't tell Noose. Noose just isn't smart enough to understand. I'll get you away from here, Peter. I'll free you so you can be who you really are.' A flicker of frustration briefly seized Peter's face. Johnson went on, 'I've waited a lifetime for this. Oh Peter, *the* Peter Smith right in front of me for all these years. All these years I've struggled to get you away from here so you could be free. I keep going over the report in my mind. If only I'd been there, been witness to it! You just wiped them all out and then stopped dead. And you knew, didn't you. Oh, you knew! You had always known. You had tried to fight it but could no longer. All that blood on you, even Noose's.' Peter's breathing quickened as Johnson went on, 'A gleeful smile fell upon your lips, those three words slipping from between them as Noose wept.' Johnson now brought the book to Peter's eyes. He looked at it, a tear rolling down his cheek. 'Now is the time, Peter. You are thirty-six, just like in the book. Just like in *I Am Dead*.'

'I am God,' Peter uttered, his first words for ten years and also the last words he had uttered ten years ago. Johnson was stunned, humbled, dropping to his knees and bowing his head. He clutched *I Am Dead* to his chest, sobbing.

'God complex,' Noose spat out from by the door. How long he had been there was not clear, though Johnson hoped he had not seen the book as he quickly slipped it back into his jacket pocket before standing up.

'No!' Johnson growled back. 'Look. I, I-' but he trailed off and wiped away his tears, trying to regain his compose.

'What, Johnson? Tell me.' Noose stepped closer to him.

'He said he was God.'

'Yes, and? I could say I was,' Noose retorted.

'You could, but you're not.' Johnson suddenly looked wry. 'Nor is Peter Smith.'

A grin creased Johnson's face and his head twitched to the left. Noose suddenly felt very uncomfortable as this doctor closed in on him ever so quickly. Peter was somehow now freed from his binds and strode from the room. He appeared to know exactly where he was going, as though he had been called in that direction by somebody, and no amount of brute force from the assortment of guards who intercepted him could stop his departure. Noose and Johnson ran after him, but could not catch up even though they were moving faster. All at once Peter was gone, called away by a figure nobody else saw, but who most certainly had been there to collect him.

NEIGHBOURHOOD WATCH

The bodies of Andrew Stevenson and Amy Noble were found in a shallow grave just off the Harnlan Path road. I should know; I was the one who put them there. The police are rather cunning and would no doubt have soon discovered the whereabouts of the missing two with their sniffer dogs and DNA testing, however deep I had managed to conceal the corpses. In fact, in another life, I may well have been quite suited to being a police officer myself. I'm rather taken with the idea of stopping others from doing what they want. The police investigation isn't really my concern here; my concern is how I ended up putting the bodies of Andrew and Amy there. Or, more specifically, how I came into possession of two dead bodies in the first place.

Don't concern yourself with my current situation at the moment. Let me instead tell you about how all this began. You see, Amy and I go back a long way. I am Stephen Noble, her brother. My connection with Andrew Stevenson also has a rather bland origin, but I won't bore you with that at the moment. That will unfold a bit later, so sit back and savour this wonderful recounting.

Amy and I had a fairly boring upbringing, to be honest. We squabbled like any family. It was often Amy who was on the receiving end of the more violent squabbles, earning me a time in the cellar. It was my own fault though; I was just so easily angered by my younger sister. I suppose, in a way, I felt a slight ownership over her, being four years her elder. Please don't misunderstand me, reader; I'm not a fiend of any sort. Maybe I felt it my duty to watch over my sister, and maybe I felt that my watchful eye had a claim over her ownership. Whatever, that is immaterial.

My parents owned me of course. They made that very clear. The incident that most sticks in my mind was when I was about eleven years old. My father had just purchased a new wall-mountable telephone for his and my mother's bedroom. I say purchase, but, knowing my father, he most probably came into possession of the phone as a result of less lawful acts.

The ceasing of a half-hour's worth of drilling indicated to me that he had finished fitting the phone on the wall next to my mother's bedside lamp and thirteen footsteps sounded as he stomped down the stairs. Mother, Amy and I were all sitting in the living room, watching television. I wasn't really interested in the gardening programme on at the time and was nearly asleep with boredom. I had been seated in the same position since we had eaten dinner almost two hours earlier. I hadn't a TV in my bedroom at the time, so I had to make do with what was being watched downstairs, there being no internet in those days either. My father stomped in. As I lay there almost asleep, I heard him call to me. I initially ignored him, wanting instead to dose off. It was the sudden thrash of his hand across the back of my head that made me listen. His intentions for me became clear; he wished me to view his handiwork upstairs with my own eyes. I, being a little naïve in approach, stated that I didn't wish to view the new phone. I instead wanted to rest a bit more, as school had been rather stressful on that particular day. This wasn't the reply my father was looking for. I didn't see his angered countenance, but did feel his hand grab the back of my school shirt. The next thing I knew, I was being dragged up the stairs against my will to see this magical installation. We ended up next to it, he telling me to look. I didn't. He told me again, and then made a threat of what he would do if I continued disobeying him. I had had enough of him telling me what to do, so I told him what I would do to him if he continued to try and force me to bow to his will. He thought he'd called my bluff when he grabbed hold of my head and moved it in the direction of the phone. I grabbed at the phone, ripping it off the wall. My father and I grappled for control of it. He began shouting out to my mother, who soon appeared at the bedroom door and helped him hold me down. He commented that I was insane and needed to be put down. I didn't comment on this, and stopped struggling. By this time, Amy had also appeared by the door and was laughing at the whole fiasco. I didn't want to give my father any more gratification than he had already earned by continuing to feed his anger with my struggling, so I merely flopped down as if I *was* dead. They moved off me and began talking about what should be done. My father suggested the cellar might teach me a lesson. With this, I leapt up and dashed out of the bedroom into the bathroom, where I slammed the door shut and securely locked it. It was some time before I was convinced to come out by my mother, who assured me that my father was downstairs asleep. He was, and I stormed out of the bathroom into my bedroom. The next day I put the incident to the back of my mind. Neither my father nor I wished to dwell on our struggle, and never spoke of it again. Maybe he didn't want to talk about it because he hadn't necessarily won the 'fight' outright. I never forgot about it, though, to this very day in fact, as I am recounting it to you, aren't I.

I am not an evil person - quite the contrary. If I am to make this sort of claim, I need to provide evidence to substantiate it. Read on, and you will be able to judge for yourself.

My mother and father had lived in our house four years before I was born. They had had another child before me, but its fate was never and has never been disclosed to me. George and Myra Noble were the names my parents had been given.

Two names which remain indelibly etched in my mind. Their privately indelicate and indubitable personas differed drastically from those that our neighbours witnessed. Considering the rest of the humdrum neighbourhood, I'd say my parents led a fairly interesting life together. I was unfazed by their constant bickering, as one is when you're used to it. The only time I felt concerned was when no voices could be heard in the house. 'Has Father finally snapped and slain Mother?' I often asked myself. Then he would drag a small number of black bags into the back garden and start digging and burying them next to the strawberry patch. My mysticisms were short-lived, however, when she always turned up again. Don't perceive my father as a wicked malicious man; quite the contrary. Only when he was aggravated or disobeyed did he feel the need to instil discipline, using violence. Otherwise he was a rather kind and generous man, often bringing home unexpected gifts for Amy and myself. This always concerned my mother. It's no wonder, looking back, that my father must have contemplated at least getting a divorce from my mother because of her constant nagging and siding with other people against him. She wasn't totally without cause, though. He enjoyed excessive gambling and alcohol abuse, often squandering away vast sums of money without even consulting my mother. Looking back, I suppose she had a very just cause for constantly nagging him and siding with other people.

Home is where the essence of this story lies. However, incidents did happen elsewhere that were to alter my life in different ways. School was one such place, and the memories of what happened there are still as strong in my mind today as when they first happened, and with good reason too.

Infant and primary school seemed to have passed by without too many glitches. Maybe the reason for this is that I can't recall any significant moments during this period of my schooling to reminisce about. It is a portion of my secondary schooling that I wish to tell you about. The following may shock you; it may even worry you somewhat that this sort of thing can happen. Let me assure you that it did happen, and it may help you answer some of the questions you will be thinking about as we progress to the incident of the two corpses.

Not much happened in the first four years of secondary school. I didn't care too much for friends, as they always seem to lie and let you down. I didn't care too much for school as a whole if I'm honest, preferring to keep myself to myself. I did have friends, or at least people I spoke to. Speaking to people of my own age group was the only way of breaking up the monotony of everyday life, and averting the concern of the teachers. There aren't any significant friends I can mention, really; just the usual collection of imbecilic and imperious fools that you try to get along with for an easier life and to divert attention from oneself. There was one lad, I suppose, who I was quite chummy with. However, he jumped out of a window and got skewered on a bus stop.

A teacher had begun to take an interest in me personally. This hadn't happened before as I had tended to shrink back relatively unnoticed in class. My chemistry teacher, a Mr Peters, began asking me to stay back after class for 'chats'. These chats usually consisted of him asking me about my family life and what I did in my spare time. I was initially not too concerned with this, thinking that Mr Peters merely admired my intelligence and wished to learn more about me. However, my intelligence didn't stretch to an incredible degree in the scientific direction his did and I soon became mystified as to why Mr Peters was continually asking me to stay behind after class or stopping me during dinnertime to talk to me at length. This continued for some time, culminating in a rather odd series of events following me leaving school. I was sixteen and it was the summer holidays before I had to go to college. I had textbooks to return to Mr Peters after finishing my exams.

When I did this, he was most interested in what I had been up to during all my spare time. I hadn't been up to anything of note, informing him thusly. He had a job for me to do at his house. He wanted to clean his pond out and get some new fish. I could help with this. I obliged. The offer of money and the intrigue of looking around a teacher's house drew me to the idea. I was wearing white trousers at the time I took the textbooks back and he took great interest in them. Fishing around in his drawer, he gave me a very smart silver pen which he said I could keep for all my 'nice chats' throughout school. I pocketed this and continued chatting. However, as our conversation wore on and the bell sounded for his next class to enter, I discovered that the pen's ink had run out in my pocket and soaked through.

'Oh dear, oh dear!' Mr Peters exclaimed.

Suffice to say, I ended up, trousers off, in his store cupboard until his class ended. He had some chemicals which, he assured me, could easily remove the ink. Alas, they only served to further spread the ink. He would have to run me home, in his smart sports car, and organise when I could go to his house. I went to his house a number of times and what occurred there was not very pleasant. Not that he told me I was not allowed to divulge the details, but he did theoretically point out that he had both the means and the motive to do away with me if he was so inclined.

As we grew up, Amy became ever more engrossed in school and social interaction, whereas I pulled back. I felt the need to distance myself from those kinds of surroundings. I am not unsociable; I just find people desperately annoying. Perhaps that is my main failing? Sometimes they can't help but be annoying; other times they thrive off the knowledge that they are annoying. The turn-the-other-cheek approach that so often worked on my father often wore thin with people of my own age. One such person was my sister's first boyfriend. He was almost my age when she was fourteen. I felt rather sickened at the thought of what went on between the two. My parents didn't, however, so I was seen as a jealous spoilsport. I always found it strange that Father did not put an end to this relationship. On the contrary, he appeared to encourage it. To use the word 'teased' would suggest their jibes at me were merely for a bit of fun, but I didn't see them as that. I felt strongly that Amy shouldn't be seeing someone at her age, let alone someone who was so much older.

'Do you want Amy to get pregnant?' I would question as my parents continued to probe me about my supposed jealousy.

'Do you want to wreck your little sister's life?' was their reply.

Did they know anything about what went on with people of our age group? Did they really believe Amy and her boyfriend wanted some privacy to help each other study for maths exams? No, they lied because they wanted to get up to other things - other things that I knew about. Mother and Father may not have bothered to fully check where Amy and Sean were going to all the time, but I did. I don't want to disclose the horrid details, but I trust you can build up a basic picture in your mind about what obviously went on. I'll take it you're not naïve, unlike some people I know of.

Sean didn't last long. Two, three months. He and his family moved away after their house was burnt down by somebody, and Sean didn't bother to keep in touch after his face was melted. I later told Amy and my parents that I had tried in vain to stop all this heartache happening in the first place, but I was told to stop interfering. I did stop interfering, for some time. I only ever, as they put it, 'interfered' when I felt interfering was necessary. As I said earlier, I felt it my duty to watch over my little sister. As she grew older, however, she felt it less and less necessary for me to keep my watchful eye on her.

There were other situations I don't wish to bother you with.

I think you have the gist of what was going on. I want to continue telling you of my life before Andrew Stevenson came into it, but I feel that this would only serve to bore you. The real interest, as that is exactly what it is, lies in the sheer mention of the name Andrew Stevenson. How he came to enter my, and indeed the rest of my family's, life is no huge mystery. He merely moved in next door. Yes, right next door. This was some years after the happening I've just told you about, and I was into my twenties.

The McGregors moved out three months before anyone else moved in. I must admit, I looked fondly upon the McGregors. An elderly couple, both struck down with agonising arthritis, and their many pussy cats. I was very fond of pussies myself. I did have one, but that isn't relevant at the moment. What is relevant is that the McGregors could no longer cope on their own since their last son had moved out. They left to go and live in the Harnlan Creek nursing home. This was a shame, since I never did find the time to visit them after the day they moved out. I heard later he had smothered her in her sleep before swallowing a load of pills. Suffice to say, he survived.

So the house lay empty for three months. Had it remained empty for much longer, I think it may have been taken over by squatters. Looking back, I think this would have been for the better compared to what we actually got. I can see myself now, staring at my fish tank when I heard the removal van bringing my new neighbour. I took little notice of the reversing van. I was too busy staring at the empty tank in front of me. I had not long since settled down in my chair after a busy day doing nothing. Several notions were pulsating through my mind, the strongest being, 'what to do next?' This internal question remained unanswered. I didn't wish to answer it. If I did, that meant I had to get up and do something. Oh yes, I haven't told you, I'm not really one of those very energetic people. I get by just doing a little at a time, usually with a lengthened gap in between each physical activity. Things could have been different, but I'd held myself back, hadn't I, and I simply had to live with my choices.

I thought for a while about my two tiny goldfish who had once swam about the tank. My two goldfish, who my cat made sure had a rather untimely end. A sigh of retrospect came over me before I rose up from my chair. Energy seemed to be the main thing I lacked. I was rather pathetic (a word which may be used frequently to describe aspects of my existence), and I staggered out of my room with a rather heavy head. Heavy from my big brain, perhaps? The reason why I stood up at this specific point in time still escapes me to this day. I somehow found the strength to make my way down the stairs, counting each step as I placed my foot on it. As I reached the last step, as ever, I counted the number thirteen.

In an attempt not to draw my mother's attention (she was the only other person in the house at the time), I crept past the living room where she presently sat. However, her hearing was sharp. I suspect she could even smell me.

'Stephen, are you making a drink?' she called after me. It was less of a question, more of a demand by how she queried.

'If you mean diluting some blackcurrant juice, then yes,' was my half-hearted response. By this time in my life, you see, the show-parents-respect idea had begun to wear a bit thin. So had my hair, incidentally.

'Better make that two, then,' replied my mother to the previous response.

Under my breath, I was muttering several curses towards her. I dare not have spoken it out aloud. I didn't wish to purposely get into an argument with her. I made the drinks.

'No digestives?' she enquired.

'No, you ate them all,' I yawned back.

We both sat there for some time, not a word being uttered. I was sat on a chair whilst my mother remained spread out on the sofa. The removal van could still be heard outside. Neither of us bothered to look at what was going on. This was unusual. My mother was usually the first person up against the window if a noise was heard outside. This, however, was not frowned upon by the other neighbours. They were all members of the Neighbourhood Watch programme.

My mother was knitting and apparently watching the TV as well. I decided to challenge her over this situation.

'How can you knit and watch TV at the same time?' I blurted out, unable to help myself.

'What I do in my own house is up to me,' she immediately responded. 'Maybe when you have your own house you'll know what I mean.'

I had heard this before, believe me. Each time she or my father said it, they somehow managed to make it sound different; as if they believed they had just that minute stumbled over a most amazing snippet of philosophy.

She was knitting a baby jumper, who for exactly I don't think I'll ever know. She was the kind of person who had ambitions for other people, but none for herself. I sipped on my blackcurrant juice. Mother hadn't touched hers. It was at this point that I felt myself sink to an incredible depth of boredom. This was not unusual. Living with one's parents when you're in your twenties isn't exactly the most riveting of practices. I could have done something about it, got a decent job and a house. Why I didn't I cannot tell you. I wish, in retrospect, that I had moved - far, far away - but I didn't. I remained with my parents in the house I'd lived in from birth.

A knock came at the door. I was less than excited at this sudden interruption, but of course I was the one who had to go and answer it. On doing so I didn't at this moment realise the significance of what was to lead from one thing to another with the caller at the door. At this moment we remained strangers, and I was never going to really get to know him. It was Andrew Stevenson. I answered the door not knowing this.

'No double glazing, thank you,' I told the mystery caller, before attempting to close the door. However, he managed to wedge his foot in it before I had a chance to close it.

'I'm not here selling double glazing, Mr Noble, I'm your new neighbour,' he blurted back.

'Oh I see. Hello, are you…' I didn't know what to say, 'wait a second, how did you know my name?' I enquired.

'Oh I've been doing a bit of research before I came. George, Myra, Stephen and Amy Noble,' he exclaimed, as if he was somehow surprised at himself. I was unimpressed, but humoured this man I knew absolutely nothing about.

'So, who are you?' I asked. His foot remained in the door.

'Mr Andrew Stevenson,' the tall mousy-haired man answered, holding out his hand for me to shake it. I was once again unimpressed, especially because he gave himself the title of 'Mr'. It was as though he was trying to suggest he was of higher status than me. This was untrue; he didn't look any better than me. He continued, 'I couldn't ask you a huge favour, Stephen?'

'Go on,' I reluctantly replied.

'Well I've got the removal van here, and there's only me and the driver. You couldn't give us a hand moving the stuff, could you?' he asked without a moment's hesitation. I wanted to say no, but I felt sure my mother was listening. If I said no, she would have shouted, 'Why not, Stephen? You're not doing anything else.' To save myself from this strangling anguish, I relented and said I would help Andrew unload the removal van. On the way down my garden path, I asked how many were moving in. He told me just one - himself.

Mother had told me to go round to Andrew's house to ask him over for a chat. I didn't understand why I had to go. Why couldn't she go? After all, it was her who wanted him to come for a chat. The reason she wanted him to come for a chat was because she was nosy. It doesn't do to be nosy. If it had been left up to me to form a friendship with the new neighbour, I would have just said good morning and good afternoon every time I saw him. I wouldn't invite him into our house so that he could have a nose around in our belongings. That's why he agreed when I asked him; he wanted to come and have a look around our house. He didn't invite me in to his house when I went across to ask him to ours. Of course, I'd been in when helping him to move his possessions in from the removal lorry, but I hadn't seen how he'd arranged things, had I? No, but he'd get to see how we had our things laid out. This is precisely what happened when he came 'over' for a 'chat'. I went round and asked him, and he said he would be over soon.

The seven-knock code came on the back door. This aggravating rendition consisted of five knocks with one-second gaps in between each one, followed by two faster knocks without any pause. He had done this the first time he'd knocked on the door to ask if I'd help him unload the removal van. This time the knock came, followed by the opening of the door. He had let himself in! I would never have dreamt of doing this, but he seemed to be quite at ease letting himself into someone else's house.

'Are you in, Mr and Mrs Noble?' he called out. 'It's Andrew Stevenson from next door.' He had evidently dropped the 'Mr' when saying his own name this time around.

'In the living room, Mr Stevenson,' my mother called out to the cankerous deviant.

He presently entered the living room. Both my parents and I were situated in the living room, my mother as ever spread over the sofa. My father and I both took up a chair each. Andrew, on entering, immediately held out his hand to shake my father's (he was seated closest to the door). He then shook my mother's hand, but ignored mine (not that I was holding it out to him, but still).

'It's nice to meet you both. I've met Stephen already. He helped me greatly yesterday,' Andrew premeditatedly announced.

'Oh, it's good to meet you too, Mr Stevenson,' my mother replied, her tone of voice uncomfortably sycophantic.

'Yes, indeed,' my father added.

'Oh please, call me Andrew, Mr and Mrs Noble,' he grinned.

'As long as you call us Myra and George,' my mother replied.

I felt this all too unnecessary. He was only a neighbour, after all, wasn't he? He'd only moved in the previous day. What did we know of this man we were socialising with here? Nothing whatsoever, and this concerned me. I wanted to know more about this Andrew Stevenson who was standing in my living room. I wanted to know even more now that he had sat down, at my mother's request, on the sofa.

My father seemed unconcerned at this new neighbour we'd acquired. He didn't seem to want to probe Andrew Stevenson at all. I realised this, and took it upon myself to do the probing. He had seemed reluctant to tell me where he was from when I asked him the previous day. What would he now tell me in the company of my parents? I was unsure, but felt I needed to push the issue.

'So where are you from again, Andrew?' I probed, 'I didn't quite catch what you said yesterday.'

'Down south, Peter, the good country!' he remarked glibly, obviously in an attempt to comically excite my parents.

'Down south, really?' I spoke with false conviction. 'A big place.'

'It is, yes. *Very* big.' He fixed his eyes on me, as if to suggest he was referring to something other than where he was from.

He was not going to tell me exactly where he was from, and I felt it unnecessary to question him further in front of my parents. I would find out using other means later on.

'Any family?' I continued.

'Oh Peter, stop asking all these questions and go and make

Andrew and us two a cup of tea,' my mother interrupted.

I smiled through gritted teeth, stood up and walked out of the living room. I indeed did make three cups of tea, and contemplated adding more than just a tea bag and milk. I naturally held back, wishing not to reduce myself to their level of intellect. Then again, I may take that back. Andrew didn't have a lack of intellect - far from it. In order to be so manipulative, he would have to have been extremely clever, which I suppose he was. Well, you have yet to see how manipulative this person was to become, so let me continue.

I carried the three cups of tea into the living room on a tray. I had placed a small bowl of sugar with a spoon in it on the tray as well. This, to my mother, wasn't enough.

'Where are the biscuits?' she angrily enquired.

'We still haven't got any left, you finished them off last Thursday.'

'Last Thursday? Isn't it time we got some in?' she pointed out.

I didn't reply to this, instead I left the three to get on with it. I preferred not to stress myself out in the company of these aggressors. Returning to my room, I slumped on to my bed and rubbed hard at my face. I felt tired and worn out, and couldn't be bothered seeing Andrew Stevenson's face again. I had already taken a dislike to him, and I hadn't known him five minutes. However, I always considered myself a good judge of character, so this helped me mellow to my frustration over our new neighbour.

I hadn't been lying on my bed ten minutes when a trampling of footsteps were heard coming up the stairs. I sprung off my bed and rushed over to the bedroom door. I left it shut though, preferring to listen to what was being said without them knowing. I always felt this was best; at least then you don't have to enter into sordid conversations with people you couldn't be bothered talking to.

My mother was talking to Andrew Stevenson. His voice

could be heard too. As they came up the stairs, my mother was giving Andrew a brief history of each one of our wall-mounted plates. This angered me even more than the door incident, but I did nothing about it. I remained listening intently. I paid particular attention to the remark made by Andrew that he was going to be sleeping in the bedroom directly behind my bedroom wall, a fact that didn't so much bemuse me as worry me. It was at this point I felt myself opening the door. I remained in my room, gripping the door tightly.

'And here is the man himself,' Andrew announced on seeing me, as if to suggest that he and my mother had been talking about me in anticipation of seeing me. I felt antagonised by Andrew's statement, coupled with that smirk that I just wanted to melt off his face. I refrained and grinned back, giving a snort before I once again closed the bedroom door.

'Oh Stephen, don't be so rude,' my mother called out.

She always had a knack for showing me up in front of other people and making me out to be the bad one. This occasion was no exception. I fully saw it within my rights to close my own bedroom door, regardless of whomever might be standing the other side of it.

'Can I get you two any more tea?' I asked sarcastically through my bedroom door.

'He can be childish at times, Andrew, I'm sure he'll mellow to you,' my mother responded.

How could she knock her own son, who she had known for over twenty years, like this in front of a neighbour she had known for five seconds? No, I take that back; she didn't even know him. None of us knew him. Where he had come from, where his family were. I could have swung my door open and stormed out there to give them a mouthful, but I knew that would only serve to feed them with what they wanted. They wanted to aggravate me; wind me up. I wasn't going to let this happen. This does seem rather ironic now, looking back.

'How about *Stephen* comes to my house to help me set up the pool table, Myra?' Andrew suggested, causing me to swallow a mouthful of phlegm in disbelief.

'Oh yes, that sounds like a brilliant idea Andrew,' my mother replied.

'Excellent!' Andrew gleamed.

Was I to have any say in this? Evidently not. I would have been damned if I were to spend time with *him* setting up and playing pool. Why did I want to get to know him? It didn't make sense. I did, though, open my bedroom door and agree that I would go to his house to help him set up the pool table. I'm not too sure why I agreed; maybe I wanted to have a nose around his house like he had done around mine.

We went across almost immediately. I became increasingly interested in discovering more about this Andrew Stevenson we all knew so little about. If the state of his house was anything to go by, he was rather lazy and hadn't yet bothered trying to sort out his boxed belongings. We hadn't spoken on the way to his house, and he spoke the first word when we arrived by his front door.

'So are you coming in, Steve? I can call you Steve, can't I Stephen?' Andrew asked, putting particular stress on the 'St' in my name.

'That's why I'm here Andrew,' I replied, putting stress on the 'A' in his name. 'And you can call me what you like.'

He looked me in the eyes and gave a smirk of satisfaction, as if to say that he had beaten me in a competition. I ignored this, and followed him in. The door was closed behind us. As I said before, his house was rather untidy. I may have admitted that I was a bit lazy at times, but I always tidied up after myself. I expected people to do the same, even if the person had just moved into a new house.

On moving into the living room, Andrew pointed out that he had a particularly clear view of my driveway and garden and could see people coming and going if he so wished. I found this rather disturbing. Who would find it interesting to watch someone else getting into a car and reversing down a drive in the morning? This man did, and my fascination (and anger) with him continued to grow as I spent more time in his company. We didn't talk much at first; he instead left me to stand in the middle of the living room whilst he dragged out the pool table. Why he didn't ask for help I don't know, maybe because the pool table wasn't all that heavy.

'You ever played pool before, Steve?' he asked me, whilst struggling to balance out the pool table with only three legs.

'Yes. Have you?'

'That's a bit of a daft question, isn't it?' he fired back, wishing to convulse my agitation. I was not moved, and instead wished to continue watching him struggle with the pool table. 'Are you going to help?' he suddenly blurted out.

Without a word being spoken, I began helping erect the pool table. After several attempts to balance out the table with a stack of boxes, I suddenly burst into anger at this person I knew nothing about.

'Look, who are you? Why do you want me here?' I raged.

'Calm down Steve, I haven't done anything,' he smiled, taking obvious delight in my anger.

'Come on, start telling me something about yourself. You already seem to know everything about me,' I continued in frustration.

'You're a bit paranoid aren't you Steve? Come on, lighten up for goodness sake. I've just moved in next door, we haven't known each other for long.'

'I don't know you, but you seem to know everything about me,' I pointed out, becoming less angered through lack of energy.

'All right then, what do you want to know?' he asked straight out.

'Well where are you from? Why have you moved here

alone? Where is your family? Where do you work?'

'I'm from London, I've moved here alone because I thought it was time I left my parents in peace and I have my own business fitting carpets. I haven't had a chance to establish it in this area yet though, it may take a while. Anything else you'd like to know?'

'It was time you left your parents in peace?' I probed further.

'Oh yes, I've lived with them all my life, and I'm into my mid-twenties now, you know. I don't think it's healthy to keep sponging off your parents at that age.'

I must admit that what he told me did sound as if it was true, and I went along with him. I was taken in by his answers. I know this may sound peculiar, but I warmed to him for some reason and came to understand that his life didn't seem that different from my own. Few words were spoken whilst we proceeded through several games of pool. One thing that did strike me was how believable he was. Through the course of that hour or so I spent at his house, I came to the conclusion in my mind that I had initially been a bit brash in my dislike for him. I had taken it upon myself to judge someone that I didn't know at all. On coming to know a bit more about Andrew, I came to feel that he wasn't as bad as I first thought. Maybe he was a bit too interested in other people's business, but that was just a fault he had. You may think I've changed my tune slightly, but on that day I decided to loosen up a bit. I also looked back on the events of the morning and thought that perhaps my mother had encouraged Andrew to behave in the manner that had annoyed me. I took it upon myself to forgive Andrew for annoying me, and decided to set about building up a neighbourly friendship with him. The only problem was I had no idea whatsoever what loosening up he had in mind.

Amy came home one evening and soon after the phone rang. I never answered the phone outright; I would always pick up the phone I had in my bedroom at the exact same time that somebody else picked it up downstairs. I did so on this occasion to hear Andrew's voice asking to speak to Amy. She came to the phone and was asked by Andrew to go to his house. She readily agreed and trotted off immediately. I felt my whole being drop. I had foolishly forgiven Andrew for his initial actions, and yet here he was goading me to reignite my hatred. I steadied my breathing and tried to forget about it.

It went on. Amy would go to his house almost every evening. Soon he came to our house and announced that they were an item. I heard from upstairs and remained so, physically unable to go down there and confront them. However, maybe this was not such a bad situation. After all, Amy's previous relationships had all been away, namely not next door. The closeness of this latest one would allow me an opportunity to spy. Andrew's bedroom was just the other side of my bedroom wall. But these walls were double brick, and a glass against them would not suffice in my prying. Something more drastic was needed. I would have to act quickly, too, I reasoned, noting how short Amy's previous relationships had been.

Under the guise of cleaning it out and laying floorboards, I had persuaded my parents to allow me unmolested access to the attic. Here I quickly set about removing the bricks in the wall leading into Andrew's attic. This was not a quick task and a number of incidents occurred during it.

I was in my bedroom one evening and was suddenly dazzled by a bright light from outside. Unable to see exactly where it was coming from because of its strength, I went into the garden to further investigate. I found Andrew up a ladder installing a security light practically next to my window.

'What the hell are you doing?' I yelled out.

'Steve, old pal. How's it going? I like your pyjamas by the way. They give you an air of adolescent innocence.'

Had his ladder not been the other side of the fence, I would have shaken him from it and brought him plummeting to his possible demise.

'You can't put that light there. It's like headlights in my bedroom.'

'Too bad. There's a lot of crime in this area.' He smiled, flicking the light on and off. 'Besides, I have your parents' permission.'

The next incident was the announcing of their engagement. Andrew staged a barbecue, to which I was forced by my mother to attend, where they divulged the upcoming nuptials. This spurred me on to break through to his attic even quicker. Indeed, I had made headway of late with my parents going shopping more frequently and allowing my noise to go unquestioned. This engagement was ever so quick, I felt, and I pondered what exactly Andrew was up to. The moment I broke through to his attic, I decided I needed to confront him on the issue in the world below.

I knocked on his door when I knew Amy would not be there. He answered it and let me in without hesitation.

'Ah, Steve. I thought you'd be round before long.'

'Oh, and why is that?' I asked as he started setting up the balls on the pool table. 'And I haven't come to play pool.'

'Well, you know. Brotherly protection and all that. You want to really suss me out, make sure I'm just right for your little sister.'

'Hmm. I suppose so,' I admitted falsely, knowing already how wrong he was for Amy.

'Come on, have a game,' he said, handing me a cue, 'we need a chat.' He positioned the white ball, breaking off. 'I know it's quick and all, our engagement. But sometimes these things happen. We're in love.'

'Yes.'

'And not the kind of love you feel for your cat. No, human love. Passion.'

'Why bring my cat into this?'

'How is Mittens, by the way?' he asked, a wry smile on his lips.

'Fine, why?'

'Just asking. Oh, and Steve,' he started, but paused, stepping closer to me.

'What?'

'I'd be careful if I were you.'

'Careful? What of?'

'I know you want to fuck your sister, you dirty little freak. But that's my job, okay? It's my job to ram her senseless every night.'

I was shocked, unable to reply. I suddenly punched him in the face, leaving immediately. The police were soon at my door, apprehending me for the 'unprovoked attack' on Andrew. Still, after a night in the cells he graciously decided to drop the charge because it was 'the right thing to do', though this did not stop the police giving me a stern warning. My parents said I should be very grateful to Andrew for not taking the matter any further. Amy, on the other hand, was livid and said she would never speak to me again. Still, she had rarely spoken to me beforehand.

The next day there came Andrew's knock on the door. I stayed upstairs, listening intently. I could hear Andrew say 'A fox must have got it' before my mother called me down. I caught sight of Andrew clasping a bin bag, which he promptly threw to my feet.

'I'm afraid it's bad news, Stephen,' my mother went, 'Mittens. Looks like a fox got her.'

'Yeh,' Andrew smirked, 'found it in my back garden. Well, some of it.'

I looked down at the bin bag.

'Nice of Andrew to scoop up the remains of Mittens and bring her home, wasn't it Stephen?'

There was nothing left to do but kill Andrew.

I was now in his attic, but it was empty. I waited for him to go out before lifting the hatch up and peering down into his empty house below. I had brought a step ladder and slipped that down the hole onto the floor beneath to aid in my task. Firstly I walked into the spare bedroom, flicking through a few of the storage boxes. They contained nothing exciting and so I moved on to the room he and Amy used. There, on the unmade bed, I found Amy lying naked and dead. It was not clear how she had died, though there were bruises around her neck suggesting strangulation. I was strangely unsurprised at this sight, having suspected that Andrew had been wrong for her all along. I stepped closer to the bed, unsure what to do. It suddenly crossed my mind that I could easily be a suspect in her murder. I had not done it, of course. It would take me some time to repair the hole in the attic wall, and there would be my fingerprints on the boxes in the other room.

I had seen Amy naked before, but this time she looked more naked than ever. She was exposed and unable to hide from me anymore. I no longer had to hide from her either. Still, I left her there and went back into the attic. In my house, things went from bad to worse as I found both of my parents similarly dead; likely murdered. Andrew had been busy. He had to pay for his crimes, so I decided to go back through the attic and lie in wait for his return home.

Andrew walked up the stairs. I could hear his footsteps, counting each one. Thirteen. He'd reached the top.

'Oh God, what have you done?' he cried as he caught sight of Amy. I charged at him, pushing him down the stairs. At the bottom he wasn't dead; he was writhing around like a newly hatched parrot. One. Two. Three. I slowly neared. Four. Five. Six. I took out my camping penknife, pulling out the mini saw on it. Seven. Eight. Nine. Andrew struggled to get his bearings as I closed in on him. Ten. Eleven. Twelve. I was almost upon him. Thirteen. I pulled his head up by his hair, attempting to thrash the saw across his neck. As I did so he pulled away and I caught only the side of his face. His neck was still intact but the side of his face was slit open. 'Oh God!' he blubbered. I went about repositioning his head to finish him off but again he struggled, somehow managing to knock me back. 'What have you done?' he called out.

'You killed them. You killed all of them!' I laughed back, lunging for him. He flopped out of the way and I fell flat on my face. As I rolled onto my back to pull myself up, I could feel something wet on my chest. I looked down to see that I had caught myself with the penknife saw. 'Look what you've done now.' I pulled it out and looked around for the man I was addressing. He was gone. 'Andrew, it is your turn. Accept that.' I stepped into the living room, a pool cue greeting me. I fell back into the hallway, the tip of the cue snapping in half over my head. But again this didn't seem to put me off, as I stepped back into the living room to be greeted by a flying pool ball. This time I ducked out of the way and hastened my pace at Andrew. I slashed diagonally at his chest and cut deep enough to knock him to the floor. There he finally lay, resigned to his impending demise, awaiting the final method by which I would bring it to a close for him. I dropped my trousers and boxers, held out my penis and took it off with the saw. Andrew, looking up at me in horror and amazement, suddenly realised he was part of something very special. Bending over him, I rammed the penis down his throat, for it no longer belonged to me, and jumped up and down as he lay choking on it.

Sufficiently dead, his corpse lay waiting for further events to occur. I pulled my trousers up, now covered in my own blood, and quickened to dispose of the two bodies. My parents could wait.

I was starting to feel pretty weak, and a little in shock from the injuries I had sustained. Nevertheless I dragged Andrew's body from the boot of his car and rolled it down the embankment onto Amy's. Sliding down with a spade, I proceeded to throw whatever I could find on top of them. I gave a moment's thought to this path I had taken in life. I could have been, or done, anything I had wanted. Maybe I still could, if there was a way of doing things again. Making alterations. But it had simply not happened for me. I was now a murderer, though a justified one. Just as I was coming to a satisfaction over the covering, I sensed somebody stood next to Andrew's car at the top of the embankment looking down. I looked up, through my eyes, to see a man waiting there. I could also see him through something else; some sort of sense I had not felt before. I hadn't seen him before, though I thought I knew him. He gestured for me to join him at the top so I dropped the spade and did so. I looked right at him, both of us remaining silent, as he turned and started to walk away. I went with him.

I'LL BE THE JUDGE OF THAT

There was always something odd about Darren Aubrey. Even as a child, it was as though he was holding himself back from something he didn't know he was holding himself back from. He was pretty smart but threw every opportunity that arose away. He kept out of everybody's way, hidden away, trying desperately to lead as small and as insignificant a life as possible. He was not without just cause. One day, when he was still in his late teens, he was snatched off the street by some hooded figures and bundled into a van never to be seen again. His parents John and Rosetta were very upset, understandably, but decided he had brought it upon himself by being inadequately equipped with sufficient self-defensive weaponry when they had managed to convince him to make a rare trip outside to the local shops.

Darren was never seen again by the outside world, because for the rest of his days he was kept sealed in a tank by these hooded figures who never showed themselves but kept him alive and every so often droned in an ancient slurred voice, 'Everything is nothing. No order, no lies. Deny your anchor, scape the goats. Everything is nothing. No boundaries, no battles.' These words were a mystery to Darren, who grew quickly frustrated at hearing them and only them on a regular basis.

Déjà vu came into play after a while. Darren just couldn't get it out of his mind. He was convinced he'd been here before and began pondering why he'd instinctively been so reticent to get on in life prior to ending up here. The answer surely lay in why he'd been brought here in the first place, and why he was being kept alive. If he'd been here before, was it in some kind of bizarre alternate reality? This was mere pondering, meandering, trying to think up some kind of solution to his predicament. Then, one day, he had suddenly cracked it. It didn't matter that he was in this tank. He was being fed, and could dispose of his bodily waste, without even seeing (let alone interacting with) those who had him here. It was all he had ever strived for in life. This, he began to understand, was what he had striven for. To be kept away from whatever it was he could possibly do were he to try. He was now content to remain here and he put to bed any further thoughts.

What Darren didn't bank on was a sudden disruption to the shared plans of himself and those keeping him here. One day, Darren having been here for either years and years by now or merely just days (for time was difficult to measure in this situation), somebody appeared on the other side of the tank. Though he had never seen those who had been keeping him here, he knew it wasn't one of them. He somehow knew who this person was and what his intentions were. He had come to disrupt the timeline of Darren remaining here for his entire life, beckoning him forth. Darren stood up and walked towards him. The tank could no longer keep him there and he walked straight through it and left with the man.

THE REASON

Tony, Jim, Peter, Stephen and Darren all found themselves in this room. It wasn't a grand room by any means, but it *was* rather spacious. As a matter of fact, it had ample space - space enough for anything it wished to hold. It did not choose what to hold, of course, but merely held what was put in it. The one who decided what to hold in this room promptly appeared in front of the five men. 'You are all mentally ill,' he announced, 'but one of you is very special indeed.'

'That'll be me,' Stephen replied, grinning, nodding at the others.

'No,' the one who decided laughed. 'Not you, Stephen Noble. It is Peter Smith.' The one who decided also looked like a man and was accepted as one by the five other men without question. Jim, Stephen and Darren now looked at Peter, instinctively knowing that was him. Tony looked at Darren, always at Darren, though he kept his distance. Peter, who couldn't look at himself, looked back at the one who looked like a man.

'Why are we all here?' asked Peter although he already knew the answer.

'You are all here because I want you to be here. You all came with me, remember,' said the one who looked like a man.

'Why do you want us to be here? And who are you?' Peter pressed.

'I am Reaping Icon.'

'And why do you want us to be here?' Peter asked again.

'I already answered that.'

Jim turned from Peter and looked back at Reaping Icon. 'No you didn't,' he pointed out, 'all you did was tell us your name.'

'Reaping Icon is not my name. Reaping Icon is who I am.'

'Yeh, and I'm Stephen Noble,' he growled, suddenly grabbing hold of Reaping Icon. 'And I'm the special one.' But he let go of Reaping Icon and dropped to his knees in agony. 'I beg you,' he cried out, 'I beg you to stop.' Reaping Icon stopped whatever it was he was doing to Stephen, who promptly crawled back to his previous position.

'Your name is Stephen Noble, yes, but that is not who you are.'

'Then who am I?' Stephen whimpered back.

'Why do you want us here?' Darren butted in.

'Because I am Reaping Icon.'

'And what does that mean?' Darren questioned.

'Yes, you're not making sense,' Jim added. Peter listened intently whilst Tony stared at Darren. Always at Darren.

'And?'

'Make sense,' Jim told Reaping Icon.

'Why?'

'So we can understand you,' Darren went on.

'Why?'

'Because we want to understand you,' Darren tried to explain.

'Why?'

'To make sense of what you are saying,' Jim helped out.

'Why?'

'Because we do. It's not fair if we don't understand what you're on about,' Stephen came in, back on his feet now.

Reaping Icon suddenly brandished a copy of *I Am Dead* and slapped each of the five men across the face with it. It kind of made sense now.

'That is the word of Peter Smith. That is the word of me,' Peter uttered, staring at the book in Reaping Icon's hands.

'So we're here to what, worship him or something?' Stephen asked Reaping Icon.

'No,' Reaping Icon laughed. 'You are here to kill Peter Smith.'

Peter stepped away from the others as they turned to face him. Apart from Tony, he just could not stop looking at Darren. Jim's head lowered, his eyes rolling into the back of it. He tried desperately to get Peter to beat himself up like he had made Inspector Kennedy, but somehow Peter knew what he was trying to do and was mentally blocking him. Stephen felt around in his pockets, finding no penis, but he did have his trusty penknife. He flicked out the saw and thrust it at Peter. Peter's hand shot out and grabbed hold of Stephen's, easily shaking the penknife from it. Darren looked around, seeing Tony. Instinctively he grabbed hold of this man, who was so much bigger than he, and demanded that he kill Peter on his behalf. Tony, who knew exactly who Darren Aubrey was, for a moment thought seriously about following his orders like he always had done. This time, though, he felt he no longer needed to. He had cast Kelly off and could cast The Dealer off too. He launched a full-on attack on Darren, The Dealer, beating him senseless. The rage was unleashed, the torment and hatred driving him on to pound and pound at Darren's being. Reaping Icon did not stop it. This was what Reaping Icon knew would happen, and was always intent on allowing it to happen. Reaping Icon always knew what was going to happen. Darren would survive the attack. Nobody died here. All that could occur here was waiting. This was a waiting room and Tony, Jim, Stephen and Darren had to wait for the right time and place in order to kill Peter Smith.

'Why are they here to kill me?' Peter asked Reaping Icon.

'You don't know? Of course you know. You *have* read *I Am Dead*, have you not? After all, it did inspire you to make claims of grandeur... and you did commit a few murders.'

Peter thought back to that fateful day when he had

discovered the book amongst the belongings of a strange man who had made his acquaintance. Up until that point in his life, he had always either felt he never knew who he was or that he had certainly lived the same life before, only differently. On occasion, Peter felt he had lived his life over and over with infinite minute alterations made to it. Upon reading *I Am Dead*, he grew to understand why and, though he realised he had created everything, everything was nothing and he wished to stop the actions of *I Am Dead* unfolding in the first place. The murders were a quick fix. He couldn't bring himself to commit suicide, otherwise he would have simply been sent back to live his life yet again. The murders had allowed him to be kept away from the life he was destined to lead. That the book fell into the hands of Doctor Johnson was immaterial; it now seemed that nothing could have stopped Peter being called forth by Reaping Icon. Indeed, Peter himself couldn't stop himself going with Reaping Icon. Nor could the others - the others now collected here to kill Peter Smith.

Tony had stopped beating Darren, who now struggled with all his might to integrate himself back into the group with as little fuss as possible. 'I haven't read the book,' he coughed, his mouth full of blood, 'will you tell *me* why we're here to kill him?'

'Ah yes, Darren Aubrey. Forever forgetful in your lives,' Reaping Icon chuckled. 'You are in the book.'

'Am I in the book?' asked Stephen, eager that he was and adamant that he should be.

'You are all in the book, but mere names shift about; they are not necessarily who you are. Darren is but a name bestowed upon this being,' Reaping Icon explained to Stephen, pointing at the beaten Darren, 'yet he is other than that. He is more than just Darren. But he doesn't know it.'

'So that means I could be other than Stephen?'

'You never know.' Reaping Icon smiled, creasing his eyes.

If they *were* eyes. They looked like eyes. 'Maybe you will find that out if and when you kill Peter Smith.'

Jim believed he had cracked it. 'So whichever one of us kills Peter Smith finds out who we really are?'

'There are many things at play here, Jim. You and your skills, for example. All will become apparent as you progress on your journey.'

'And when does this journey begin?' Jim asked.

'He's gonna say it already has,' Stephen interrupted.

Reaping Icon, smiling and never frowning, tapped his nose with his index finger and winked.

'I will sense his presence,' Jim purred, holding his twitching eye. Stephen had noticed Jim's twitching and thought to mock it, mimicking it. Jim looked down at where Stephen's penis had been. 'I once had a friend who was so convinced he was the re-incarnation of Hitler that he sliced his scrotum open and scooped one ball out.' With this, Stephen promptly stopped the mockery and felt self-conscious about his stump.

'Look, are we four going to work together to kill Peter Smith?' Darren asked, stepping in between Jim and Stephen. Tony kept behind them, looking on in silence.

'I've been asked to do things before. I usually do them alone,' was Jim's reply.

'I'm generally a solitary killer too,' Stephen chipped in. 'But hey, this is something different, isn't it?'

'I guess it is,' Darren replied.

'It won't be as easy as that, my friends,' Reaping Icon interrupted.

PART TWO

BICYCLE MAN

ONE

It was absolutely glorious spring weather. The vast fields surrounding the country lane were open and blazing a myriad of bright greens. Sweet birdsong filled the air above as not a car raced by to disturb them. And then, as if unknowingly, a man rode past on a bicycle. There was something strange about this man. He looked surprised, shocked even, and came crashing off the bicycle as though he'd just found himself on it. Indeed, as he picked himself up off the ground, he realised he *had* just found himself on it. Where had he come from? What had he been doing before he found himself on the bicycle? He didn't know the answers to these questions. He didn't even know who he was. What he did know was that he wasn't riding a bicycle down a country lane mere moments ago, though he didn't quite know what he *had* been doing. Nevertheless, now he was riding a bicycle down a country lane. Or at least he had been before surprise had torn him from it.

He leant against the saddle and felt his face. It was rather rough with stubble. Who was he? He must be suffering from amnesia or something, he thought. He felt his hair; dirty, shaggy. And yet, he was wearing a smart brown suit. It fit him quite well - bespoke, even. But it looked rather old-fashioned for a young man such as he. There were muddy stains on it. From these clues, he deduced that he must have been knocked out or something by a passing car and left in the ditch for a while. He felt his head, but there was no lump.

He shifted his shoulders up and down, feeling a slight weight upon his back. It was a rucksack. He removed it from his shoulders and opened the zip. In it lay a single piece of paper, with a name and address written upon it; 'Mrs Parsonage, Kittiwake Cottage, Harnlan Lane, Myrtleville.' Looking somewhat bemused, he glanced up and surveyed the countryside around him.

Another man, physically similar in many ways but certainly in possession of more confidence, strode past on the opposite side of the lane, carrying a green bag.

'Excuse me,' the man off the bicycle asked the other.

'Why, what have you done?' he answered, coming to a stop.

'I'm a - well, I'm lost.'

The man, matter-of-factly dropping the green bag on the ground, stepped up to the bicycle man. 'Go on, pal.' He lit a cigarette.

'I think I'm trying to find a cottage.'

He blew smoke in his face. 'Plenty of them round here, mate.' He showed him the address. 'Hmm. Not far from here. Want me to draw a map?' he asked, the cigarette dangling out of his mouth.

'Will you?' asked bicycle man, smiling. 'Cheers. Thanks.'

'Yeah, you got a pen or summat?' asked the man who had just dropped the green bag. Bicycle man searched in the pockets of the brown suit, coming across a nice fountain pen with the initials S. S. engraved on it. He handed it to the man. 'Cheers.' The man began sketching on the back of the address paper, looking very thoughtful. Bicycle man tried to take a look at the unfolding map but a slight of hand obscured his view. 'Hey, you wouldn't mind fetching my bag, would you?' bag man asked, flipping the cigarette in his mouth to point in the direction of the bag.

'Certainly.'

Bicycle man strode confidently across the lane to do as the

helpful man had asked. However, when he turned back with the bag, the man was riding off on his bicycle with his rucksack on his back. Bicycle man tried running after him, but it was no good. He was gone.

It was now cloudy and tall buildings dominated the skyline as bicycle man negotiated his way across the busy road towards the police station. This felt uncomfortably real for the man who didn't know who he was, but he knew he'd have to report the theft. It was the right thing to do. Though cars whizzed to and fro in his way, he did somehow manage to end up the other side of the road; the right side for where he wanted to be. He came to a halt outside the police station, looking up at the entrance. It did look familiar, though man-made structures always did, he quickly thought. There was a certain logic to them, a shape. A square shape. A box.

He walked up to the reception desk just as another man pushed past him and started banging on the perspex screen protecting a police officer sat behind it.

'Get me Noose!' the man yelled, intermittently flailing his arms to the heavens and continuing to pound at the screen.

'Come on Neville, Inspector Noose is busy. And would you kindly refrain from provocatively bashing my protective screen?' asked the officer under attack.

'Get me Noose!' Neville repeated.

'I've told you, he's busy.'

Neville continued his banging as the officer sighed before asking politely: 'Would you like to be arrested, Neville?'

Neville immediately stopped banging and paused for just a second before turning, dropping his trousers and waving his bum at the officer. He started to smack each cheek as though they were bongos, singing 'Get me Noose! Get me Noose!'

'So be it. I only wish you'd asked for *the* noose.' He picked up a telephone on his desk, 'Jim... Neville again.'

Almost immediately, two young officers Jim and David appeared from behind a set of double doors and marched over to Neville, taking a firm grip of him. The officer on reception gave out a yawn, checking his watch.

'Take your hands off me!' Neville suddenly exclaimed, affecting a posh accent. He slipped from them and spun around, grabbing hold of bicycle man. He was not really startled, for he was not yet that familiar with the way of things again since his memory had failed. 'I didn't do it!' he yelled at him, the two men's eyes fixed on each other.

'You didn't?' asked bicycle man in all earnestness.

'You are my witness... I'm guilty of no crime...' Defiant, Neville let go of bicycle man and raised a finger into the air.

'Is there a law against bad breath?' asked bicycle man.

'You'll eat those words,' replied Neville.

And suddenly, as the two officers came to restrain Neville once again, one of them seemed to recognise bicycle man, for he froze in either terror or joy and stared at him. 'God, it *is* you!' he blabbed.

'Sorry, do I know you?' bicycle man responded.

'Of course you do.'

'Who are you?'

'What?' the officer asked, puzzled. 'David.' He gave out a knowing, disappointed sniff. 'Still ashamed?' He shook his head.

'Who am I?' asked bicycle man. But Neville was struggling, and Jim and David had to take him away through the double doors before bicycle man's question could be answered. Still eager to resolve the bicycle issue, bicycle man stepped forward.

'Officer O'Toole, Myrtleville Police Station. How can I help?' said the officer who had just been exposed to the latest attack from Neville. Before bicycle man could relate his tale, however, a tall blonde woman appeared at his side and seized O'Toole's attention.

'Trouble all abound today, hey!' she joked, turning to glance at bicycle man as O'Toole gurned at her. He looked back at her, feeling he somehow knew her.

'All in a day's work, Lauren,' O'Toole replied.

At this, bicycle man felt a sharp shiver right down his spine, causing him to spasm slightly. Lauren took another, more studied, look at him. Her profound, pointed face overwhelmed him for some reason. He could not understand why as she was what some would likely call plain. To him, she was beyond all others. She herself seemed to find something profound about bicycle man as it proved difficult for her to move her sight away from his, but she did and awkwardly continued on her way.

'So, who've you murdered then?' O'Toole yawned, interrupting what could only be described as apoplexy on bicycle man's face.

'I haven't murdered anyone. I don't think. Hmm. No, I want to report a stolen bicycle.'

O'Toole shook his head in disappointment. 'And I joined the police for this?'

'Did you really?'

O'Toole handed him a form. 'Just fill this in, wise guy.'

'Oh, another thing...' bicycle man started, not actually knowing what he was going to say.

'Was the bicycle made of gold, *Sir*?'

'Gold?'

O'Toole stood up and walked over to the filing cabinet behind him, flicking through some documents as he tried paying as little attention to bicycle man as possible.

'Look,' bicycle man went on, still not knowing what words were about to be unleashed from his lips. 'I a, I heard you mention Inspector Noose.'

'Yes.'

'Well I was wondering whether I could see him.'

'Didn't you hear what I just told that mad man?'

'I'm different.'

'You've got that right.' With this, O'Toole turned to face bicycle man and, relenting, came back and flopped at his desk. He picked a phone up and pressed a button on it. 'Name.'

'Who, me?'

'No, the pig in a tuxedo behind you,' O'Toole replied in anguish. Bicycle man actually turned around to look, further infuriating him. 'WHAT IS YOUR NAME?' he shouted slowly.

'I don't know.'

'Oh for God's sake.'

'See, I don't know who I am.'

'Sir,' O'Toole spoke into the phone. 'I think maybe you need to come out here.'

There was a loud noise as the double doors flew open and Inspector Noose, slightly tubby and disguising the first stages of thinning hair, caught sight of bicycle man.

'You! YOU! Oh God,' he yelled, pacing up and down before coming to a stop and fixing his glare at bicycle man.

'You must be Inspector Noose.'

'Of course I am. What do you want this time?'

'This time?' bicycle man asked, perplexed. 'You mean you know me?'

'You really are unreal, aren't you? Try anything I suppose.' Noose stepped up to him, spotting the green bag he was carrying. 'What's that?'

'Oh yes, this is the thief's. The thief who stole my bicycle. Well, the bicycle I was riding.' Noose snatched it off him as he continued. 'I can do one of those e-fits if you like.'

'No.'

'Everyone's very grumpy around here,' bicycle man sighed, 'except that Lauren. She seemed very happy indeed.'

'The super's just been arrested for fraud. Don't you read the papers?' Noose replied, recoiling as he looked in the green bag. 'They're scrutinizing the whole damn station.' He pulled out a pile of old, wet socks, looking putrefied at his macabre discovery.

'That's the exact same face I pulled when I put *my* hand in.' Bicycle man made eye contact with Noose. There was an awkward silence as they studied each other. 'Who am I?'

'What happened? Have you really forgotten who you are?'

'Just tell me.'

'You're Peter Smith.'

Peter, expecting some kind of instant complete realisation of himself, felt strangely sad. 'Ah,' he responded, no wiser than before. 'And who is Peter Smith? I mean, all I know is I am a man who was on a bicycle. Now I don't even have the bicycle.'

'Well, what more can I say? Maybe you had a blow to the head or something. I don't know,' Noose replied.

'I'll have to be off. I think I have somewhere to be. An address. Might see you again, you know. Socially.'

'Yes... no. I'll have to see, Peter. Been a long time. A lot of harm was done.'

'Harm? What harm?'

'I need to go too. See you round.' With this, Noose disappeared back the way he'd come.

Peter turned to O'Toole. 'I'll, I'll fill this in again. I need to be somewhere. I think I need to be somewhere.' O'Toole rolled his eyes as Peter turned to leave. 'Just one more thing,' Peter suddenly came back at him, 'please.'

'Let me guess, somebody dropped a banana skin and you slipped on it?'

'Not that I recall. No, this is about that woman. That Lauren.'

'What about her?'

'Who is she?'

'Lauren.'

'Lauren who?'

'That, my mysterious bicycle man,' O'Toole grinned knowingly, 'is our trainee pathologist.'

'I see.'

With this, Peter exited.

Peter strolled past the row of cottages on Harnlan Lane, intermittently glancing between them and the piece of paper with the address on it. Mrs Parsonage, Kittiwake Cottage, Harnlan Lane, Myrtleville. Who was she, and why was her name and address on a piece of paper in a rucksack Peter had on his back when he appeared from nowhere? This thought process caused him to pass Kittiwake Cottage even though he'd seen the name on the old gate. Stopping abruptly, he turned and headed back to correct his error. Whilst doing this, however, the driver of a car attempting to gain access to the driveway of the cottage next to Mrs Parsonage's had to slam his brakes on to avoid knocking Peter over. Peter seemed unaware that he had almost been knocked over and continued gallantly on his way. Michael the driver, a rather short man who was most certainly in his late forties if not fifty, wound his window down and stuck his head out.

'You stupid fool, I could have killed you!' he yelled, waving a fist.

But Michael's words didn't seem to have gone in. Peter merely waved back to acknowledge him. 'Lovely day, isn't it!'

'I'll give you a lovely day in a minute… You stupid idiot!' With this, Michael accelerated into his driveway and came to a screeching climax as Peter opened the equally noisy garden gate of Kittiwake Cottage. The garden was overgrown and wild, feral grunts seeming to emanate from its grassy depths. But this didn't interest Peter; he was more interested in the twitching net curtain in the front window of the cottage ahead. As he neared, the twitching abruptly stopped and it was time to ring the bell. It didn't work so Peter gave a knock at the glass panel on the door. It smashed. He looked in through the broken panel and spotted the hunched figure of an elderly lady shuffling forward in the yellowy darkness.

'Hello,' he called out, pulling away just in time to miss being skewered by a thrusting walking stick. It rattled in the new hole, removing the rest of the broken glass.

'Who's there? I'll call the police on you,' the old girl called back ferociously. 'I've got a mobile phone, you know. I could call them from this very spot.'

'There's no need for that, Mrs Parsonage,' Peter replied, attempting joviality in his speech.

'Why not? Who are you? Why have you smashed my door in? How do you know my name?' she reeled off without an intake of breath. Peter bent down and looked through the broken panel again.

'I'm sorry about the door. I believe I'm called Peter Smith.' He held out the piece of paper with the name and address on. 'I believe you must be called Mrs Parsonage.'

'Who? I belong to the Church of England. Go away.'

'No, no. I'm Peter Smith. Yes, and I think I'm meant to have come here,' he persisted.

'Oh, it's you,' the old girl sighed. 'You're late.'

'Late for what?'

'You're not the sort to get lippy, are you?'

'Goodness knows... No, Mrs Parsonage, of course not.'

'I'm Mrs Parsonage.'

'Yes. Yes, you're right.'

The old girl seemed pleased that Peter had agreed with her, for this instilled the trust she clearly required in order to unlock and open the door. Peter could now see her features. She was rather short and rotund, though could easily have been tall and slim in her time. Still, her time was yet up and she beckoned Peter in by shuffling to one side. Equally, this could have been to avoid having her grey skin dawdle in the sun for she made sure she was in the shadow of the door. However, Peter didn't seem to get the body language and remained standing outside.

'Come in, come in,' the old girl demanded. 'Yes,' she said, eyeing him up and down. 'Must be you. You've got a reputation as a fool, Peter.'

'I have?' She did not reply. 'Then what on Earth am I doing here? Why was I supposed to come here?'

She put her hand on his shoulder and made the mighty effort to angle her head upwards to catch eye contact. 'A cheap fool, Peter. You're a cheap fool.' She slammed the door shut behind them as Peter stepped into the hallway, the sound of crunching glass beneath his boots. Boots and a suit. He supposed this was standard dress for Peter Smith. For him.

He caught his face in the mirror and studied it. Yes, it did look somewhat familiar. Like a new song from an established band. He didn't remember ever seeing his face before, but it was not completely alien to him. It was, perhaps, just bland. He looked down at the glass and, feigning a cough to cover the sound of its crunching, purred, 'Oh dear, how clumsy of me.'

'Fear not, my simple-minded chimp,' she chuckled, slapping his cheek playfully but still rather hard, 'the repair bill will be docked out of your wages.' She turned and began the journey into the depths of Kittiwake Cottage with her new pet, he who was formerly known as bicycle man, following behind. 'Now,' she went on, 'I hear that you're not exactly the easiest person to trust, Peter.'

'Where did you hear that?'

'Look,' she stopped and turned to face him, 'I'm prepared to give you the benefit of the doubt and overlook the warnings people have given me. People I hold in high regard. If you're punctual and do a good job, you'll get paid. Both parties will be happy.'

'Thank you Mrs Parsonage.'

'Now, come along. I'll show you what I want doing.'

The two disappeared from the hallway.

Next door, Michael stormed into his living room, where his

wife Cynthia, twice the weight of her weedy little husband, was sprawled on the couch watching TV. The room was minimalist in content, not looking very lived-in. A single ornament cabinet seemed the centrepiece of this room, despite sitting to one side.

'Some idiot's just gone next door,' Michael yelled, pacing the room. 'Nearly knocked him over for crying out loud.' Seeing he hadn't got his wife's attention, he stepped in front of the TV.

'I'm watching that,' she yelled back.

'I should have run him down, taught him a lesson,' Michael pondered, rubbing his chin.

'Do you mind going in the other room to rub your chin?'

'Hah, there's nothing else in here I want to rub. Road safety, hah. Makes you laugh!' Cynthia, however, sat doing a good impression of Buster Keaton. 'Nobody listens these days, do they?'

'You've got that right.'

'What the hell are you on about now?' He stepped closer, almost threateningly so, leaning in with a pointed finger. 'Always sarcasm with you, isn't it?'

Cynthia rolled her eyes and, taking hold of the TV remote, turned the volume up. Michael marched off up a set of rackety wooden steps leading into a converted attic bedroom that housed a model train track. Here he picked up a pair of binoculars off the windowsill and quickly brought them to his eyes to scan Mrs Parsonage's garden next to his below. There, in the garden, stood Peter and Mrs Parsonage, surveying the horrendous mess the garden was in. There was grass where there really shouldn't have been any grass and weeds galore.

Peter spotted a rotting shed to one side of what was a lawn. The old girl passed him a key and nodded towards said shed.

'You'll find all you need in there. Now, do you take sugar in your tea?'

'Sugar? Erm, hmm. No thank you,' he replied, somewhat unsure really.

'Noooo,' the old girl rolled lazily, 'you're sweet enough!' She grinned a rather peculiar grin, somewhere between sarcasm and a seizure, as Peter stood silent as though waiting for further instruction. After a moment or three, she grew tired of this. 'Well, what are you waiting for? You have your instructions. Clear the weeds!' With this, she turned back towards the house and hobbled away.

As Peter made his way through the two-foot high grass to the shed, something caught his eye in the attic window of the next cottage to the left. A reflection - the sun catching something. A figure pulled away. It was Michael. Peter gave this little thought and unlocked the shed to start his work.

'This fool's arrival could prove beneficial,' Michael purred, now stood back from the window and fingering his binoculars.

'I hope you ain't perving on that old bag next door again,' Cynthia yelled from downstairs, 'there's a name for people like you.'

'I can think of a few for you an' all,' Michael growled back.

Peter and the old girl were sitting drinking mugs of tea in her kitchen.

'This is a very nice cup...' Peter started.

'That is a mug,' she interrupted, raising an eyebrow and chewing her gum.

'A very nice mug, Mrs Parsonage.'

'Young man, we might just get along after all.'

'I hope we do.'

'Yes,' she went, lowering the tone of her voice, 'I don't see many friendly faces nowadays. My son's only after my money, and the neighbours.' She sipped at her tea, frowning. 'Such wretched people.'

'It's funny you should say that,' Peter replied. The old girl leant in to hear more, but Peter prolonged her wait with a sip of his tea.

'Yes, yes?!' she eagerly encouraged the young man.

'Well, the man next door. I'm sure he was watching me in the garden.'

At this the old girl sat back again, perhaps disappointed.

'Yes, Michael, and that insane wife Cynthia. We've been in a legal entanglement for two years over the fence.' She began gyrating somewhat in her chair. Angry, maybe. Excited, definitely. 'I swear down on my life that he's tried to kill me before now.'

'Interesting,' Peter responded, grinning into his mug of tea. 'He hasn't been successful, obviously.'

'Quite the contrary,' she shot back, enjoying the attention, 'and I shan't allow him the satisfaction of doing me in in the future, either.'

'I *am* glad,' Peter came back at her, his attention turning to a plate of biscuits. Suddenly the old girl picked the plate up and moved it onto the sideboard behind her. Peter accepted his biscuit-less fate and smiled stoically.

'Oh, and you'll find a piece of wood for the door in the shed. I doubt I'll get it repaired professionally today,' she went on.

'Oh right. I'll get onto it.' He stood, drinking his tea faster.

'You do that.'

The sun was now low in the sky, hiding behind a tree and casting Peter in mere grey. The garden was looking a lot tidier now. Peter had been working hard but it was evident that he had not yet finished the job. He put his jacket on before wiping a garden fork clean with his gloved hand as the old girl appeared at her back door. Peter carried the remaining tools back to the garden shed and, having put them inside and locked the door, innocently pocketed the key.

'Time, young man!' she called out.

She waved Peter off as he made his way down the path.

'Oh Peter,' she called after him. 'Where have you put the shed key?'

'Oh, nearly forgot...' Peter started, putting his hand in his pocket. But something flashed through his brain. 'I a, I left it on the kitchen table.'

'That's fine. See you tomorrow!'

'Yes, will do! Bye, bye.' He waved to her and went.

Meanwhile, Michael next door was peeping out of his front window. Cynthia was, as ever, rooted to the sofa watching television.

'What are you doing? Who are you looking at?' she demanded of the thin man hovering at his window.

'Quiet! Will I never be rid of your incessant whining?' he shot back at his vast wife.

'Will I never be rid of *yours*?!' she yelled in response.

Michael grabbed the telephone, thrashing at its numbers, all the time his eyes fixed outside at Peter walking away. 'Geoff,' he spoke into it, 'yeah it's me. Look out of your window now, over at the witch's cave.'

Geoff lived across the road from Michael and Cynthia. He was a much bigger man than Michael, perhaps a better match for Cynthia. Sat in a chair facing the window, with telephone in hand, he lurched forward and picked up a pair of binoculars.

'Interesting,' he uttered, catching a closer perspective of Peter as he raised the binoculars to his round, moist eyes. He panned across to Michael's front window and caught sight of the short thin man peeping out. That wasn't his interest, however. His interest was Cynthia, and he edged forward in his chair again as he adjusted the focus on the binoculars to grasp a sharper image of her.

'Michael,' he whispered, the telephone now pulled away from his lips, 'Cynthia is wearing an awfully low-cut top today.' He cleared his throat, seemingly overcome with some kind of unexplainable desire.

Michael and Geoff were not the only nosy neighbours. In the cottage the other side of Mrs Parsonage lived another elderly lady, Mrs Lester. Her front room was dark and misty. All that could be seen in this dim light was the figure of a short, grey-haired buxom figure pulling back the net curtain on her window to peep out at Peter. She released a wheeze from between her lips, intended to disperse the mass of bluebottle corpses strewn on her windowsill. They merely shuffled about somewhat, a number of them dangling from cobwebs. Resigned, she left them to it and disappeared from the window as her net curtain fell loosely back into place.

Peter strolled down the lane, fingering the shed key in his pocket, serenely unaware that he was the centre of attention now. Geoff had moved on to thoughts of Cynthia and Mrs Lester was preparing for an evening of lonely obscurity, but Michael was busy making notes.

Peter walked past a cake shop window and glanced in. What lay on display made him stop dead in his tracks and take a second look. Such wondrous, magical varieties of cake. He fished around in his pockets for money, but found nothing. All he had was Mrs Parsonage's shed key. He was so hungry. He hadn't eaten all day. In fact, he couldn't remember when he had last eaten. He couldn't remember anything. All he now knew was what he had been told. He had been told that he was Peter Smith, and he had been instructed by a note to go to Mrs Parsonage's cottage. He had done this, and was expected to return tomorrow to finish off before he was paid. What then? Would his memories ever return? Perhaps Noose could help bring back his memory. Noose did, after all, recognise him and he had in some strange way recognised Noose. He would have to see Noose again, perhaps tomorrow afternoon, if he finished his work at Mrs Parsonage's quicker. Perhaps then he could begin to feel that he was himself, and not just this random unknowing thing.

It was getting late and, with nowhere else to feasibly stay, he resolved to head back to the old girl's shed and sleep in there.

He crept up the lane towards the old girl's cottage, passing Mrs Lester's on the way. Reaching her gate, he opened it gingerly. Before walking through, he looked over at Michael's cottage. It was in darkness. He thought he'd better look around a bit more and turned to glance at Geoff's cottage. That too lay in darkness, though the curtains were not drawn. He continued through the gate, gently closing it. Instead of heading to the front door, he headed across the garden to the side of the cottage. Another much higher gate awaited him. He opened it and, after looking around yet again, walked through it slowly so as to make as little noise as possible. It was also deadly dark and he was relatively unfamiliar with the ground which lay ahead so found it easier to shuffle along somewhat. He found it best to keep a hold of the fence which separated Mrs Parsonage's land from Michael's, as this helped lead the way to the goal of Peter's endeavours: the shed.

Eventually he reached the shed, unlocking it and creeping inside, pulling the door closed on himself and locking it from the inside. He settled down for the night, conserving what little energy his fasting body had left.

In the early hours of the night, the old girl got up for a drink. She, in her flowery nightwear, wobbled into the kitchen and struggled to find the light switch. In need of a glass of water, perhaps, or a trip to the toilet, she was unaware of an outstretched garden fork moving towards her from behind. As she finally found the light switch and flicked it on, the garden fork was thrust into her back. She gave out a perishing squeal of agony. The garden fork was removed.

Mrs Parsonage fell to the floor on her stomach. With her last ounce of strength, she turned back to confront her killer eye to eye.

'You!' she gasped in horror and surprise.

The garden fork came crashing down on her once again. She was now well and truly gone from this savage, savage world. A gloved hand switched the light off. The room was in darkness and Mrs Parsonage was no longer the old girl; she was the old dead girl.

TWO

The early morning sun shone through the shed window onto the sleeping Peter's face. He looked quite serene, quite comfortable, leant against a garden fork and various other tools and bric-a-brac. His work in the garden the previous day could now be more appreciated in this light; it could even be said he had a knack for gardening. The two police officers, Jim and David, stepped out of Mrs Parsonage's back door and walked over to the garden shed. Both peered inside through the window, spotting Peter. They knocked on the glass before trying to open the door. After a bit more noise, Peter slowly began to stir. He yawned, stretching, rubbing his neck where it had been lying against the fork handle. As his wits returned, he turned to see where the noise was coming from. Upon spotting the two officers, he jumped up and, brushing himself down, unlocked the door.

'Good morning, officers. Can I help you?'

David stared long and hard at Peter for acknowledgement, as though he desperately wanted to be recognised. Peter did not reciprocate; he couldn't. He didn't even know himself, let alone anyone else.

'Maybe we can help you. We have reason to believe you may have witnessed or been involved in the murder of one Doris Parsonage,' Jim announced, holding onto the shed door in readiness to throw it in Peter's face were he to try to escape. Peter merely chuckled.

'Good one, very convincing.'

'I don't think you understand the gravity of the situation, Peter,' David came in.

'Yes, you. David, isn't it? You recognised me yesterday at the police station.'

'So you're acknowledging my existence all of a sudden then?' David shot back, his face reddening.

Peter shook hands with them both. 'I believe I must have amnesia,' he concluded. 'Though I have been told my name is Peter Smith by Inspector Noose. I suspect this Mrs Parsonage being dead thing is some kind of joke by him. Am I right?'

'You know the inspector?' Jim asked, flipping his notebook open.

'Of course I do,' Peter yawned, stretching his back. 'I met him yesterday. Well, we may have met before that. I simply can't remember. You could say the inspector knows me.' Peter stepped out of the shed and looked around the garden, rubbing the sleep from his eyes.

'He's in the kitchen right now with forensics, examining Doris Parsonage's battered corpse.'

'Battered like cod?' Peter joked, an unbelieving smirk on his face. Jim and David remained grave. 'I see. You wouldn't mind me going to take a look then, would you?'

Peter pushed past Jim and David and made his way towards the back door. David took hold of Peter's arm and pulled him back.

'It would be rather foolish to allow the suspect to visit the scene of the crime,' David said as he stared at Peter's lips. Peter felt a bit queer and pulled his arm from David.

'Look lads - officers - the joke is beginning to wear a bit thin. What's going on?'

Noose appeared at the back door.

'Dear God! See what I mean, you're in the village five minutes and already we have a murder... and you're on the scene,' Noose exclaimed, rubbing his mouth.

'You're not joking, are you?' Peter replied, realising Mrs Parsonage really had been bumped off. He felt sure he hadn't done it.

'Come and have a look for yourself,' Noose invited, stepping aside for Peter to enter. Jim and David looked at each other in shock.

'But Sir, it's against regulations,' Jim pointed out.

'Regulations! What do I care?'

Peter, shock and disbelief playing equally on his tired face, slowly entered the cottage. Michael was, of course, watching through the window next door. He picked up his cordless telephone and speed-dialled Geoff's number.

'An interesting development,' Geoff replied to Michael from across the road, again sat in his chair. 'Asleep in the garden shed? Perfect.' He sipped at a cup of tea, his legs spread wide apart.

Meanwhile, Mrs Lester walked over to the front window and opened her curtains. The busy presence of police outside did not seem to catch her attention as she refused to acknowledge them and immediately sat down in front of the television.

Mrs Parsonage, lying dead face down in a pool of her own dried blood, was being examined by Lauren. Noose walked in and, standing aside to let Peter pass, looked down at the slim figure of Lauren. Peter walked in very slowly, keeping his eyes firmly on Noose. He gave out a pained sigh.

'Stabbed in the back. I can't be too sure quite yet, but I'd say it was a garden fork. Facial mutilation was with the same weapon.' She looked up at Noose, smiling. 'You've got one sick nutcase on the loose, Inspector.' She and Noose both turned to look at Peter. He took a quick look at the body before smiling at Lauren.

'Hi, Lauren. I'm Peter Smith, I believe. We met briefly yesterday.'

'Congratulations,' she shot back, 'Are your parents proud?'

Peter took in a deep breath before rubbing more sleep from his eyes. Maybe this was how women treated him. He couldn't be sure. He looked back at her, forgetting to register on his face what she had said. She did, however, with her cheeks reddening as she broke eye contact. 'Sorry.' Peter smiled at this apology, trying to keep his eyes on Lauren and not the corpse lying between her legs.

'I was talking to her yesterday. Now she's dead.'

'I think you need a drink, Peter,' Noose offered, stepping over to the worktop and switching the kettle on.

'Do you mind, Inspector? You could be destroying vital evidence.'

'Bloody early this morning isn't it?' Noose continued talking to Peter, yawning. Peter looked around for a clock, forgetting he had a watch.

'The killer was very thorough tidying up,' Lauren relented, turning to and rummaging through what looked like a fishing tackle box. 'Won't find much outside either. It rained heavily last night.'

'There will be something to go on, surely. There always is,' Noose came back at her, suddenly now registering her words.

'Always?' Peter added, a bit puzzled at Noose's surety.

The kettle began to boil.

'Yes, you're right,' Lauren replied, less resigned than before.

'Early morning cleaner stumbled on her body, Peter. Has her own key. She probably did it,' Noose went on, opening a cupboard in search of some cups. Lauren looked again at Peter, but turned away when he looked back. She stood up and began looking up and down the blood-smeared wall.

'Mugs are in that drawer,' Peter pointed out, 'And there's no sign of forced entry?'

'The front door glass. Been smashed in, cleared up and crudely covered over with a badly-cut piece of wood,' Noose explained. Peter scratched his head and turned his back on the body.

'Ah yes, I did that.'

'Figures. That, with everything else, indeed secures your place at the top of the suspects list.' Noose was very matter-of-fact, now searching happily for some teabags.

'It would seem so.'

Lauren looked over at Peter, and in particular his relatively clean, albeit creased and muddy, clothing before looking back at the blood-smeared wall. She nodded to herself. Noose reached into his old creased jacket pocket, bringing out an equally tatty notepad.

'Garden fork. Hmm. You again, Peter.' He scribbled something down in the pad. 'We'll have to put out a search for the weapon.'

'Can I have a look at the front door?' Peter asked, heading towards the corpse through the kitchen before waiting for a reply. Lauren stood in his way, clearing her throat and looking over at a vacant and tired Noose.

'Aren't you in the slightest bit concerned about destroying vital evidence?'

'I'm middle-aged, balding and divorced,' he retorted, 'nothing concerns me anymore.' Upon this announcement, Jim and David entered.

'We're gonna have to start giving statements to the press soon, Sir,' Jim announced, frowning over at Peter who was busy negotiating a path around the corpse.

'Let them come to us I say,' was Noose's lazy reply.

'I'll just nip and take a look at the front door then...' Peter mumbled, ignored. He stepped into the hallway.

The key was already in the lock of the front door. Peter unlocked it and took a look at the wooden panel over the broken window from both sides of the door. He had attached the panel, via screws, from the outside. Perhaps he should have screwed from inside he thought. He looked closer, noticing that one of the screws was missing. A quick scan of the floor beneath his feet showed up the missing screw. He bent down and picked it up. Suddenly Noose appeared behind him.

'Found something?' he queried, not in the slightest bit suspicious of his good friend Peter.

'A screw. This is how your killer got in.'

Noose studied the door as Peter had done.

'They stuck their hand in and unlocked the door on the inside.'

'The key is still in the lock on the inside, look. Very foolish of Mrs Parsonage,' Peter pointed out.

'You'll have to come to the station, you know.' Noose stood straight, slightly above Peter, looking down at him. A flicker of some emotion flitted past his expression, though Peter could not read it. Peter couldn't remember Noose and was thus untrained in understanding his slights of facial movement. He merely nodded to Noose in reply, who stepped closer. 'Listen, Peter...' he started but stopped abruptly as Jim and David entered the hallway. Noose quickly stepped back from Peter and turned to face his officers. 'Ah, Jim, David, could you escort this man to my car please?'

Jim took hold of Peter as David held back, his focus on Noose and Noose's on his. His eyes almost welled up, though he held off as he followed Jim and Peter past Noose and outside.

In the lane Peter was on full display for the neighbours, who watched as he was put into the back of Noose's car. Michael was watching avidly, his eyes like pinpricks at the window as he clutched his phone to his ear.

'They've put him in a car. I think we're safe,' he whispered down the phone. Cynthia, spread-eagled on the sofa watching television, raised an eyebrow.

'What you been up to? What's going on?' Though her curiosity had been raised, she did not make the effort to stand up and look outside. Michael turned to his wife, growling.

'The pigs are snorting about all over the place and all you

do is sit there like a slug watching shit on the TV. Why don't you get off your fat arse and take a look for yourself?' He turned back to see Noose's car driving away as a uniformed officer began cordoning off Mrs Parsonage's front gate.

'It's a wonder they haven't been round here yet,' Cynthia came back at him, a sly streak to her voice, 'asking what we've seen.'

'We haven't seen nothing, right,' her husband shot back, lurching over her.

'Whatever you say, Boss,' she purred, grinning.

'I've had just about enough of you.' He stepped even closer, perhaps a bit too close for a husband to be next to the wife he so loathed.

Noose pulled up outside the police station with Peter, Jim and David in the back. The journey had been rather uncomfortable for David, who gave it all away with a pained and prolonged stare through the window the whole time as Peter, who apparently did not remember him, sat right next to him in the middle without uttering a word about their past. Now they all vacated the vehicle, ambling into the station as Peter seemed to be giving little thought to his predicament. Now may have been the opportune time to question Noose, or even David, about who he actually was. Perhaps they could re-jig his memory by divulging what they knew about him. But he did not ask. He did not even seem to be thinking about asking. There was, in his silence, the air of indifference to that which his current mindset did not have access. Noose and David, in turn, were not eagerly offering up any titbits about Peter's life. Maybe they did not believe his amnesia claim, or maybe they simply hadn't had the time to fully register the implications of him turning up in their lives again and with such a dramatic series of events following.

Inside the station, O'Toole chuckled from behind the reception desk as his eyes caught sight of Peter being led in. Noose marched up to him.

'Anything troubling you, O'Toole?' Noose asked him sternly.

'Not at all Inspector, Sir, just that guy who was in here about his bike.' He could not help himself, he burst out laughing. 'What did he do, steal it off himself?'

Noose did not seem remotely amused. 'We're conducting a murder investigation,' he shot. The easygoing Noose of earlier seemed to be struggling to remain, with an altogether harder, less tolerant Noose coming to the fore at the sight of this irksome officer before him. O'Toole flopped back in his seat, swivelled in it and sighed.

Peter was escorted through the double doors.

'Great, and I'm stuck behind a desk answering the phone,' O'Toole yawned.

In the grey corridor beyond the double doors, Jim and David signalled for Peter to enter an interview room. David opened the door for Peter who simply nodded his gratitude at this afforded luxury. David now bit his lip, his hands shaking as some mental torment overcame him. He held back, no doubt for the purposes of professionalism, but this Peter Smith was tearing his mentality to shreds. Still, there was nothing he could do. He and Jim left Peter and Noose to it, heading back to reception.

The interview room, just like the rest of the station, was grey and dull. It was difficult to tell whether the walls had actually originally been white or a pale blue. Neglect, or simply lack of light from the single barred window up high in the wall across from the door, set this box in a difficult shade.

'Take a seat,' Noose told Peter, but the softness of his voice made it sound more like a suggestion. There were chairs in the centre of the room, around a table with a tape recorder on it. Peter obliged, sitting down as Noose joined him on the opposite end of the table. 'So, how you been keeping?'

'I don't know.'

Noose leant forward, smiling. 'Anything changed on your

part? You still in lodgings?' There was no reply from the puzzled Peter. 'Why don't you just go home, Peter?'

'What do you know about me?' Peter suddenly blurted out, in a way wishing he hadn't asked but not having any control over the urge to want to know.

'Seriously? You seriously cannot remember who you are?' Noose rubbed his chin. 'I thought it another of your games. It still might be.'

Peter looked down at his hands.

'I just appeared on that bike. I appeared from nowhere. I have no memories whatsoever.'

'Hmm.' Noose, wanting to believe him as he always did, took in a deep breath. 'Well, it might not be a bad thing.'

'What do you mean by that?'

'Perhaps you had an accident of some sort,' Noose quickened, altering the direction of discussion. Before they could bond further, the door swung open and in stepped Sergeant Stephen Noble. Young, as always, and with moist eyes that upset every heterosexual man who was unlucky enough to catch a glimpse of them, he stood still for a moment for the two seated men to take in his fine, sharp suit and well-groomed visage. He could have any woman he chose, and the woman he chose would feel lucky to have been bagged by him. 'Ah, Noble. Where have you been?'

'Sorry Sir, I got held up with the new super,' Noble replied with perfect diction. Peter looked at Noble, but Noble did not look back.

'Oh no,' Noose jumped up. 'Where is he now?'

'She, Sir, is in her office down the hallway.'

'Superintendent Williams, isn't it?' Noose's heart sank and also skipped a beat.

'That's right,' Noble replied, oblivious. Noose's jaw almost dropped off. His stone-face tinged even greyer, blending perfectly with the walls. He took a very deep breath indeed.

'I… oh no, please not… Nicola Williams?'

'Got it in one. You already met her or something?'

'I need to pay someone a visit.' He bounded out of the room.

For some unforeseen reason, Peter suddenly thought about sex. He didn't know why and he couldn't decide whether he'd ever even had sex. However, it was enough to make him chuckle to himself. Noble caught wind of this - it sounding more like sniggering - and he now turned to look down upon Peter. Peter felt a little uneasy, as though for a brief nanosecond there shot through his brain a glimmer of memory. Was it about Noble? Surely not; he felt above all else that Noble was the least of his interests. Nevertheless, he stood up. Noble put his hand on Peter's shoulder.

'Stay right where you are.'

'I'm Peter Smith.'

Noble stepped back, blocking the door and folding his arms. 'I know who you are.'

'You've met me before?'

'Not that I recall.' Noble shook slightly, as though a memory he could not remember was just out of reach. He rubbed his temples, sure that he had never met Peter in his life. He had not lived other lives, though. Had he? 'I've read your file.'

'Ah. Have you also read up on Nicola Williams?'

'No.'

'I thought not.' Peter rubbed his teeth with his tongue, wondering what he could say next. He had, in a way, been on auto-pilot, allowing whatever his brain wanted to come out of his mouth. 'You clearly don't know who she is, and what connection she has to Inspector Noose.'

Noble came to sit down across from Peter. 'And you do?' He gave him a long hard stare, sniffing.

'I never said that.'

Noble jumped up, stretched over the table and pointed right in Peter's face. 'Listen up,' he spat, his ever so well-spoken voice strained, 'Noose may be a pushover but I'm not. I don't want the likes of you sending this station even further into the abyss.' Peter, experiencing unease as though for the first time, looked either side of Noble's close face. 'I know who you are and what you do. I've read all about you in the file. You've gotten away with too much.'

Peter pulled away from Noble, pondering upon the precise response. Should he punch him or pat him on the shoulder? He decided neither was adequate, and settled upon no course of action at all.

Meanwhile, Superintendent Nicola Williams was sat at her new desk. Her office was bare, apart from an empty fish tank sitting under the window. Williams was, like Noose, in her forties. She had been, and remained, an attractive woman physically. Mentally, that was in the brain of the beholder. The masculine suit she donned lent itself to sophistication and intelligence, though monkeys could be put in a suit. However, she was a bit more evolved and demonstrated thusly when a knock came at the door. Noose entered. Williams kept her melted brown eyes on her work as she scribbled on some paper.

'How long has it been, Henry?'

Noose closed the door behind him, but stayed standing near it.

'Not long enough,' he snorted. Williams looked up. 'Why are you here?'

'I'm here because Superintendent Hastings has been arrested for fraud. I've been sent to sort out the horrendous mess this place is in. There aren't even any fish in the fish tank!' She slammed her fist on the desk as Noose glanced over at the empty tank. A grim smile played about his lips before he once again frowned. 'And what happens the first day I arrive? An effing murder!' Noose looked surprised. 'Luckily I have a competent Detective Inspector to *fish* out the doer of this dastardly crime… ' She smiled ever so warmly, perhaps a little too warmly.

'I am more than competent, Nicola. You of all people should know that.'

'Superintendent Williams. Or Ma'am.' She chuckled. 'No, not you.' She stood up. 'I'm talking about Norman.'

'Trout? Norman Trout?' Noose, his jaw gaping once more, fumbled.

'Inspector Trout to you, Henry.' She lifted a box off the floor and dropped it on the desk, leafing through the contents. 'And seriously, don't call me Nicola on duty. Sir will be fine!' she chortled.

Suddenly the door swung open, nearly knocking Noose to the floor, and Trout waltzed in. Tall, like Noose, and well-built, he closed the door behind him and, with a jerk, spun around to face Noose.

'Ah, Noose! How's it hangin', old pal? Life in general, not your scrotum!' Trout laughed. He stepped closer to Noose, raising an eyebrow. 'You still have a scrotum?'

'Why wouldn't I have a fucking scrotum?' Noose screamed back, shocking even himself at his outburst. Trout, getting the reaction he wanted, swaggered to Williams' desk.

'Language, Henry,' Williams yelled back.

'You just said the F-word yourself,' was Noose's feeble, child-like excuse.

'No, I said effing.'

'Divorcees are often left scrotum-less, Noose,' Trout went on. 'I don't know, bitten off or something. It's metaphorical, isn't it.' Trout sat on the edge of the desk, Williams glistening behind him.

'Nicola...' Noose paused, 'Superintendent. You cannot seriously be putting this dick on the case.'

'Now there's no need to be like that, old boy,' Trout went on jovially.

'Old boy? There's every need to be like that!' Noose angrily responded.

'Now now, boys!' Williams waded in, chuckling, 'no squabbling.'

Trout studied the fish tank whilst Noose rubbed his temples and paced the room. Suddenly he stopped and pointed at Williams.

'I'm on this case whether you like it or not,' he told her.

'You are not, Henry. This station cannot afford another slip-up.'

'You listen to the super, Noose,' Trout added, his eyes still on the fish tank, 'she speaks words of wisdom.'

'Stay out of this,' Noose screeched. He was perspiring and jittery. He just couldn't believe the situation.

'I'm afraid,' Williams concluded, 'you're not on the case, Henry, and that's final. Sergeant Noble has also been assigned to Norman.' Noose eyed Trout up and down, the wrinkle-making frown of hatred on his face. He turned to face Noose, winking. 'Now go, both of you, out of my sight.' She ushered the men out.

'Does Noble know about this? He didn't mention it,' Noose pondered as Williams opened the door. 'Look, you cannot do this.'

'I can and I have. End of story. Henry, you're on a week's leave, go and enjoy yourself. Take a lady friend on a few nights out.'

'I don't believe this. I was on the scene, you stupid woman. I've started interviewing.' Noose almost stamped his foot in frustrated bewilderment. 'This is madness.'

'The whole notion of life itself is madness!' Williams shot back, sterner than before. 'What can you do?!' With this Noose stormed out, pulling the door from Williams' grasp and slamming it shut. Trout turned to face her, smirking. 'Don't push your luck, Norman. Get to work and solve that murder.' The smirk fell from his face and he left, albeit more quietly than Noose had just done.

Peter was still sat at the table in the interview room. Noble was now stood next to the door, which presently flew open to accommodate Noose's marching entrance.

'Good luck Peter, I'm off the case.'

'What?'

'Oh yes, that's right, Sir,' Noble chipped in, 'I was going to tell you about that.'

'Never mind,' Noose responded, but he would not look at Noble. 'It's happened now. See you around.' Noose abruptly left. Peter stood up to follow, but Noble stepped forward once again. For the first time, worry and concern appeared to fix on Peter's face. It now registered with him that he was being interviewed about a murder. Was he a suspect?

No sooner had Noose exited, Trout sauntered in, closing the door behind him, carrying a police file. He threw it down on the table and, swishing his smart navy jacket aside, sat down across from Peter. Noble came to sit down next to Trout.

'Do you have a solicitor, Mr Smith?' Trout began.

'Not that I am aware of.'

'Oh dear, that is a shame.' Trout spun the file around slowly on the desk, keeping his eyes on Peter.

'Have you?' Peter replied. Trout looked rather displeased. 'Aren't you supposed to record this?' Peter added, glancing down at the tape recorder on the desk.

Angered, Trout yelled, 'Who's in charge here?'

Unaccustomed with procedure, Peter continued with, 'By your tone of voice I take it you are insinuating that you are?'

Trout looked at Noble and bit his lip.

Meanwhile Noose, who was getting a strange feeling of rejection for some reason, burst through the double doors into reception. Lauren stood at the reception desk.

'Some saliva on the carpet doesn't match the victim's DNA. Might be the killer's?' she called across as Noose continued past.

'Not my problem.'

'Huh?'

Noose stopped at the exit, turning briefly. 'This isn't my problem anymore. It isn't my case.' O'Toole lifted his head, licking his lips in readiness for a smart quip. 'Don't say a word,' Noose warned him.

'But that's ridiculous. You were the first on the scene,' Lauren replied.

'Go tell that to the new super.'

'Ah!' Now Lauren understood. 'Well, where's Stephen?'

'Hah! Oh don't worry about lover boy, he's still on the case. He's Trout's bitch now.' Noose pushed the door open with his foot and stormed out.

Lauren seemed bemused and concerned at Noose's out-of-character behaviour, but was not angry. In fact, she was still concerned about the way she'd spoken to Peter earlier. There was something about him, she thought; something she couldn't possibly discuss with Noble.

'Who needs TV eh,' O'Toole chuckled, 'when you can pop down to the local police station.'

'Oh shut up.'

But he continued his chuckling. Lauren now thought about her Stephen, Sergeant Noble, who was still sat next to Trout interviewing Peter. She *was* in love with him, she thought, and this entered her head right now for some girlish reason. But no, it didn't feel girlish. It felt like her mind was trying to convince itself that she was in love with him. She had never questioned it before; it had always just been so. What she felt for Noble existed and seemingly always had done. How they got together, and what they got up to, seemed hazy and far-off though, as though it was just some kind of automatic thing. Something that had been programmed into her. This was too deep, she thought, shaking her head and walking on to continue her work.

'So where did you hide the murder weapon, Peter?' Trout asked him in the interview room. Noble was fixed by his side.

'Once I was done, I carefully cleaned the weapon, which we all know is a garden fork, and put it in the shed. I then, instead of making my getaway, proceeded to spend the night in the shed to ensure capture the following morning when the body would inevitably be discovered.'

'The actual fork used isn't in the shed. We haven't found it yet, you psychopath,' Noble responded, seemingly deeply hurt on a personal level by Peter's out-of-place humour. But Peter didn't know the etiquette.

'I don't think I'm a psychopath, just a very tired, hungry and thoroughly fed-up-o-path.'

'I don't think you realise the gravity of the situation,' Trout pointed out, quite comfortable in his chair, 'It's looking very grave for you. Confess and it will all be over.'

'Very grave? I doubt that. Your evidence, if any, is all circumstantial. Where's the DNA, the fingerprints?' Peter had heard these words before, in the time his brain could not or would not remember. 'You haven't even taken my clothes for examination to see if there's any blood on them. There's no proof whatsoever that I killed Mrs Parsonage.' Peter folded his arms and sat back. Trout grinned, opening the file on the desk.

'Mr Peter Smith. Dear me.' He flicked through the file, comically gaping his jaw in shock and awe at its contents. 'It seems you've pleaded your innocence before.' Even though Peter could not remember what Trout was referring to, he still felt agitated for some reason. Perhaps his subconscious could remember what Trout was referring to, even if his conscious had forced it away. 'Lucy Davies,' Trout purred, looking up from the file.

'Who?' Peter asked, oblivious. He tried to look at the file but Trout flipped it from his view.

'Do *not* play that game with me,' Trout came back at him, fierce, all trace of humour extinguished. 'You were arrested for her murder four years ago.'

'I was?'

'It's in your file, isn't it?' At this Peter remained silent. 'You even stood trial, did you not?' Trout continued. 'You were acquitted, of course. Some last-minute new evidence coming to light. Convenient. The *real* killer was never brought to justice, naturally.' Trout leant closer to Peter. 'Could it be, Peter Smith, that you are indeed the killer of Lucy Davies, and that any last minute piece of evidence was pure trickery?'

'I don't know. I simply don't remember.'

'I guess I'll have to ask your bum chum Inspector Noose. He did, after all, *find* the CCTV tape of you at the railway station at the time Lucy was murdered.'

'I see.'

'Video can be tampered with, Peter, but never mind, *that* murder is not why we are here, is it? We're here because it appears that lightening has struck again. Yet another body turns up in the vicinity of the legendary Peter Smith.' Trout turned to Noble and gave his eyes an over-exaggerated roll.

'I did not kill Mrs Parsonage.' Peter thought for a moment. 'And I did not kill Lucy.' He thought long and hard again but simply could not remember.

'It says in your statements at the time that you claimed to have been engaged to her. Nobody else could back this up, of course.'

'Maybe I was. Maybe I asked her to marry me the last time I saw her, and the only person who saw her afterwards was her killer.'

'That's indeed what you claimed at the time. You asked her in the morning then had a meeting to attend in the afternoon so had to leave her alone. Then when you returned you found her dead. Rather strange; all her friends simply said you had an unreciprocated crush on her.'

'Ah.' Though Peter could not remember, his body appeared to be reacting emotionally to this event in his past. He could feel his heart pounding, his cheeks burning. He clenched his fists.

'Your crush on her resulted in the crushing of her skull.' Trout sat back, smirking. Peter's breathing deepened. 'Dear me, had you indeed married her she'd have only gone from a Davies to a Smith. How low-key.'

Peter could not stop himself. He leapt up, throwing the table aside, grabbing hold of Trout and tossing him against the wall.

Noble pulled him off Trout, twisting his arms behind his back.

'What in God's name is going on in here?' Williams demanded as she appeared at the door in the midst of the commotion.

'We have our murderer,' Trout valiantly announced. 'He just attacked me. Unprovoked.'

'But...' Noble tried to add.

'Unprovoked,' Trout called over him. Noble looked at Trout in disapproval. Peter no longer resisted, easing up in response to Noble's trained strength. He thrust him towards the door. 'That's right,' Trout kept on, straightening his tie. 'Lock him up for a few hours. Calm him down.'

Peter turned to Williams as he was led past her. 'Can I have something to eat, please? I haven't eaten for some time.'

'Life's a tough egg to crack sometimes, isn't it?' Williams remarked, patting him on the back. Peter did not have time to contemplate this as Noble pushed him on. Williams turned to Trout. 'I hope you know what you're doing, for your own sake as much as mine. You wouldn't want me to have to bring Henry back in, would you?'

Trout squinted back.

Meanwhile, Noose was enjoying his time off work by pulling up across the road from Mrs Parsonage's cottage. Eating an apple, he wound his window down and kept his eyes on two police officers standing outside.

Peter found himself in a cell with Neville. Perhaps

remembering their encounter the morning prior, Neville sat staring directly at Peter. His face was expressionless, registering little more than an acknowledgement of animal life. Peter kept his gaze off him, facing instead the cell door. Suddenly Neville cleared his throat.

'You said I had bad breath,' he uttered, almost with a touch of sadness. Peter looked up to the ceiling, wiping his moustache stubble. Before he had to respond, the serving hatch in the cell door opened. Lauren's face pointed in.

'Peter?'

'Lauren?' He stood up and walked to the door.

'I believe you Peter. I believe you're innocent. Whoever killed Mrs Parsonage would have been covered in blood, on their clothes and face. Clearly you haven't washed your face for a while.'

'Clearly.'

'They say you're being held for breaking and entering, assaulting a police officer... and possibly murder.'

'Oh dear.'

'Your DNA is on the database. It doesn't match with anything found near the victim.'

'Does that mean I'm officially innocent?' Peter played with a wry smile.

'Maybe.'

Neville started whistling. Peter turned to see that Neville had now taken up his space on the bed and was lying flat on his back with his hands supporting his head.

'I am dead!' Neville called out, flopping his tongue out of his mouth and rolling his eyes back.

'Look, is there anything I can get you?' Lauren asked, getting Peter's attention back. She didn't need to try too hard for that.

'Anything remotely edible would be nice.'

'I'll see what I can do.' She smiled before closing the hatch. Peter stood upright and turned to face Neville once more. He thought of Lauren. It was as though she had never smiled before, and yet had always been smiling. Her face seemed so new and unused to him.

'You're in there, my son,' Neville called out.

'Sure,' Peter, unbelieving, replied, raising an eyebrow. Neville, deadly serious, jumped up.

'I AM DEAD!' he screamed, flailing his arms.

'What does that even mean? How can you be dead?' Peter questioned the fool.

'I,' Neville screamed once again, 'AM DEAD!' before he flopped back onto the bed in exhaustion.

And, in the very place where bicycle man had first appeared from nowhere the previous day, there was all of a sudden another figure that was not there before. Unlike Peter, however, Tony was stood still and knew exactly who he was and what he had to do. He had to kill Peter Smith. For some reason.

THREE

Noose wrapped the apple core up in a tissue and shoved it in the glove box before fixing his stare once more on the two police officers stood outside Mrs Parsonage's cottage. One was surveying the front door, before opening it and calling the other inside. This was Noose's chance, who jumped out of his car, carrying a box, and darted across the lane to Mrs Lester's cottage. Swinging the gate open, he strode up the path and rang the door bell. Mrs Lester, seemingly out of breath, opened the door almost immediately.

'You just caught me as I came to check for the post, else I'd have been quite some time,' she gasped.

'Are you not well?'

'Oh good lord, no! Heavens above.' She squinted, suspicious. 'Are you here to murder me?'

Instead of a weapon, Noose brandished his warrant card. Mrs Lester squinted further at it. All this squinting revealed the origins of her facial lines. That and too many years.

'I am Inspector Noose. I'm,' Noose took a breath, 'working on the case, Mrs Lester.'

'Dreadful business, isn't it Inspector?'

'What is?'

'The murder of Mrs Parsonage! Poor old bat.'

'Oh yes, quite dreadful.' Noose, afraid of being spotted, kept looking around behind himself. He was quite safe.

'I don't understand why nobody has come to see me sooner,' Mrs Lester explained.

'Well, we are busy down at the station.' Noose edged forward, suggesting that he should be invited inside.

'Because I know who the murderer is!'

Mrs Lester wobbled into her living room as Noose followed closely behind. He looked around at this rather airless box. For him, unused to such zones, it felt like he had suddenly fallen into a vacuum and he had to clear his throat to ensure there was enough space in it to take in as much air as possible. What air there was.

'Cup of tea? I hate mugs.'

'No thank you, Mrs Lester. I need information.'

'Oh yes, please, sit down.'

Noose sighed, but complied. 'What exactly do you know?' he pushed.

She too sat down, opposite Noose, and put her feet up on a small padded stool.

'Corns. On my feet.' A pause. Noose rubbed his nose. 'What I know is indeed intriguing. Are you all ears?' Noose did not reply. 'Are you all ears?' she demanded.

'Yes, of course. Please, go on,' Noose encouraged, hiding his frustration at her lack of speed.

'You see, Mrs Parsonage was going to change her will, leaving all of her money to a cat sanctuary.'

'A cat sanctuary?'

'A cat sanctuary. Where they look after unwanted cats.'

'Yes, I know what a cat sanctuary is. But what does that have to do with her murder?'

'My point is, Inspector, that her son Roger Parsonage was effectively going to be cut out of said will, thus receiving nothing.' Impressed with herself, Mrs Lester stretched her neck and tilted her head sideways as she closed her eyes.

'I see. And exactly how, pray tell, did you come by this information?'

'I'm an old woman, I get to know a lot of things with a little curtain twitching.'

'Very well.' Noose stood up. 'Oh yes, before I forget.' He opened the box he was carrying and pulled out a small device. 'This is an attack alarm. It is wired straight to the police station and my car. If you're attacked, we'll know all about it. It's silent, so you won't provoke an attack if an intruder does... Well, I don't want to worry you.'

Mrs Lester took the device and studied it.

'That is a comfort for a frail old woman such as myself. Do you fear more murders may occur then?'

'I can't say, but it's better to be safe than sorry.'

'Of course.'

'Oh yes, just press this button if you are attacked.' Noose pointed the button out to her.

'Thank you Inspector, I can rest a little easier now.'

Peter was stood at the side of the door as Neville sat on the bed, staring that vacant stare.

'You have no idea, do you?' Neville whispered.

'What?'

'You really must read it. It'll reveal you to yourself.'

'Read what? What will?' Peter was more annoyed than intrigued. He thought - no, he knew - that Neville was just a fool.

'I've read it. I tracked Noose down, never thought I'd come across you though. You're Peter Smith, aren't you?'

'So I've been told.'

The cell door unlocked, opened and an ageing police officer entered, carrying two trays of dinners. Though hungry, Peter instinctively grabbed him from behind and sent the dinners flying into the air. He threw the startled man to the floor and darted out of the cell, slamming the door shut just as the doddery officer tried to regain his wits. However, Peter turned the key in the lock and ran down the corridor. The officer's yells echoed down it as he began banging for help on the metal fortress.

'Back up! Back up! Escaping prisoner! Stay right where you are!'

His demand fell on deaf ears as Peter continued on his way. He heard Jim and David ahead and dropped back into an alcove just in time to see them sprint through the double doors from reception. As they approached him, he jumped out and bent down in front of them. Unable to stop in time, they both tripped over him and fell in a heap on the floor. Kicking the double doors open, Peter shot through reception. O'Toole yawned as Jim and David headed after him.

Peter kept going down the road and around the corner. He turned to see who, if anyone, was after him. He slowed down and ended up walking at a normal pace as he realised they had failed to catch up.

'You stupid nancy!' Jim yelled at David, before looking somewhat embarrassed. 'Sorry. You stupid,' he paused to think. 'Clown.'

'Shut it!' David replied, playful, wanting to laugh off any awkward slight.

'You go left,' Jim decided, 'I'll go right.'

'So you're giving the orders now?'

'Just do it, for God's sake.'

The two separated and went in search of the escapee. Now standing across the road, looking on at the station, was Tony.

That was Jim and he has clearly forgotten himself, Tony thought of the different life of Jim. It will be much easier for me to be the one to kill Peter, he surmised. Sensing he was being watched, he turned to look behind himself. There was nobody, not even his best mate *Tony*. That was the other Tony, the Tony he sometimes confusingly thought wasn't him. He was a little nervous after the run-in with The Dealer earlier, though he had succeeded in overcoming him that time. Now he was back in reality, the only one of the four who knew himself. He knew he was Tony and he knew he had to kill Peter Smith. He had a new independent strength and an advantage over the others.

Noose checked his watch as he stood facing Michael's door. Michael soon opened the door. Wearing pyjamas, he stood silently and stared at Noose.

'Yes?' Noose spoke awkwardly, 'Michael Evans?'

'Yes.'

'I'm Inspector Noose, here about the unfortunate turn of events that lead to the brutal demise of Mrs Parsonage next door.' Noose looked past Michael and into the hallway. It felt cold; ghostly. Something was off.

'Oh dear, the bitch is dead,' Michael replied, compassionless. In fact, devoid of any emotion. 'Come in Inspector, Moose.' He stood aside.

'Noose. It's *Noose*.'

'Noose? Like the rope? Nordic name, is it?'

'Could be.' He stepped inside. Michael slowly closed the door behind, looking over at Geoff's cottage as he did so.

Noose entered the living room, closely followed by Michael.

'Do you sleep naked, Inspector?'

'I beg your pardon?' Noose was rather taken by surprise. He turned to face his questioner.

'I haven't slept naked since Cynthia started gaining weight. I liked it at first, the weight. Kinda fed her, you know.'

'I see.'

Michael stepped up close to Noose, undoing the top button on his pyjama top. Noose scratched his head, turning sideways. Michael scratched his genitalia.

'A man's home is his castle,' Michael added.

'Is it?'

'Mrs Parsonage caused a lot of heartache for my wife and

I.' He once again stepped up close to Noose, who had managed to manoeuvre himself away slightly. 'Let me cut to the chase, Inspector. Had I killed that wrinkly old hag, I would have been the first to admit it.'

'I was not accusing you, Mr Evans.' Noose eased himself away a fraction. Michael suddenly stepped away, doing his button back up. He walked across the room.

'I'd have happily murdered her had somebody else not beaten me to it. I'd be hailed a hero in this shit-hole.'

'Is that so?'

'The question for you is not who *did* kill her, but who didn't. You give me the name of one person in this neighbourhood without a motive and I'll eat my hat... and I don't even own a hat.'

Noose caught sight of the binoculars and notepad on the windowsill. 'Where is your wife Cynthia, Mr Evans?'

Michael scratched his nose. 'Dunno. She left early this morning. Hasn't returned yet. I take it as a blessing, Inspector, I really do. Perchance she's run away after slaying Mrs Parsonage?' He grinned, almost dancing as he moved back towards Noose, eager to implicate his wife in the slaying.

'Perchance.'

Williams sat at her desk with her head in her hands. Jim, David, Trout, Noble and the old police man were stood in a line, facing her.

'You do realise how close this pitiful station is to being closed down?' she sighed, almost holding back tears.

'They can't close down a police station!' David exclaimed.

'Silence, you buffoon!' she shot. David turned his head away and mouthed a swear word. She did not see. 'Trout, why are these inept twits working here?'

Trout stepped forward. 'Because they're trained police officers.'

Williams stood up, prompting Trout to gulp and stand back.

'*Because* everything about this station is stupid! For crying out loud, what is the serving hatch in the cell door for?'

'So you don't have to open the door?' Jim pointed out, desperate to feel impressed with himself.

'So you *don't* have to open the door!!! Then why in God's name did this pitiful excuse for a police officer open the damn door?' she pointed at the doddery one who stood sulking, his arms folded.

'Technically, the trays the food are served on are half an inch too wide to fit through,' David remarked.

'I'm this close to serving *you* through a little hatch,' she yelled, making a gesture of small size with her finger and thumb. David eyed her hand up, wondering what it had touched in its time. 'Oh, just get out. Get out of my sight, the lot of you.'

Jim, David and the old one walked solemnly away down the corridor as Trout and Noble loitered just outside Williams' office.

'I'm this close to serving *you* through a little hatch!' David whined in a girly voice. 'I'm this close to drowning her in that fish tank,' he continued in his own voice. Jim laughed. They left the old one to his withdrawn disappointment as they headed for reception.

Trout put his hand on Noble's chest. 'You do know what this means, Noble? We now have a murderer on the loose.'

Noble brushed his hand off. 'According to DNA found at the scene, Peter isn't our killer.'

Trout turned his back on Noble and rubbed at his face. 'DNA, huh! You saw how he went for me, there was evil in his eyes.'

'You did provoke him, Sir.'

Trout spun around to face Noble and pointed right in his face. 'He attacked me for no reason whatsoever. That is how it happened, right?'

'I know what I heard.'

Trout stormed off down the corridor. 'And that was nothing. I'm hungry, time for food. Come along, Sergeant.'

In reception Jim and David came face to face with Tony. The big man looked suspicious and Jim and David approached him with caution.

'Can I help you?' Jim asked Tony.

Tony did not reply. He could not talk.

'Reporter, eh?' Jim decided, pushing him aside. 'Peter's gone. Print that, why don't you? Escaped.'

Tony took hold of Jim's arm but he pulled away from his grip. 'Touch me again and you'll spend the night in the cells.' Jim and David continued on their way, leaving Tony to his devices. Perhaps Jim is playing a game, Tony thought. Perhaps he knows exactly who he is and who I am. Tony's best mate *Tony* appeared.

'Perhaps we should kill Jim first,' he told Tony.

Peter crept over Mrs Parsonage's garden fence and ducked behind the shed, edging slowly along it to peep out at the cottage. Happy he had not been spotted, he made his way along the side of the garden under the fence to avoid detection. He reached the back door and opened it carefully, sticking his ear in to hear for any voices inside. Nothing. He gingerly slipped in, closing the door behind himself.

At the front of the cottage, Noose was getting into his car as Noble drove up beside him. He was alone.

'Ah! I've been caught,' Noose said in a sweet whine. Noble jumped out of his car and approached the Inspector.

'Your pal has escaped.'

'Come again?' Noose stood straight, leaning on his car door.

'Peter Smith, he's escaped from the cell.'

'He ain't changed one bit,' Noose chuckled.

'I'm glad you find it funny.' Noble shook his head in disappointment at his superior. 'They're not liking it much down at the station. There's a suspected murderer on the loose and we've got a bunch of reporters drooling over it all.'

'Peter isn't the killer, that's Trout putting ideas in your head. Where is he by the way, your new best buddy trout face? Shouldn't he be taking swabs for DNA?'

Noble shook his head again. 'Having brunch. He's a bit useless, to be honest.' At this Noose sneered in agreement. 'Trout provoked Peter. Mentioned a Lucy from years back.'

'Trout is such a prick.'

'Look, I have my money on Williams putting you back on the case. Hell, Trout hasn't even interviewed any neighbours yet or looked into other suspects. He's even stopped the search for the garden fork.'

'There are plenty of suspects. Michael and Cynthia Evans, to name two, and she's missing today. That Mrs Lester mentioned Mrs Parsonage's son, said he was pressuring her not to change her will. She was gonna cut him out and give it all to some cat home or something.' Noose shook his head, rubbing his chin. 'I don't know.' He started across the lane towards Mrs Parsonage's cottage. 'Come on, let's go and have another look at the scene.'

Noble followed.

Peter was inside, a wall cupboard door open as he munched on a cake from within. He rummaged through several other food products, picking them up and pushing them aside. There was nothing as good as cake. He turned momentarily to look at the blood-splattered walls and red-soaked carpet, rubbing his top lip and sniffing indifferently. He heard the front door opening and the voices of Noose and Noble. Startled, and with half the cake still in his mouth, he looked around for a quick hiding place. Shutting the cupboard door, he dived under the kitchen table. Noose and Noble entered. Peter watched as their shoes, Noose's dull and Noble's shiny, pulled up right by him.

'Of course,' Noose laughed, 'she was quite the love machine back in the day.'

'Oh yes? Go on,' Noble encouraged.

'She'd have kept going all day long if I'd allowed it... I got ulcers with the stress of it all.'

'And she ends up your boss!' Noble now too was overcome with laughter. Peter tried his best to swallow a piece of cake in silence.

'And this is between you and me, Stephen. That woman helped break up my marriage.'

'I'm not surprised. You must have been banging her all day by the sounds of things.'

'Half a morning with Norman Trout and you're already referring to love-making as *banging her*. Dear me!'

'I'm just saying,' Noble pointed out, holding back more laughter.

'Well don't,' Noose came back, stern for a second. 'The teeth marks have only just healed!' Both rolled about with laughter. 'Come on, let's check the other rooms.'

Noose and Noble walked back the way they had come. Peter crept out from under the table and, seeing that the two men had gone far enough away, stepped over to the fridge and opened it. In it he found a bottle of apple juice which he pocketed before leaving.

He crept out of the back door, eyeing his surroundings with suspicion. Even the grass now looked at him with concern, perhaps afraid it would be slaughtered with the mower. But Peter wasn't here to work. He now thought of the work he had done and not been paid for. Mrs Parsonage's death was indeed an inconvenience. The wind changed direction and he caught the faint noise of an argument coming from Michael's cottage next door. Peter made for the dividing fence, climbing over it as quietly and quickly as he could. As he dropped into a bush the other side, he removed the apple juice from his pocket and unscrewed the lid. He sipped it, not enjoying it much, as he crouched down and listened in on the unfolding argument within the building.

Inside, Michael and Geoff were in the midst of a rather heated, if not steamy, debate. Michael had been distracted and was looking out of the back window.

'What are you doing now?' Geoff demanded of the man half his weight and height. He tried to pull Michael away.

'Keep your voice down, I thought I heard something. The place is swarming with filth.'

Geoff swung Michael around to face him. 'I don't care if it's swarming with shit,' Geoff howled, 'if you've done anything to Cynthia, I'll-'

'You'll what?' Michael barked back, 'Stab me with a garden fork as well?'

Geoff turned his back on Michael and walked away. 'I did *not* kill that old bitch.'

'You don't think, if I'd killed Cynthia, I'd have chosen a more convenient time when the place wasn't buzzing with pigs?'

Geoff turned back to Michael. 'I haven't seen her leave the house this morning, so where is she?'

'How should I know? You seem to care more about her than I do... Why's that Geoff, eh, why the hell is that?' Michael jabbed his finger into Geoff's chest, who promptly thumped him in the face in response. Michael flew across the room and landed on his dining table, tossing over a bowl of bananas. 'You'll pay for this Geoff,' he moaned, clutching his bloodied nostrils.

'No Michael, *you'll* pay.' With this, Geoff stormed out. Michael wiped away the blood from around his mouth as he got up, turning once again to the back window as though he sensed somebody's presence outside. But he could not see the silent, unmoving Peter. Peter, bemused and suspicious of the commotion he had been privy to, sipped more on the sour apple juice. Deciding he definitely didn't like it, he poured the rest away in the bush.

In the front, Noose and Noble headed down Mrs

Parsonage's garden path, chatting and joking. They hadn't heard the commotion next door and failed to register Geoff jogging across the lane back to his cottage. A car screeched up the lane and slammed to a halt at Noose and Noble's feet as they reached the gate. Williams leapt out of the passenger side as Trout casually stepped from the driver's side and folded his arms on the roof, a smirk on his face.

'I should have known!' Williams stormed at the men.

'You *should*?' was Noose's flippant response. He kept walking, heading to his car and opening the door. Noble stayed stood in front of her.

'I knew I'd find you here.'

'That's what I said,' Noble whimpered.

'Shut up!' Williams demanded, turning to Noose. 'You're off the case, Henry, go home or I'll suspend you.'

'My house is empty, Nicola. I have nothing left but my work. Do not take that from me as well.'

'Touching!' Trout mocked. Williams turned to him.

'If you don't have anything useful to say, just shut up.'

Trout's grin disappeared.

'Look, I haven't got time for this. I have a murder investigation to solve and not even my superior officer is going to stop me.' Noose got in his car.

'At that you're quite wrong. Drop this or you'll be suspended indefinitely.'

'Fine, okay. I give in, you dominate once again.' Noose looked over at Noble, who tried not to laugh. 'I'll go home, Superintendent. Yes, I'll go home.' He started the ignition and slammed the car door shut. 'Farewell!' he called as he sped off, waving with two fingers.

'As for you, Stephen,' Williams turned to him, 'I am most disappointed. Good job Norman came to tell me of your disappearing act in the café.' Noble stared at Trout, who once again smiled slyly back. 'Norman, in the car.' Reluctantly Trout got back in, as did Williams. 'Come along Sergeant, stop messing about.'

'What about taking DNA samples?' Noble questioned, staying still by Mrs Parsonage's gate. He knew what Noose would do.

'We let them stew first. Besides,' she spoke out of the open window, 'we need to put all our energies into finding Peter Smith. His escape is just one too many blunders for my liking.'

'Lauren found some DNA at the scene. Peter isn't a match. If we take samples from the neighbours, we might pinpoint who-'

'Just get in the car, Stephen,' she interrupted. Noble gave up, getting in the back. The car pulled away.

'And what if Peter comes back here?' Noble pointed out.

'He may be a lunatic,' Trout laughed, 'but he's not stupid.'

As the car turned out of the lane, Peter appeared, crouching, from behind a hedge. Soon enough, Noose drove back up the opposite end of the lane and stopped in the exact spot he was in before. Peter spotted him, scurrying towards the car.

'Suspend me! Huh. Yes, I'll get myself suspended, Nicola, if that's what you want,' Noose whinged to himself. Suddenly his passenger door opened and Peter got in.

'Talking to yourself, Inspector?'

Noose was initially startled, but relaxed once he saw it was Peter. 'I never thought I'd say this Peter Smith, but it's good to see you. About the only friendly face around these parts at the moment.'

'Friendly face? You mean we're friends?'

'Hmm,' Noose pondered. 'Pass me the binoculars out of there, would you?' He pointed at the glove box. Peter opened it and passed him the binoculars. 'These are handy for spying on people.'

Peter saw the kitchen paper parcel and picked it up to investigate. In it he discovered the rotting remains of the apple core. He wrapped it up again and put it back. Noose handed the binoculars back to him, so he took a look through them.

'Did I kill Lucy Davies?' he suddenly blurted out, lowering the binoculars from his eyes and looking directly at Noose.

'Oh God.' Noose rubbed his temples. 'No, you did not.'

'Then who did?'

'I don't know. Nor do you, Peter. Well, the Peter I know doesn't. The Peter with a memory.'

'They never did find her killer?'

'No. Though we looked, Peter, you and I both looked. Then...' but Noose trailed off.

'Then what?'

'It was just too much for you, Peter. Lucy wasn't the first.'

'The first?'

'There was another girl as well, before her. Perhaps the trauma has only just caught up with you and this is why you're blocking all the memories.'

Before they could continue, the car police radio came on. It was Jim's voice, giving Williams, Trout and Noble information. Noose and Peter sat back and listened.

'Superintendent, Inspector, guess who's just dropped by the station for a visit?'

'We're not here for guessing games, Jim. Spit it out,' Trout demanded.

'Roger Parsonage. He's Mrs Parsonage's son.'

'We're well aware who Roger Parsonage is. Is he there now?' Williams chipped in.

'He sure is. Oh, and guess what, we've been in touch with Mrs Parsonage's solicitor.'

'Have you indeed?'

'You're never going to believe this...'

'If it's coming from a solicitor, I don't suspect I will,' Williams quipped.

'Well, get this. Her solicitor says she was about to change her will, cutting her son out of it.'

'Indeed fascinating. A motive if ever I heard one.'

Noose turned to Peter. 'That's exactly what Mrs Lester told me.'

Roger, middle-aged and gaunt, sat at the table in the interview room with his head in his hands. Jim and David were facing him, their hands on their lips and their elbows on the table.

'I hear my mother has been murdered, so I come down to the local police only to find that *I'm* the one being accused of her murder,' Roger, distraught, wept.

'You must admit, it does look a bit suspicious,' Jim pointed out. Suddenly, for the first time he could remember, his eye twitched. It was an odd, uncontrollable sensation, and he rubbed at it. Luckily, he thought, nobody had seen it happen and he quickly forgot about it.

'So next time one of my family is killed, maybe I should stay at home doing cartwheels… Should I?'

'It's a little suspicious that you just happened to be in the area when your mother was murdered, despite actually living a hundred miles away,' David added.

'It's also a little suspicious that, on the eve of your mother's will change to cut you out of it, she was murdered,' Jim went on.

'This is rubbish!' Roger cried, shaking his head in shock.

'Why was your mother about to cut her only child out of her will, Mr Parsonage? And who was she about to make the new executor?' David pushed the weeping wreck.

Roger suddenly stopped crying and lifted his head to look up at the two officers. 'Are you two really the inspectors around here?' he asked them.

'Interview suspended,' David suddenly announced, standing up. Jim remained seated until David knocked him and signalled to stand up.

Jim and David stood facing Williams, Trout and Noble in reception. O'Toole listened in from behind his desk.

'You let him go? You just let him walk out of here?' Williams screeched.

'Ah,' was Jim's weak response as he scratched his cheek and looked at David.

'I see. So, let me get this straight. You let a murder suspect just walk out of here before we could even interview him?'

'When you put it like that,' Jim responded, nudging David.

'That is correct,' David acknowledged, sulking.

Williams threw her arms up in the air and flopped down onto a chair. 'We're doomed, we're all doomed!' she sighed.

'He did say he'd be back later,' Jim tried to console her.

'Yes, after he's concocted an elaborate alibi!'

'He said his wife had been with him when the murder must have taken place.'

'Did he! Well, where is she, then? Maybe she was holding his mother down as he thrust the fork in.' Williams shook her head in despair.

Jim, pleased with himself for some reason, folded his arms. 'Back home,' he answered, 'Roger left to drive down here early morning.'

'So she's still at home? And this is a hundred miles away?' Williams stood up.

'Yes.'

'We want a statement - in person. Jim, David, you two can drive down there and get it. If he is the murderer, they might already have sorted out his alibi.' She paced up and down, counting on her fingers. 'We want statements from neighbours… Who saw him leave early this morning? Did he leave yesterday? Could he have been here to kill his mother?' Jim and David both sighed in tandem. 'Come on, move, move… Time is not on our side here.'

Noose and Peter were still sitting in his car across from Mrs Parsonage's cottage. Noose was looking out of the side window over at Michael's cottage whilst Peter appeared to be asleep. Suddenly, Noose nudged him.

'Wha... oh,' was Peter's dazed response.

'Look,' Noose pointed towards Michael's abode. Michael was busy reversing out of his driveway. 'He put something in the boot.' The car drove past. 'We're gonna follow him.'

Suddenly, Geoff drove past as well.

'Looks like we've been beaten to it,' Peter remarked. As Noose turned his ignition on, another car pulled up at Michael's cottage. Roger stepped out. 'Who's this?'

Roger jumped out and ran up to Michael's front door. Looking around, he took a key from his pocket and unlocked the door.

'I suggest you go and find out,' Noose suggested. Peter obliged, stepping out of the car just in time for it to pull away in search of Michael and Geoff. He made for Michael's cottage, knocking on the door. There was no answer. He checked the door; it opened. In he went, somehow unaware of fear, shutting the door behind himself.

'Knock, knock, anybody in?' he called out down the hallway. He stepped into the living room to find Roger rooting around in a drawer. 'Find anything interesting?'

Roger turned to face him. 'Who are you?'

'I was just gonna ask you the same thing.'

Roger kept rooting. 'Michael killed my mother. I'm looking for evidence.'

'In a drawer?'

'You gonna call the cops, then?'

'No I'm not, Mr Parsonage.'

'So it seems we're both trespassing.'

'Trespassing? You have your own key.'

'Long story.' Roger stopped briefly, looking sideways.

'You'll have to fill me in sometime.' Peter pondered what to do, or say, next. The automatic speech he had so relied upon until now seemed to be failing him. 'So Michael killed your mother? What makes you so sure?' he found from somewhere, quite happy with it.

'Who the hell are you, anyway?' Roger turned to face him, looking him up and down.

'Your mother was about to change her will, making sure you didn't get anything.'

'What? I don't know what you're on about,' was Roger's seemingly genuine response.

'I think you do, Roger. The only thing standing in the way of you getting your hands on your mother's assets was her. And now she isn't here, is she?' Peter stepped closer, which was the wrong thing to do. Roger turned back to the drawer and grabbed hold of a decorative, and very sharp, letter opener. He waved it in Peter's face with intent.

'You saying I murdered my own mother?'

Peter, looking at the letter opener, seemed not to fear it. For some reason, he felt safe. As though he could not be harmed. 'I don't say anything. I merely insinuate.'

'You some kind of private investigator?'

'You could say that. I dig for the truth. In fact, your mother hired me. She, erm, she was suspicious of Michael.' Peter kept thinking on his feet. He was good at making things up. 'Thought her life was in danger.'

Roger slowly lowered the letter opener. 'I see. Now we're getting somewhere.' He removed a folded piece of paper from his pocket and handed it to Peter. 'I found this in the drawer just before you got in. Recognise it?'

Peter opened it. On the paper was the message 'YOU ARE EVIL. YOU WILL PAY' made from magazine cut-outs.

'Recognise it?' Peter questioned, confused.

Roger snatched it back and folded it up again. 'My mother received one saying the same thing. Surely she showed you?' He looked suspiciously at Peter.

'Of course.'

'Well, this is proof that Michael made and sent it.'

'Why is it?'

'Well he was obviously gonna send this one as well, but then he must have snapped and killed her sooner than he had planned.'

Peter snatched the paper off Roger this time. 'Maybe he was sent this too, by the same person who sent it to your mother.'

'I hadn't thought of that.' Roger sat down, his face reddening with grief. 'Michael must be the killer, though.'

'I'm keeping an open mind myself. I'll take this to the police.'

'I'll keep it for now.' Roger jumped up and snatched it back, pocketing it.

'What about the man across the road?'

'Geoff?'

'Yeah, what's his story?'

'Cynthia has been the source of many an argument around here,' Roger started. Peter gestured for him to carry on. 'You're a private investigator, you should know all this already.' He pushed past Peter, ready to leave.

'Maybe I do.' But, Roger was gone and Peter wasn't keen enough to go after him.

Noose was in hot pursuit of both Michael and Geoff. Their cars were quite a way in front and Noose found it tricky winding in and out of the busy traffic. Traffic policing had never really been his thing; he was interested in the proper stuff, as he saw it - the rapes and murders. He had dealt with plenty of those in his time. The gap between his car and their cars widened even more and all of a sudden traffic lights put paid to his plans. He thumped the steering wheel, looking sideways at an elderly couple in the car next to his. Dismay was on their faces. Noose forced a smile through gritted teeth.

Tony watched as Jim and David drove off. He had missed his chance to do away with Jim first. Never mind; Peter Smith's death would have to come sooner than planned. It would be easy, though, because Peter Smith didn't know who Tony was and wasn't expecting to be murdered by him.

FOUR

Noose marched straight through reception and through the double doors. O'Toole, sitting at his desk as ever, yawned and checked his watch. Noose wasn't interested in seeing him. He wanted Williams. He *really* wanted Williams and didn't even knock on her office door before barging in. The woman of his intentions appeared to be startled and attempted to sit up straight as she bundled something into her desk drawer.

'What on Earth do you think you're doing?' she shot at him, shutting the drawer.

'Let's cut to the chase here, you've taken me off the case because you can't handle seeing me,' Noose blurted out.

'What are you on about now?'

'Go on, tell me you don't still have feelings for me.'

'Oh, what childish nonsense. Get out!' She stood up and strode past Noose, opening her office door. 'Go on, you're off the case. End of story.'

Noose pulled the door from her grip and closed it. She found herself standing against it, facing him. He moved in closer and their eyes met. Passion seized the pair and they thrust their lips on each other. She took hold of his hand and placed it on her bum. He squeezed her bum, running his fingers down its centre and between her legs. Suddenly a knock came at the door. Noose and Williams jumped apart just as Trout opened the door and stuck his head in.

'Someone's just seen Noo-' he saw Noose for himself. 'Oh, I see.'

'Didn't your mother ever teach you to wait outside until you were invited in?' Williams blasted as she adjusted her hair. Noose straightened his tie. Trout stared long and hard at the pair.

'Why do I bother?!' he finally asked himself, slamming the door shut. Noose turned to Williams once more. But this time she was having none of it and opened the door with more intent.

'Just go. I don't want to see you here again,' she told him without making eye contact. Noose reluctantly, and uneasily, left. She, shaking somewhat, closed the door again and flopped against it as she let out a huge gasp of air.

In the corridor outside, Trout was stood, arms folded, facing Noose. Noose merely walked past, rather slowly, staring back with a grin. Once he had gone, Trout knocked on Williams' door once again.

Peter was walking along the pavement looking somewhat, if not thoroughly, fed up. A car drove past and stopped before reversing back to him. He was worried, by now realising he wasn't in the safest position in the world, until the passenger side electric window went down to reveal Lauren in the driving seat.

'Well, well, well if it isn't Mr Naughty,' she called out jovially. A bit too jovial, perhaps, considering the circumstances in which they had met. Peter stopped, happy.

'I suppose you're going to escort me back to the station now?'

'If that's what you want.'

'Not particularly. I'm innocent.' Peter started walking off. Lauren trailed him in her car.

'You've certainly made yourself look guilty by escaping,' she pointed out.

'Well, I'm sure it'll all come out in the wash soon enough, when the real killer is revealed.'

'Not too far away, by all accounts. Look, where are you headed?'

Peter stopped again. 'Dunno really. Haven't got anywhere *to* go. Nowhere I can remember, anyway.'

'Jump in,' she offered, 'looks like you need a wash.'

Peter opened the car door and got in. 'Nice of you to notice.'

'You can come back to mine if you like and freshen up.'

'You're not afraid I'll try and kill you?'

'That's the first time I've ever heard that chat-up line.'

'Oh no, it wasn't a… Oh, never mind.'

Lauren smiled, pulling the car away and heading off. 'Just remember,' she concluded, 'don't try anything funny. I know karate.'

'I'll keep that in mind.'

Lauren lived in a flat. It was small but sufficient. Everything was within easy reach of everything else - not that everything wanted to grab everything else.

'You really are looking rough, you know,' Lauren went on, unlocking the flat door to let the stranger inside with her. But he wasn't really a stranger, was he? Somehow, Lauren felt this. Subconsciously, she felt she knew Peter.

'That's really lifted my spirits, thank you.'

She placed a bag down on a table near the door. 'And that beard thing, or whatever it is, has just gotta go.'

'You think?' Peter questioned, spotting a mirror on the wall. He eyed up what was quickly turning into a beard on his chin and neck. 'I thought it was quite stylish.'

'In which century?'

Peter examined the rest of his face, paying close attention to his eyes.

'Peter Smith?'

By now, Lauren was in the living room. 'Look, I've got some old clothes you can wear whilst yours are being washed… Or burned!'

'Am I really that bad?' Peter asked as he followed her into the living room. She paused, blushing somewhat, looking back at him.

'Go and have a shower, put your dirty clothes in the washing basket and I'll go and fish out something for you to wear. I'm sure they'll fit.'

'What, your clothes?'

'No. Not unless you want to?'

Peter could not tell whether she was serious or not, so laughed. She too laughed and that was that.

Not long afterwards, Peter found himself rummaging through the bathroom cupboard with a towel wrapped around his waist. The lingering pong had diminished and the brown suit was nowhere to be seen. He felt like a new man all over; a new man with no past he could remember and with a future he need not even consider. He took out a brand new toothbrush and opened it. Whilst cleaning his teeth, he came across a woman's pink electric razor and surveyed his beard in the mirror. He turned to the clothes hanger on the door. A smart black suit awaited him, all pressed and ready to be worn. He took it down and, upon smelling it, decided that it was good.

Lauren was busy filling in paperwork at her kitchen table. Well, it was also the living room table in a way. Peter entered. He was clean-shaven and looked ever so smart in the clean suit.

'Wow. Look at you. You've scrubbed up well,' she noticed. She couldn't help herself. She found the man appealing somehow.

'This is all very kind of you. I don't know how to repay you.'

'By not telling anyone!'

'Don't worry, I'm good at keeping secrets. I think.'

'Yes,' she responded with knowing frustration, 'men generally are.' She stood up, gathering her papers together. 'Look, I've gotta get back to the station. Work to do, bodies to dissect!' She held out her keys for Peter.

'Oh no, I couldn't.'

'I've got a spare set. Get yourself together, get something to eat. When you're done, just lock up and put the keys through the letter box.'

'Well, if you're sure.'

'Yeah, course I am. Even if you are some crazed thief or something, you won't find much of value in here.'

Peter took the keys, chuckling slightly. Lauren dashed out, smiling back as she went.

Peter headed into Lock Lane pub with a fiver he'd come across somewhere. Presenting it to the woman at the bar, he asked for a pint of ale. She obliged, pulling one with a nice head and taking his money in exchange for it.

'You from round here?' she asked him.

'Just passing through,' Peter replied, not really wanting to enter into a conversation with her.

'Yeah, you don't look familiar. What's with the suit? You a copper or something?'

'Far from it.' He leant forward. 'In fact, I've just pinched it.'

'I see,' replied the bemused woman. There was an awkward silence before Peter decided to move to a seat away from her.

The pub was rather quiet, but Peter decided to sit right in the corner. He caught eyes with another rather smartly-dressed man who was sat in the opposite alcove to him. What Peter didn't know, or couldn't remember, was that this was Darren Aubrey, or The Anarchist as he liked to call himself in this guise. Peter took his eyes from The Anarchist, sipping his pint of ale. It was rather refreshing for the man who didn't realise he liked alcohol so much. A newspaper lay on the chair next to him. He picked it up and read the front cover headline, 'OAP BUTCHERED BY CRAZED GARDENER'. Suddenly Trout and Williams entered. Luckily Peter looked up and saw them before they saw him. He ducked behind the newspaper.

Glancing to the side of it, he watched the uneasy-looking

Trout and Williams walking over to The Anarchist. They sat down beside him and began talking about something or other. Peter couldn't hear what. Before long, Trout removed a padded brown envelope from an inside pocket and handed it to The Anarchist, who pocketed it and shook hands with them both. They abruptly stood up and left the pub, walking straight past a hidden Peter. The Anarchist, his work done, downed his drink and also got up to leave. Peter instinctively felt he had to follow him, to uncover whatever it was that was going on. He got up to follow as The Anarchist departed.

However, when he got outside, he had vanished. Before Peter could do anything else, Williams, Trout and Noble drove past.

'Well I'll be!' Williams called out as she spotted him. Trout slammed the breaks on as Peter caught eye contact with Williams and frowned. 'Stay right where you are, young man!' she demanded. However, Peter turned and ran in the opposite direction straight down the middle of the busy high street behind Lock Lane pub. 'Go after him!' Williams ordered Trout and Noble. They both set after him, but Trout soon had to stop as he clutched at his chest.

'Don't let him get away,' he yelled after Noble. Peter leapt right over a bench obstructing his path and darted around a corner. It was a one-way back alley and he paused for breath as Noble shot past. Not fooled, Noble turned and came back, ready for a struggle.

'Don't worry,' Peter relented, gasping for air, 'you've caught me fair and square.' He sat down on the ground and held his arms up in the air as Trout came limping around the corner into the alley. He took hold of Noble's shoulder from behind.

'You should exercise regularly, Inspector,' was Noble's response.

'You should keep you mouth shut, Sergeant,' Trout gasped back. 'Oh, what a clever and cunning disguise,' he went on, looking down at Peter. 'Shaving his beard!'

Noble took a second look at Peter, askance. 'Where did you get that from?'

'Get what from?'

'My jacket… Wait a second, you're wearing my clothes.'

Noble dragged Peter to his feet and pulled the jacket off to take a closer look.

'No I'm not.'

'Yes you are, you're wearing my damn clothes.'

He spun Peter around, pulling at the trousers.

'Do you mind!'

'I left these at my fiancée's.'

'Your fiancée isn't Lauren the pathologist, by any chance?'

Noble gripped Peter by the throat. 'What the hell have you done to her?' he spat.

'Oh dear, what *have* I done!' Peter howled in confusion.

'Hello. My name is Peter Smith. I am dead,' Neville preached, sat facing Peter in the cell. Peter, now in an old prison uniform, faced his cellmate.

'Who are you? What do you know about me?'

'The Prosecutor had chosen the corporeal form of my brother Stuart,' Neville went on.

The cell door opened. Trout and Noble entered, with two hefty officers stood just outside. Trout arrogantly swished his jacket around before settling for a comfortable pose. Noble stood next to him, silent and blank, holding a file. Trout held his hand out and Noble handed him the file.

'Louis Sellers and James Harrington, both murdered,' Trout read aloud from the file. 'Two members of a Museum Club.' Trout looked up from the file. 'Aren't you a member, Mr Smith?' he asked coyly.

'I could be.'

'I see. It says here that you are. Interesting how your past is littered with murders, isn't it Peter?'

'Fascinating.'

Trout clicked at Noble and pointed for him to leave. Reluctantly Noble obliged, stepping out of the cell. Trout gently shut the cell door and stepped closer to Peter.

'Tell me Peter, man to man,' Trout started, noticing Neville was staring intently at him. 'You had a part to play in those two murders, didn't you?'

Peter stood up and stepped up close to Trout. 'Oh yes,' he replied sarcastically, grinning. Trout sensed the sarcasm with disappointment.

'I'll get the evidence, Peter, and I'll put you away for a very long time.' Trout turned to leave but Peter grabbed hold of his arm and pulled him back.

'I was in the pub, Trout,' Peter pointed out.

'Take your hand off me.' But Peter wouldn't.

'You and Nicola Williams, the superintendent.'

Trout looked concerned. 'What did you see?'

'Enough. I know there's something going on in this place and I intend to find out what.'

'You don't know the half of it,' Trout sneered, pulling his arm away and storming out. The cell door was slammed shut once more.

'Inspector Norman Trout, yes,' Neville trilled from the cell bed. Peter turned to him.

'What do you know?'

'I know what *wasn't* in that envelope he gave to The Anarchist.'

'The Anarchist?'

'Money, that's what wasn't in it. It was supposed to be documents proving that The Major killed his wife, but Frank swapped them for blank paper. You see, this is all interlinked.'

'Interlinked with what?' Peter was becoming rather agitated at knowing nothing. Neville lapped up the attention.

'The briefcase caper. You and Noose solving the murder of

Susan and Derek. Oh, and Rosetta Aubrey.' Neville jumped up, excited. 'But tell me, why on page 159 do you call her Rosetta Harden? There are inconsistencies.'

'I don't know what you're on about, for crying out loud,' Peter wept, pulling at his hair. This was the first time he was really beginning to get angry at his predicament.

'*I Am Dead*,' Neville exclaimed, 'you really must read it. It'll solve all your problems.' Neville flopped down once more, lying flat out and closing his eyes.

'You're insane,' Peter shot back, pacing the room. Exhausted, he came to a stop and slid down the wall to lie in a heap on the floor.

Williams, slotting something into her filing cabinet, was disturbed by Noose once more. He, intent on doing a bit of slotting himself, slammed the door shut and approached her with extreme intent as she sighed at the sight of him.

'You really are trying my patience, Henry.'

'Peter is innocent.'

'Maybe. However, the safest place for him right now is that cell. He's admitted to stealing Lauren's flat keys and going there to steal Stephen's clothes.'

'Odd. How did he manage to steal the keys?'

'Must have been before he escaped this morning.'

'Come to that,' Noose pondered, the detective in him coming to the fore, 'how did he know where she lived?'

'You're the detective, go find out.'

'Coming from the one who took me off the case.'

'Oh for the love of-' Williams began, but was interrupted by a ringing phone. She grabbed it. 'Williams... I see...'

'What is it?' Noose pestered. Williams put her finger on Noose's lips as she continued to listen. Noose hadn't felt her finger on his lips for a while.

'Thank you, David.' She put the phone back down. 'It

seems we have a significant development, Henry; it appears our grieving son Roger Parsonage lied about his alibi. His wife stayed with friends last night, not at home like he said.'

'Do we know where he is now?'

'No idea. Oh, and Jim's taken a funny turn apparently. Had a bit of a twitching fit or something.'

'A twitching fit?'

'He couldn't control a facial spasm. It was quite an episode.'

'Is he alright now?'

A sharp knock sounded on the door.

'Come in,' Williams called out. Nothing. 'COME IN!' she yelled.

Trout stormed in, slamming the door. 'Bastard!' Trout spotted Noose and stopped dead. 'What's he doing here? Can I have a word, *please*, Superintendent?' Noose crossed his arms. 'In private?'

'Okay Henry, later. Go home,' she told him. He dragged his feet out of the room. 'What is it, Norman? Storming in here like an irate goose!'

'Peter Smith knows something. He saw us in the pub.'

'Don't be stupid.'

'He knows something!'

'We've come this far, we cannot have our plans ruined by a meddling do-gooder now. Sort it out. Deal with Peter Smith.'

Trout grinned. 'Done.'

In the corridor outside, Noose had his ear pressed up against the door. From the fragments he had heard from within, he was perplexed. Trout suddenly opened the door and Noose made busy, pretending he was reading the notice board. The two rivals gave each other the evil eye before Trout stormed off down the corridor. Noose charged into Williams' room once more, slamming the door shut again. Williams gave out a huge gasp of air and rolled her eyes.

'I'm *really* getting tired of this.'

'Ditto,' Noose shot back. 'Look, don't play the fool with me. Let's cut to the chase, shall we?'

'Alright, alright, I *do* still have feelings for you,' she responded, coming to him.

'I wasn't on about that.' Noose gulped. 'You do?'

She smiled seductively, tilting her head so as to look up at him with her deep eyes.

'Oh yes. There hasn't been anybody else for me… Not in a long time.'

Noose looked somewhat childlike now as Williams fed her fingers through his hair and brought his head down to kiss him on the forehead. Passion kicked in once more, their lips locking. Williams pulled away, putting her finger on his lips. She spun around and slid the lock shut on the office door. Noose grabbed her and they flew onto her desk, knocking everything off. He was hard for her, so hard. She had always been the temptress to his foolish lust for skin. And she, for some reason, was moist and ready for him, and they went at it right there.

In the morning, Noose woke up in the reception of the police station as O'Toole was standing on a chair next to the one his feet lay on. Noose was dazed and rubbed at his eyes to regain his sight. He struggled into a sitting position as O'Toole merrily pinned a piece of paper onto the notice board.

'What?' Noose asked either himself or the world in general, looking around the room.

'Wakey, wakey, rise and shine!' O'Toole joyed in merriment. Noose either didn't hear him or didn't want to. 'Bad night, Inspector?'

'Bugger off!' Noose exclaimed, covering his face. O'Toole sniffed indifferently, used to being treated this way. 'Oh God, what have I done?' Noose asked himself, burying his face further into his hands.

There was something odd about what Peter was doing, though it seemed ordinary enough. He walked through the front door of this place and into the hallway. It was dark here, the curtains drawn, though it was not night outside. He pulled the curtains open, walking into the living room. A grizzly sight awaited him. There lay Lucy Davies dead, sprawled on the carpet and covered in blood. Peter dropped to his knees, weeping, attending to her corpse.

But this was not a present event, for Peter suddenly wakened from his nightmare flashback and tried to sit up. Realising the hard floor of the cell had done nothing for his back, he struggled to his side. He thought about the nightmare. He knew she was Lucy Davies, he could just feel it. Was his memory returning, or was his brain merely playing tricks on him?

He pulled himself up with the concrete bunk, coming face to face with Neville who appeared to be asleep. Without opening an eye, however, Neville spoke.

'This is what it's like. They forget about you. They lock you up for no reason at all then forget. Nobody knows you are here, nobody misses you. Well, me at least. People know you. You're Peter Smith.' He opened his eyes and turned to smile at Peter. 'You know what I mean?'

'Sure,' Peter replied, pulling himself to his feet. He stretched a painful stretch.

'Bad vision?'

'No. A nightmare.'

'Ah, just a nightmare. Not The Space then.'

Peter, tired of asking Neville questions, did not rise to this one and remained silent instead. It was as well he did, for Neville was not the most forthcoming with straight answers.

Noose was still sat with his head in his hands when Williams and Trout floated past.

'Ah, Henry, good morning!' she beamed, wide awake and full of life. 'Did you have a rough night?'

'You could say that.'

'Oh dear.'

'Look,' Noose started, standing up and trying to pull her aside, 'about last night.' She brushed him off.

'Well, you better sort yourself out. You're helping out with the case again.'

'What? But...' Trout exclaimed.

'We need as much thinking power on this as possible,' Williams explained. 'There's no time for trivialities.' Noose gave Trout a big grin. Trout gave a sly grin back. 'Right, we've received a warrant to search Michael Evans' house. Use it!'

'Right away,' Noose, perking up, responded.

'Right away,' Trout mumbled. Williams headed off towards the double doors, turning back briefly to look at Noose. He looked at her as she winked before disappearing. Noble appeared from behind them. 'Are we going or what?' Trout nudged, marching off towards the main entrance. Noose and Noble followed.

'You look rough as toast,' Noble remarked. Noose did not respond, preferring instead to eye his sergeant with mild contempt for the cheeky observation.

The three men approached Michael's cottage and noticed the door ajar. They pushed it open and stepped inside. An awful sight confronted them in the living room.

'Oh shit,' was Noose's first utterance at the sight of Roger Parsonage sprawled on the floor with multiple injuries. He was quite clearly dead from them. There looked to have been a ferocious struggle, with Michael's belongings completely trashed around the room.

'You should have taken DNA samples,' Noble tutted at Trout, 'we could have avoided a second murder.'

'Is he dead?' was Trout's response.

'Well he's not doing the bloody can-can is he!' Noose spat back in anguish.

Time passed and Lauren had been and done her work. She now stood in the hallway and spoke to Trout and Noble. 'Well he didn't kill his mother, anyway. The DNA never did match up and now I know for sure.'

'When was he murdered?' asked Trout.

'At this early stage, I couldn't be absolutely sure. Six to eight hours ago, probably.'

Noble bit one of his fingernails and looked at Trout. 'Peter's been banged up all night.' Trout raised an eyebrow and yawned. 'Innocent. Sadly.'

'Of this one. Two different killers, you see.'

'This is the same killer.'

'Who's the Inspector here, Sergeant?' With this Trout stormed off.

Noble turned to Lauren. 'What went on with you and Peter?' he asked her, looking her square in the eyes.

'Hmm?' she responded, pretending not to have heard him properly.

'Did you let him in the flat?' he pushed. She turned to walk away but he grabbed hold of her arm. 'Oh come on, Lauren. You shut me out last night and you're shutting me out now. He was wearing my suit. How did that happen, huh?'

'I'm working.'

She pulled off him and walked back to the body.

'You're just like Amy, you are,' he called after her. 'You women never let me into your little worlds.' With this comparison of Lauren with his sister over, Noble too stormed off.

As he came in search of Trout outside, he spotted Noose across the road talking to Geoff.

'You heard nothing, right?' Noose asked Geoff for confirmation.

'That's right.'

'Did you see…'

'I saw nothing.'

But Noose was unconvinced.

Noble cleared his throat and spoke to Trout. 'Same killer. We have to let Peter go, as much as I'd like to see him go down.' Trout gritted his teeth, watching Noose.

'Why were you following Michael yesterday?' Noose asked Geoff.

'I wanted to ask him about Cynthia. She's missing. He's done something to her, I know it.'

'Why follow him?'

'Michael is a strange man; he may have attacked me had I stepped onto his precious land. In public, I could challenge him unmolested.'

'I see. And did you?'

'Did I what?'

'Challenge him?'

'No, I lost him,' Geoff rubbed his lips. 'At some traffic lights.' He grinned. Noose scratched his chin. 'Isn't it a little odd, however,' Geoff continued, unprompted, 'how he goes missing the day after the murder of his next door neighbour, and the day *before* a dead body is found in his house… The son of the murdered neighbour!'

'I am aware of what has happened.'

'Of course you are,' Geoff chuckled.

'Stick around, Geoffrey, I'll be taking a DNA sample from you.' He turned to walk back across the lane.

'Shame you can't take Michael's and Cynthia's,' Geoff called after him. He, now very smug indeed, sat down on his garden wall and kept watch over the ensuing action across the lane.

'Better check on that Mrs Lester,' Noose spoke to Noble, ignoring Trout.

'Er, don't forget here Noose, you're not in charge of this case,' Trout interrupted.

Noose stepped up to Trout. 'You're really beginning to piss me off.'

Trout in turn came closer to Noose. 'Me pissing you off, eh?'

Noble stepped in between the Inspectors. 'A mother and son have been murdered within the space of two days. I dunno what the hell is going on in this bloody lane but I want us to find out before anyone else gets killed.'

Trout turned and put his arm around Noble. 'You're right, Stephen. Come on, we'll go and speak to Mrs Lester.'

Noble and Trout headed for Mrs Lester's cottage together as Noose followed behind. As they walked up her path, she opened the door and stuck her head out.

'I am a poor old lady, I have no money hidden under my mattress,' she called out in a timid strain.

'We're not here to rob you, Mrs Lester,' Noose called back.

Trout blocked Noose's view and spoke over him. 'We're here to ask you some questions about last night.'

'Last night? Why, what happened last night?'

Noose pushed past Trout and greeted Mrs Lester with an attempt at a warm smile. She squinted, perplexed at what came out as a grimace. 'There's been another murder,' he told her, 'in Michael's cottage.'

'Oh poor Michael, or was it Cynthia? They both live there, you know.' She removed from her pocket a snot-soaked hanky and dabbed her eyes pointedly.

'We're well aware of that,' was Trout's frustrated response.

'It was neither of them,' Noose continued, 'it was Roger Parsonage.'

'My word,' the shocked Mrs Lester responded, 'I thought it was he who killed Doris!'

'It would appear not. We have a suspect for Doris Parsonage's murder,' Trout shouted out, believing the old woman to be hard of hearing, as he poked his head around Noose's shoulder. 'We were wondering, did you see him about on the night she was murdered?' He slipped in front of Noose.

'See who?'

Noose slipped back in between Trout and Mrs Lester. 'Peter did not do it! You're getting out of hand, Trout.'

Trout pushed Noose. 'If you want the killer brought to justice, let me do my work.'

Noose pushed Trout back. 'Of course Peter was around the other night, he slept in the shed.'

Mrs Lester stepped out of her cottage and fixed her frame between the two inspectors. 'Have you any further questions? My back isn't half giving me gyp!'

'Yes, actually,' Noose responded, 'you mentioned Roger Parsonage to me yesterday. There was no sign of forced entry at Michael's house.'

'Well he had a spare key, didn't he, from years back.'

'Oh?'

Trout rolled his eyes.

'Yes of course,' Mrs Lester lapped it up, 'it's public knowledge. Roger and Cynthia had an affair years ago. Roger hasn't shown his face much since. Who would? Have you seen Cynthia Evans? Dear Lord.'

'I see,' Noose replied, nodding at Noble. Trout yawned.

Peter was still in the cell with Neville. Suddenly the door opened and Tony stepped in before the door was locked behind him.

'Ah, here we go,' Neville chuckled, lying on the mattress. Peter stood up and turned to face Tony.

'What you in for?' Peter asked him, but Tony remained unresponsive. He just stared, as if waiting for a cue to do something. With no reply forthcoming, Peter turned his back on the big lad. This was rather foolish as Tony promptly put his hands around Peter's neck and started strangling him. Taken by surprise, and overcome with Tony's brute strength, Peter could do nothing but submit to this attempt on his life.

'Help!' he whimpered at a frozen Neville.

The cell door opened once again and a surprised Trout dashed in, trying to pull Tony off Peter. Tony merely thumped him across the face and sent him flying. Noble was the next to enter, but he too froze, unable to act on the spot. Two more hefty officers entered and pulled a raging Tony off Peter just in time. Peter flopped in a semi-conscious heap as Tony was restrained and led off.

'What was that all about?' Noble asked, unsure whether he was questioning Tony's attack on Peter or his own unwillingness to intervene.

'You're free to go, Peter,' Trout grimaced as he got his breath back. 'On the charge of murder. Don't leave the town though, you're gonna be in court for breaking and entering and assaulting me.'

'I didn't break and enter,' Peter mumbled. 'I stole a key and entered.' He struggled to stand, but could not. Trout grabbed him and pulled him to his feet. 'He was in this cell five seconds. Is that how long it takes to make someone want to kill you?' Peter did not reply. 'Just get out of my sight.' Trout pushed the floppy Peter towards the open cell door.

Peter sat slumped on a chair in reception. Noose entered and, spotting his friend, darted over.

'Peter.'

'What the hell's going on here?'

'Peter, I think I'm in love with Nicola.'

An ear-wigging O'Toole spat a mouthful of coffee out.

'What?'

'Something happened last night between us.' Noose sat down next to Peter and sighed joyously.

'I thought you were gonna find out about this fraud business or whatever it is? You know, getting the other Superintendent suspended. Williams and Trout in the pub with the brown envelope?'

'We embraced, Peter.' Noose, hazy-eyed, rolled his head about the room.

'I'm not hearing this.' Peter struggled to his feet. 'Don't get sucked in. We've gotta find out what's going on, whatever you feel for her.'

'Roger Parsonage is dead, you know.'

Peter found the forensic laboratory and gingerly pushed the door open. He slowly walked up to the slab with Roger's corpse lying on it.

'Lauren,' Peter called out, glancing away from Roger. He could hear voices oozing from another room. He walked towards its door. 'Lauren? I was just wondering if you'd washed my clothes...' Before she could answer, Noble opened the door and stepped out, looking rather angry.

'What?'

Lauren, lurking behind Noble, skulked away.

'Oh dear. I mean, I'm a, I'm sorry for stealing your keys and letting myself into your flat.' Peter scrunched his face up and turned to leave.

'You lied to me Lauren,' Noble yelled, 'you just said you left your keys in reception.'

'I'm sorry, Stephen, I thought you'd go mad if you knew what happened.'

'What happened?' He went to grab her. 'What did you two do?'

'Hey, watch what you're doing,' Peter shot back, grabbing hold of Noble's arm. He spun around and whacked Peter to the floor.

'Shut your face,' Noble grunted.

'Stephen,' Lauren tried again, 'nothing happened. I just saw him on the road and felt sorry for him.'

Peter got to his feet.

'Oh really? How nice. How very Christian of you.'

Noble stormed off, pushing Peter over again.

'I'm really sorry Lauren.'

'He's always tossing his toys out of the pram. He'll be right as rain in an hour.' She sighed and turned.

Noose closed the file he was reading on his car roof and chucked it in the backseat. As he was about to get in, Trout appeared behind him.

'What's all this about you and the super?' he asked Noose with a grin on his face.

'Piss off, Trout.'

'I hear you're all loved-up.'

Noose turned to face Trout. 'I hate you, Trout. I don't want to have a conversation with you.' He sat down in his car.

'You must be pretty desperate for a quickie if she's the best you can do,' Trout goaded him.

'I know your sort, Trout. You're sick. Sick in the head.' Noose slammed his car door shut and wound the window down for some air.

'Not too sick to attract your wife all those years ago.' Trout's grin widened. Noose crossed his head in disbelief at this being brought up again. 'I may have dumped her years ago, but at least she chose me. She chose me over you, you fat balding state.'

'It didn't work like that. You meant nothing to her.'

Trout rested his arm on Noose's car roof.

'She meant the world to you, and you can't handle the fact that I've had her.'

'If she meant the world to me, why did I cheat on her? I cheated on her, so she cheated on me,' Noose pointed out. 'End of story.' Trout stood back and folded his arms.

'Then why do you hate me so much?'

'You're scum. You are a terrible police officer and an inadequate detective. This latest case has only served to prove that to everybody. Go and flap back to your pond.'

Trout laughed. 'Then why did Williams put me on the case and take you off? Answer me that, genius.'

'You and her are up to something and I plan to find out what it is.'

Peter was now dressed in his own clothes again. Well, the brown suit. He was sat quite happily on a park bench behind the police station, watching the world go by around him. Lauren appeared and approached the bench.

'Mind if I sit down?' she asked, smiling warmly. This was a very warm smile, warm enough to make Peter jitter with a flash of lightning down his back. He could not remember this Lucy Davies from his past, but he could remember this Lauren from his present. She had nothing to do with his past, he thought, but could be brought into his future if he so wished.

'Of course not. Sergeant Noble might, though.'

She sat down anyway. 'Life, eh!' was her conversation starter after a moment's silence.

'You don't pull any punches, do you?' Peter smiled back.

'I suppose not. I haven't known you long Peter, but somehow I feel I do know you. It's very strange.'

'Is this where you tell me you're my long-lost sister?'

'No, not quite!' she laughed. 'You intrigue me.'

'You intrigue me! A beautiful young woman spending all her time examining corpses.' Lauren blushed. 'Did you always want to be a pathologist or whatever?'

'I don't know. It just kinda happened, I guess.' She pondered. 'It's peculiar really, I sometimes get this odd feeling I should have worked in a bank.'

Peter chuckled. 'That's even worse than a pathologist.'

'Jeez, thanks!' They sat silent once more, but she spoke again. 'Anyway, what's your story? Turning up here, an old face with Noose but not remembering who you are. What's that all about?'

'Hmm, good question. I wish I could remember my past. We all live in the past, don't we? Except me. You can't really live in the future, 'cause it hasn't happened yet. If you try to live in the present, if soon becomes the past. I guess I'm creating a new past. A past I can actually remember.' Peter paused, but Lauren seemed to be so drawn to his words that he was desperate to continue and keep her attention. 'Stephen's probably told you about Lucy Davies - and whatever else is in my file. Something about a museum club, too. I just can't remember.'

Though he could not remember, his body automatically produced tears which now trickled down his cheeks. Lauren moved in and wiped them away. He looked into her eyes, lost in some haze he suddenly felt was a future memory. But that could not be so. The future had not yet happened. She moved in, wetting her lips and opening her mouth.

'Thanks for saying you stole my keys, by the way.'

'Oh yes, sorry I dropped you in it before.'

'Oh, don't worry. We're always fighting.' She played with a ring on her finger. 'Been engaged two years now.' She looked up at Peter again and touched his cheek. Suddenly Noble appeared.

'I don't believe this!' he screamed.

'Stephen,' a startled Lauren called back, quickly pulling away from Peter.

'Talk about rubbing my nose in it! And I insisted that you were innocent of murder,' Noble continued to screech. He grabbed hold of Peter and thumped him square in the face, sending him tumbling over the back of the bench.

'That is it!' Lauren screamed back, pulling her ring off. 'I've had it with you!' She threw the ring at Noble and ran off.

Peter looked up at Noble from behind the bench, holding onto his throbbing jaw.

'Hello Mrs Lester, can I come in?' Peter asked her as he stood rather glumly on her step. He looked jolly, so she accepted his request and allowed him to enter.

He sat down on her sofa as she wheeled in a tea tray laden with goodies.

'Oooh, that cake looks lovely Mrs Lester,' he remarked, admiring a delicately-decorated little pink cupcake.

'It is, young man.'

She flopped down in her chair and poured out two cups of tea.

'I didn't really have a chance to finish Mrs Parsonage's garden, what with her being slain and all, but I would still like to do some work in the neighbourhood.' He took the cup and saucer of tea from her. 'Lovely, thank you.'

'Well, I've got a big old bush down there in the garden and I do find it difficult to maintain these days.' She took a sip of tea. 'Your help would be greatly appreciated.'

'Why thank you, Mrs Lester.'

Peter and Noose were sat in a café. Noose looked impatiently around. He checked his watch.

'Twenty minutes we've been waiting.'

'Shush, they'll hear you!' Peter, finger to his lips, tried to calm his companion.

'That's the idea. Twenty minutes for a round of toast. Ridiculous!' He flopped back in his seat as a waitress casually strolled up to their table and dropped a plate of toast each in front of them. 'At last!'

'Thank you,' Peter addressed the waitress. She ignored him and walked on, chewing on gum.

Noose took a bite, chucking it back down on the plate in disgust. 'Cold! It's damn cold.'

'Look, I've come here to discuss this Trout and Williams thing.'

'Yeah…'

'Well, what have you heard?'

'Nicola, she - she said something about not wanting a do-

gooder spoiling their plans. Something like that.' Noose lifted the plate to his nose, sniffing the toast.

'Look, I don't think Noble is involved. He was waiting in the car when I saw Williams and Trout in the pub.'

'He's too slow to catch a cold.'

'This fraud, what do you know about it?' Peter questioned further, fancying himself as a bit of a detective. Noose smiled. Perhaps he and Peter had solved mysteries before, and would do in the future. But Peter couldn't remember.

'Well, a load of money went missing from the police treasury. Some of it was found in Superintendent Hastings' account. Not all of it though - he must have put the rest somewhere else.'

'Unless he was stitched up,' Peter pondered, 'by Trout and Williams.' Noose yawned and checked his watch, before gazing out of the window. 'You just don't seem interested somehow.'

'I've got a lot on my mind.' Noose picked the toast up and started nibbling a corner off.

'We all have. Well, I have somewhere to be.' He too took a bite out of his toast, grimacing, and putting it down again. 'Oh yeah, before I forget - Roger and I found a threatening letter in Michael's house.'

'What? Where is it?'

'I left it with Roger. It was for Michael, saying he'd pay for being evil.'

'Well, we haven't found it.'

'Looks like Michael's taken it with him. He must be the killer, it all fits together.'

'Yes. Roger and Cynthia had an affair years ago, that must be where he was the other night whilst his mother was being murdered. Cynthia is missing, perhaps Michael has killed her too. Perhaps he found them in the midst of their passion!' Noose sank back in his seat, his glazed eyes staring up into space.

Peter stood up. 'Right, I'm off back to Mrs Lester's. Jobs to do.'

As Peter walked down the street, a man bumped into him, carrying on at pace down the road. He caught only a brief glimpse of his face, but he was in no doubt. It was the smartly-dressed man from the pub who had met with Williams and Trout. The Anarchist. Peter decided to follow him. He went on for some time, leaving the residential area of the town and leading Peter towards a warehouse. He kept in pursuit until The Anarchist turned down an alleyway. It was dark and dodgy. Peter prepared to walk on past it, unwilling to risk going down it himself. He could wait further on, in the light, for The Anarchist to re-immerge. However, as he walked past the opening to the alley, The Anarchist leapt out with two hefty muscle men and pulled Peter into the darkness.

'Well looky what we got here, boys,' he cackled, throwing Peter at the wall.

The hefty men grinned before one of them stepped closer, raising his fist in the air. Peter made a dash for it, but the other struck him from behind. He fell to the ground, unconscious.

FIVE

Peter had a pain in his neck and his head was flopped back. He opened his eyes slowly, raising his head, moving it around to try and ease the stiffness. He looked down at his body, unable to move it. He was bound to a chair, in the centre of a sparsely-filled warehouse. Some wooden crates sat to one side, a single door next to them. Suddenly The Anarchist stepped into view from behind Peter, his bright white teeth shining and his brilliant auburn side parting distinguishing his already slim, toned features.

'I reckon we waste him,' he whispered, taking out a gun and putting it to Peter's head. The two hefty men appeared the other side of him, stood together. Peter looked at them, trying to smile.

'Now, now my friend, not so hasty,' he replied as The Anarchist leaned in to examine him further.

'We know who you are and who sent you,' he continued.

'Oh?' Peter replied, 'And who's that?'

The Anarchist crossed his head, looking at the two hefty men before grabbing hold of Peter's hair, pulling his head back and forcing the gun down his throat.

'Don't be stupid, my friend. We're very close to ending your sad little life.'

'Come on now, we're all grown men here,' Peter gagged. 'Surely we can sort this out without the need for violence.' The Anarchist laughed. 'Okay then. So you know why I've been sent?' he went on, playing into his hands.

'We've done our research,' he went on.

'I see. And I've done mine,' Peter added. The Anarchist looked on, puzzled. But now Peter froze, unable to come up with anything more to say.

'Go on,' The Anarchist pushed, totting the gun.

'Erm, yes,' Peter thought fast. 'I know who you are and what you're up to.'

The Anarchist stepped back, smirking at the hefty men. 'Cut the crap,' he growled. 'You can tell Trout that he's playing a very dangerous psychological game with us.' He straightened his back, putting his finger to his lips. Peter eyed up the gun. He clicked his fingers, prompting one of the hefty men to step forward and pass him the brown envelope from the pub. He opened it, taking out a wad of blank paper the same size as bank notes.

'Is that supposed to be money?' Peter asked, trying to keep up.

'Money?' The Anarchist laughed. The hefty men cackled. 'What on earth would we possibly want with money? We want what Trout owes us.'

'Well if it's not money, what is it?'

Laughter once more. The Anarchist pointed the gun at Peter again. He pulled the trigger. A 'BANG' flag popped out. There was more laughter as Peter squirmed, one of the hefty men striking him from behind again. Darkness.

Peter awoke, sprawled on a park bench. He started to get his bearings, rubbing his head and looking around at people. Pounding, pounding. An old woman walked past with a dog.

'You boozers make me sick!' she exclaimed, 'Serves you right when you choke on your own vomit!' She marched on, raising her nose in the air.

Peter managed to struggle into a sitting position, catching a glimpse of his watch. He jumped up. 'Mrs Lester!' He was late for his job. With this sudden movement he felt light-headed and dropped to the ground.

He jogged straight past a bus stop, passing it as a black car with tinted windows pulled up. He checked his watch impatiently. He had to get to Mrs Lester's. She would be angry by now.

Peter perched somewhat awkwardly on Mrs Lester's sofa, ready, if not all that willing, to consume more tea. She wobbled in, pushing the tea tray. On it was a pot of tea, two cups and saucers, and yet more nibbles. Gone, however, was the fancy cake from last time. Peter had already consumed that.

'More tea! Lovely!' Peter exclaimed falsely.

'You can't beat a good cup of tea,' Mrs Lester replied. She sat down and poured the tea, handing Peter a cup and saucer.

'Thank you very much.'

'Manners, how refreshing.'

'Well, it doesn't cost anything to be polite, does it?'

'My sentiment exactly. I just cannot tolerate people with no manners.' She suddenly seemed rather angrier than was necessary. 'I was angered when you turned up late, boy, but you're slowly making up for it.'

'Erm, thank you, Mrs Lester.'

'Yes,' she continued, her face reddening as she clenched her fist. 'I abhor ignorance of manners... deviancy in all its manifestations.'

Peter, a little confused at Mrs Lester's vagueness, glanced down at a stack of magazines. 'Oooh, a gardening magazine.' He put his cup of tea down and bent to pick the top magazine up.

'Don't!' Mrs Lester called out to him, but it was too late. Cut-out pieces fell from within the magazine. 'I told you I abhorred ignorance of manners. You should have asked me first!'

Peter picked the pieces up off the floor. '*You* sent the threatening letters?'

'That I did,' she admitted, holding her head high. 'Plain

and simple, they are all horrid people. It is hellish living amongst them.'

'But why send them the letters? People will think you're the killer now.'

'I imagined the letters would scare them into flying straight and bucking up their ideas.' She put her feet up. 'I didn't realise they would become embroiled in a murder mystery.'

'Well, part of that mystery has now been solved.' Peter finished his tea.

'I do not regret sending the letters, even after Doris and Roger's murders. Quite frankly, I believe they deserved a sticky end.' She sat back in her chair and nibbled merrily on a biscuit.

'Am I the only one who thought they were alright?'

'You're not a very good judge of character.' She sat up, leaning forward and pointing her finger at Peter. 'Any trouble that woman could cause, she'd cause it. As for her son! Are you aware he had an affair with that Cynthia?' Peter looked around the room before re-focussing on Mrs Lester. 'That's why he moved. Michael threatened to kill him.'

'This thing gets weirder by the minute.'

'Anyway, enough chit chat. Back to work for you!' She stood, prompting Peter to do the same. She sidled up to him. 'I trust you'll keep my part in this charade a secret… the letters. You do want to get paid, don't you?'

'What letters? I've seen nothing!' he exclaimed.

'Ah! I see what you did there. Very good.'

Peter walked through to the kitchen, opening the back door into the garden. Mrs Lester followed. Outside he picked up the small garden fork he'd been digging with and stepped back into the kitchen with it.

'Oh Mrs Lester, do you happen to have a larger fork please? I can't seem to get deep enough with this one.'

'Of course.'

She ambled towards a small door in the kitchen that led into a storage room, opening it. Peter peeped around her into it as she picked up a much larger fork next to a spade. She turned and passed the fork to Peter.

'Thank you!' Peter turned to exit, glancing down at the fork. A crusty reddish-brown substance covered its prongs. 'That's odd, that's not soil.' He turned to face Mrs Lester once more only to be met with a spade crashing down on his face. He collapsed to the floor as Mrs Lester lifted the spade up high into the air above Peter's neck, ready to decapitate him. Luckily, the door bell rang. Calm and collected, she gently placed the spade down and ambled out of the room.

At the door she met Noose, smiling wryly.

'Oh, sorry to bother you Mrs Lester, but Peter said he was gardening here. I just want to have a word with him, please.'

'He is busy, come back later.'

'Is he very busy?'

'Flat out!'

'I see,' Noose relented, 'oh well, goodbye then.'

'Goodbye.' She slammed the door shut. The doorbell rang again. She pulled it open. 'What is it, you impetuous man? My cup of tea is getting cold.'

'Oh, just one more thing... You're under arrest for murder.'

Two other officers stepped out from either side of the door. 'Oh, really?!'

Peter sat slumped at Mrs Lester's kitchen table, holding a bag of frozen peas on the top of his head. Lauren attempted to attend to his bruising.

'Let me take a look,' she demanded as he squirmed away.

'It stings.'

'You're lucky to be alive, let alone conscious, you know.'

'I might have been better off dead,' he responded, full of self-pity. Lauren smiled comfortingly. Noose entered. 'Knocked out by an old woman.'

'How do you think Roger Parsonage felt, being brutally battered to death by her? And Doris Parsonage…'

The officers brought Mrs Lester through into the kitchen, her hands cuffed behind her back. Peter lifted his head up and looked her straight in the eye. She stared back, her head held high, defiant in defeat.

'Why?' Peter asked of her.

'You discovered I was the killer, you had to be silenced.'

'Not me. Why kill an elderly lady and her son? It doesn't make sense, it's cruel.'

'Cruel? You have no idea. Putting them out of their misery, I'd say.'

'Quite insane,' Noose chipped in.

'I shall be pleading insanity, Inspector.'

'You'll die behind bars whatever happens.'

'A small price to pay for peace of mind!' she chuckled.

Peter stood up and leered at her. 'Peace of mind? You're a murderer, for crying out loud.'

'Oh please! Each and every one of us is capable of murder. Even you! I know what goes on in this village. It's about time somebody started tidying up all the mess.'

'Tidying up the village? By slaying an old woman?'

'I don't have to explain myself to you people, but I'll say this one thing and one thing only; Doris and Roger Parsonage have caused me nothing but grief for the last thirty years. I am quite pleased that I murdered them in the end.'

'And what did they do exactly? Park their car outside your house? Drop litter?'

'I saw that Roger, coming here when Michael was away. Fiddling about with Cynthia he was. Roger's death was more of an accident, though. I was after Michael, you see. I was stitching Roger up for the murders. I planned to wipe out the whole lane. Kind of scuppered my plans a little. Oh well. I may get to live my life again and do things more efficiently.'

'We only get one life,' Noose retorted. It was this that Mrs Lester found most amusing.

'Do we indeed?' she laughed.

Peter stood surveying his work in Mrs Lester's garden. He looked up at the sky as Noose came to join him.

'Lucy's out there somewhere, Peter. Looking down.' He put his arm on Peter's shoulder.

'You believe all that, do you? Heaven?'

'I don't know. What I do know is that we'll find her killer. Trust me. I know you can't remember it now, but when you get over this amnesia thing it'll be top of your priority list.'

Peter smiled, sure he would be keen to bring Lucy Davies' killer to justice if he had his memory and could remember having been in love with her. However, his affections had now been cast upon another - another he could remember. He turned and looked through the cottage window at Lauren inside. She was plain and yet somehow so beautiful. She was the perfect woman for him. He wanted her so bad, but she was tied to another man.

Mrs Lester was being put into a police car when Williams, Trout and Noble pulled up. They stepped out as Noose and Peter walked down Mrs Lester's front path. She called out to them as they walked past her.

'Hey, you two. One thing I don't understand.'

'You mean you want *us* to clear something up for *you*?' Noose laughed.

'Well, I'm bemused. If Peter found out I was the killer, how come you rang on my bell moments later and arrested me?'

'Ah, you see, the mysteries of life I'm afraid,' Noose teased, slamming the car door shut on her. He tapped on the roof as it drove away before walking over to Williams, Trout and Noble. Peter removed the silent attack alarm Noose had given Mrs Lester from his pocket.

'This gadget saved my life. Hold your finger down, it doesn't make a sound and the police can hear everything!' Peter exclaimed.

'Lauren did say you were lucky,' Noose added.

'All cleared up it would seem,' Williams chirped ahead of them. 'And with your help, Peter!'

Peter shrugged his shoulders. Williams took hold of his hand and shook it but he pulled it sharply away from her.

'Not only did I solve two murders today - well stumble upon a murderer - I also had a gun held to my head whilst tied to a chair.'

'What?' Williams questioned, confused.

'Oh yes. I have a message for you, Trout, and you, Williams. The man from the pub wants what is owed him. Somebody told me he was called The Anarchist, I don't know.' Peter walked between them and off down the lane.

Geoff came running over.

'What's happened? Was that Mrs Lester in the cop car? Is she the killer?' he cried out in joy and excitement.

'Go away, man,' Williams cried back, trying to head after Peter.

'I demand answers!' Geoff shouted, getting in her way.

Noose got in his car and drove up the lane after Peter, who got in. They drove away. Lauren stepped out of Mrs Lester's cottage with a bag of evidence. She and Noble caught sight of each other. He stared for a moment at her before turning his back. She looked down at her ringless finger, not knowing what to do.

Peter sat alone in the police station reception. O'Toole was busy rustling papers in a filing cabinet behind his perspex-screened room. He exited the room and disappeared somewhere. Peter stood up and walked up to the screen, looking at the door that O'Toole had just gone through. Something possessed him to discover how to get into the room and behind the desk. He walked through the double doors and searched for the door, soon coming across it. He walked in, sitting on O'Toole's swivelling chair on casters. He spun around and up and down, smiling. Oh, for small pleasures.

Peter's attention was now focused on the computer on the desk. It was off. He switched it on, but nothing happened. He looked under the desk to see if the computer was actually plugged in. Suddenly, O'Toole came back in with a coffee in his hand.

'You won't get it to work.'

Peter turned to him. 'Why not? It should do, it's plugged in.'

'Superintendent Hastings removed the hard drive and mutilated the inside. It contained all his dodgy dealings.'

'Ah, I see.' Peter stood up.

'Yes,' O'Toole continued, coffee clutched, 'they found it in his house. It's been taken away for examination.'

'Why haven't they removed the computer too?'

'I don't know. No need to, really.'

'Well, why not remove and replace all the computers? Surely they're on a local area network or something?' Peter amazed himself at how the forgetting brain could remember facts yet not personal memories.

'Yes,' O'Toole explained, 'but his dodgy files could only be accessed from this computer. He had them password-protected or something.'

'Hmm. Sounds very complicated to me.'

'Anyway, what are you doing in here?'

'Oh, I solve mysteries now,' Peter proclaimed arrogantly. 'Anyway, it just all sounds a bit odd to me.'

'What does?'

'Well I mean, you're always on reception. It's you who uses this computer all the time. Surely Hastings would have used his own computer? Presuming he had one.'

'Look, they found the money in his account and the hard drive in his house, he's guilty,' replied a flustered O'Toole. He had dropped his previously jokey demeanour.

'Only some of the money,' Peter pointed out.

'What? Who told you that?'

'What if he was framed? Think about that.' Peter grinned at O'Toole, impressed with himself. Suddenly, however, O'Toole threw the coffee in his face and thumped him. Peter cried out at the burning pain as O'Toole pulled him up and got him in a headlock. 'I wasn't accusing you,' Peter cried out, 'I was accusing Trout and Williams.'

'You're too nosy.'

Peter broke free and darted for the door. O'Toole blocked his way and punched him again. Noose appeared at reception and saw the unfolding thrashing.

'What the hell?'

'I want to be rich! Sitting behind a desk day in day out isn't gonna get me far, is it?' O'Toole spat out as he launched for Peter again. But Peter was sick of being beaten all the time and gave his attacker one massive smack across the chops. O'Toole fell to the floor, unconscious. He turned to see Noose through his burning eyes.

'He framed Hastings!'

The investigation was over and Peter had no more instructions to follow from the rucksack he had found on his back a few days previously. He still could not remember himself, but had managed to survive several attempts on his life. He sensed there was more to come, though, and he sat on the park bench for a moment with Noose to contemplate his next move. He simply had to try and remember.

'I wonder what happened to Michael and Cynthia,' Noose pondered before Peter could ask him any questions. 'I guess they got scared and ran away or something.'

But that was not quite the case. Only Geoff knew their ultimate fate. For he *had* caught Michael up during the car chase when Noose had been stopped by the traffic lights.

Michael's car eventually came to a halt on a bridge and he jumped out of his car to open the boot. Inside was a huge roll of carpet. This little man struggled to heave it out, but he managed. The immense weight dropped with a tremendous thud to the ground.

'I warned you Cynthia, I really did!' he told the carpet, before dragging it to the edge. As it plopped into the river below, Geoff's car pulled up and he got out with an air rifle in his hand. 'If you tell the cops, I'll say we planned it together,' he told Geoff. But Geoff raised the air rifle to Michael's face.

Geoff pulled the trigger and blasted Michael's life away. 'Don't worry, it can be our little secret.' Michael's body, and what remained of his head, dropped to the ground. Geoff kicked him over the edge after Cynthia.

Peter walked along the country lane he had first appeared in, hoping to somehow regain his memory in the place he had lost it. Coming towards him, in the distance, was the man riding Peter's bicycle. The man who had stolen it from him. He even still had Peter's rucksack on his back. Peter darted into a ditch and searched for a stick. As the man rode past, Peter jumped out and whacked him with the stick he'd found. The man flew off the bicycle into a ditch himself.

Peter sprinted up to him and pulled the rucksack from his back, jumping on his bicycle and riding off. The startled man got his bearings, waving his fist after Peter as he rode off into the distance. After a time, Peter's legs tired. The lane seemed to have no end the opposite way. He must now have been quite far away from Noose and the other inhabitants of Myrtleville. He came to a stop and suddenly realised his rucksack felt weightier than before. He opened it, wondering what the strange man had put in it. There were more wet socks, for some strange reason, and under them a rather battered old book. Peter's heart nearly stopped when he saw what it was called. *I Am Dead*. He felt somehow he shouldn't read it, for he had heard so many fractured mentions of it in the last few days. It had rather put him off in a way, even though Neville had said it would reveal himself to himself. Just as Peter was about to open the cover to look upon its contents, a group of hooded figures came charging at him from up the lane.

'NO!' they howled together.

Peter jumped on his bicycle, still clutching *I Am Dead*, and desperately pedalled away from them. But he could not get away. They enveloped his very being and he felt himself being drawn back. He didn't know what to do, but the final decision on this occasion was made by the sudden appearance of a big upright box in the middle of the lane that had not been there a second ago. He slammed into it, torn from the bicycle. The hooded ones ensconced him, drawing him away from this place. In a moment he, they and the box were gone. Only the bicycle and rucksack remained. And *I Am Dead*.

Tony sat alone in the cell, all alone. He, the only one who knew himself, had failed in the task to kill Peter Smith. He would get another chance, he thought. There would be ample opportunities in the future so long as Jim, Stephen and Darren remained forgetful. But Tony wondered why Reaping Icon had even instructed them to do so in the first place. Why couldn't Reaping Icon just kill Peter Smith himself? Maybe he was unable to. All this thought of Reaping Icon presently brought the one who looked like a man to this cell and he stood over Tony.

'Oh, Tony,' Reaping Icon said. Tony tried to stand but could not. 'You have failed my task. Tony, of usual impeccable loyalty.' But, Reaping Icon always knew what was going to happen, didn't he? Then he knew that Tony would fail, surely? Perhaps the future wasn't as set in stone as first thought. But, he hadn't rested all his efforts in Tony's attempt. There was still the awakening of Jim, Stephen and Darren to come. 'He who kills Peter Smith usurps his link to The Space,' Reaping Icon explained to the hapless Tony. 'As the most mentally malleable, you had the first chance. You failed, Tony.' With this, Tony dropped to his knees. Reaping Icon placed his hand atop Tony's head and drew the life from him until there remained nothing but the dead empty shell that fell to the cell floor. Tony was dead and Reaping Icon left.

PART THREE

SLIP

When your memories aren't true

INTENT TO MURDER - PART TWO
THE FOLLOWERS

'It all happened so suddenly. It really did. But I forget exactly what it was, so I will get back to it later. In the meantime, there's something else you should know about me. You might not want to know it but I'm going to tell you anyway. I say you might not want to know it, but that's maybe a bit presumptuous of me. Presumption has always been my weakness. Let me down, it has. I underestimate, no, overestimate people. Presume they're in the know when they're not. Sometimes they are in the know. Very occasionally, of course. Thus, on the whole, I jump to a misjudged conclusion based on presumption. I say a lot of words too but don't really say much,' he laughed, 'if you know what I mean. A lot of words, but not a lot actually being said. Anyway, I had something to tell you, something you might not like to know. My name is Stuart Smith.' He paused for a response from his listeners, but he got nothing. 'A once faceless nobody, I have through no fault of my own risen, or should that be fallen, to infamy by proxy. The brother of Peter Smith. I am defined, forever labelled by history, as the younger brother of Peter Smith. A name which brings grown men to their knees in terror. But it wasn't always that way.' Again he paused for a response or, at the very least, acknowledgement. Nothing. 'It's amazing how quickly you can become annoyed by something so simple as the way somebody walks,' Stuart continued. 'Just by being in their company too long. It was the beginning of the end of my time under that roof. I had to escape. Dad was dead, you see, and Peter and Mum had this thing going on. I could see it. Sort of an inescapable rut. It wasn't for me. I wanted to get out and do something. Of course, Mum was apprehensive, wasn't she. She wanted me to go out and do something, but she was still nervous. She couldn't fully commit to my plans, but didn't try to stop me. She had him. And he was never going to leave her, was he. God knows why. She would always belittle and humiliate him. We all would. She'd say he had no job. He'd say he was a writer. She'd say he'd never had anything published, though. That sort of thing.' He paused to allow his brain to retrieve further memories. 'He had no go in him. He always said he had plenty of go, but he just couldn't go. Something was holding him back. Something neither he nor I could put our fingers on. Maybe it's because he was dead. Dead metaphorically; dead inside. Kind of a self-indulgent type thing. Not as dead as Lauren from the bank, and Lucy from way back when. Maybe that's why he had no go. He had gone before and it had lead to murders. And there were others too. Murders seemed to follow him around. That Inspector Noose was always on his side though, really chummy for some reason. God only knows why. What got me was how Pete was able to block these things from his mind. Well, I dunno really. We were all able, I guess.' Stuart had a tickle in his throat and presently cleared it with a little cough. 'I used to get so bored - bored out of my tiny little mind. So much to do, plenty to do - I just didn't want to do any of it. I guess I could have lead a completely different life had I not fought against this and gone out into the big bad world. Sometimes you just have to have strength of character. And a will. I got a job and a wife, and my son Zak came along soon afterwards - ended up Consultant

Supervisor at the cake factory. Funny thing, my boss calls himself The Cake. Funny chap. But anyway, I forced myself to walk down a different path to the one I could have gone down. Peter was forever drawn back home. Maybe that was the best place for him. Every time he did go out, something bad happened. Somebody somewhere just didn't want him to leave Mum. It was almost like, had Pete sacrificed himself and stayed at home forever, everyone else would have been spared.' Stuart looked around again at his audience. He felt he was running out of things to say. 'I guess if you really want an insight into my mind, I'd say only this: there's nothing more beautiful in this world than the sight and smell of freshly-laid tarmac. So uniform, so splendid. All pressed down as it is. I truly believe that. Odd, isn't it. I dunno what else to say to be honest.'

'You say on page 193 of the sacred text,' Doctor Johnson uttered, flicking to the section in *I Am Dead*, 'that you feel there is some catastrophe coming, involving yourself. What about that? Tell us more, brother of the final link.'

'*Felt.*' Silence. 'I felt like there was some catastrophe coming.'

'It has come?'

'No. I don't know. I am not quite the Stuart Smith of the book, am I. Things have changed, I'm an alternate version.' He wanted to laugh at his sheer audacity, but knew these people believed this stuff. He was making money from this appearance. 'We all are. Peter changed things. Perhaps the catastrophe I sensed was Peter changing things. Closing The Space.'

Doctor Johnson leapt up. 'Yes, yes! You said humanity wasn't just doomed, but over. You foresaw it coming. You, Stuart Smith, can reach The Space.'

'I can? But humanity isn't over, is it. We're here right now, aren't we?'

'We must prepare.' Doctor Johnson, shaking but sturdy, turned to the rest of the gathering and nodded. They all stood up together and stepped towards Stuart. 'The Space begged you to save it. You failed, but were singled out. And you heard the calling. You will reach The Space for us.' Doctor Johnson grabbed hold of Stuart and threw him at the rest of The Followers. He stumbled down, lost in the mass as they consumed him.

Stuart was hanging upside down in the centre of a circle of Followers, his thick blonde hair hanging, torn down by gravity.

'You will no longer prosecute the final link,' Doctor Johnson preached at Stuart, 'you will join him as a link. Today,' he turned to face his fellow Followers, 'we will create our own link. We, my brothers, are servants of Peter Smith. We will become a new collective for him. We will be as great as the Great Collective itself.' He turned back to Stuart. 'I know that somewhere this very moment exists a further reality beyond this one, being created right now by the one who lead Peter away. I was there when Peter was called and went with the man.'

'So was I,' a voice called out. Doctor Johnson turned to the circle of Followers just as Noose stepped forth from within them. He came to Doctor Johnson and raised a gun to his head. 'I'm officially ending this shit.'

'I was quite enjoying my bullshitting until they took me so seriously and strung me upside down,' Stuart revealed as Noose drove, his bottom lip protruding as he sulked.

'You're lucky I came when I did.' Noose looked in the rear-view mirror. Doctor Johnson was close behind. 'They'll never give up.'

'Who, and until what? I mean I've read *I Am Dead* too, but it's just the ramblings of my mad murdering brother, isn't it.'

Noose glanced sideways before fixing his eyes back on the road ahead. 'For ten years, I struggled to understand that night Peter went on his rampage. It just didn't make sense to me. Then, when he broke from his restraints and vanished with that other man, I had to look into it further. I read *I Am Dead* and it all started slotting together.'

'Yeah, I read it too, as I said. Everyone has. It's the rambling notes of a madman, printed to sensationalise and profit from Peter's notoriety since his escape.'

'No, not at all. An ancient copy appeared to me. I was just strolling down a country lane in Myrtleville one day and there it appeared. It was so old and worn out, as though it had been printed centuries before.'

'Don't tell me you believe it's a sacred text as well?'

'It *is*, Stuart, and there's something we must do to stop Johnson and his Followers succeeding.'

'Succeeding in what?'

'Peter only killed those people in desperation. Something snapped inside him and he saw no other way of breaking from the inevitability of *I Am Dead* unfolding.'

'So did *I Am Dead* happen or not? Did Peter destroy and re-create the universe or what?'

'It did and it didn't, and he did and he didn't,' Noose explained.

'What? I don't understand.'

'*I Am Dead* did happen, because I can remember it happening. The Space has shown itself to me.'

'But in *I Am Dead*, Peter closed The Space. How can it show you something if it's closed?'

'Peter has re-opened The Space by undoing the events of *I Am Dead*.'

'You're not making sense,' Stuart shouted, getting quite angry now.

'Listen,' Noose raised his voice to the level of Stuart's, checking his rear-view mirror again. Doctor Johnson was still behind. 'The events of *I Am Dead* did happen, but they must continue to play out to remain constant. The only way to undo the events is to fight against them. Peter has stopped them with his actions. He changed history, stopped it unfolding. Johnson and The Followers want them to remain as in the book.'

'Why?'

'Because they're crackers. They believe in their book. Nothing can challenge that, not even the one person they follow. Their god became their enemy.'

'So,' Stuart tried to make sense of this, 'you're telling me *I Am Dead* happened, and when Peter finally realised that he had closed The Space, he tried to change it by murdering a bunch of people?'

'Something like that.'

Noose slammed the brakes on and turned the engine off.

'Where are we?' Stuart asked, nervous, looking around at the country lane.

'We're where I found *I Am Dead*. We are here to face our destiny.' Noose picked his gun up and pointed it at Stuart. 'Get out of the car.'

'Hey man, we're on the same side.'

'There are no sides. There is only something we must do to ensure The Followers cannot gain access to The Space and use it to bring back the events of *I Am Dead*.'

Doctor Johnson's car pulled up behind Noose. He stepped out slowly, his hands in the air. Noose got out of his car too, with Stuart following.

'Things must occur as they do in the book. There must be stability,' Doctor Johnson called over to Noose.

'Never. Peter did not want it. If you truly follow Peter Smith, you will accept his new path.'

'Don't make me laugh, you foolish man,' Doctor Johnson replied. 'Why do you think he was taken away?'

'To stop you succeeding?'

'No! Because Peter himself had done wrong. He was taken away to be punished.'

'You're insane, and *I Am Dead* will never unfold again.'

Noose, still pointing the gun between both Stuart and Doctor Johnson, removed the book from his pocket and threw it to the ground. 'This is where I found it. This is where we die.'

'Die?' Stuart asked, filled with dread. 'No, that's not happening. I've got a wife and son.'

'And you always will have, right now in the new reality where Peter is. We all exist there too, but we must remove ourselves from this one to ensure he has the best chance to extinguish *I Am Dead* for good.'

'No, you can't do this.'

Stuart turned and ran. Noose pulled the trigger and shot Stuart down.

'I'm so sorry, but it must come to pass. Peter must not be torn between these realities.'

'You stupid man,' Doctor Johnson shouted at Noose. 'If you undo Peter's work here, the events will unfold anyway. I win.'

'Peter is a murderer in this reality, but he is not that man. He is a good man, I know it. I will not have him cemented in history as that murderer. He is a great man, a wondrous man who has the potential for such compassion and kindness. If there is the remote chance he can be that person in the next reality, then I am willing to sacrifice all this for that.' He held the gun up to Doctor Johnson. 'The Great Collective had crumbled, when It came, but Peter Smith had closed The Space and saved it from ebbing away any further. Love. Friendship. Respect. All had returned. Now The Space has been re-opened, and all is in flux. We must fix that which shifts about.'

'That is one of the things I could never solve, what It was. What is It?'

'It is yet to come for us. Peter will save us all.' Noose pulled the trigger and shot Johnson down. But he was still alive; the bullet missed his heart.

'You must listen to me,' he cried out, in one final attempt to halt his impending demise. 'There were others called away, by the man. I traced four others from the book who were taken.'

Noose did not care; he had made his mind up. He fired again, finishing Doctor Johnson off. He then dragged both bodies to the very same spot he found *I Am Dead* and put the gun to his own head. 'I AM DEAD,' he yelled, before pulling the trigger. His lifeless body dropped on top of the other two. Nothing happened, because Peter Smith was no longer in this reality and nothing here mattered. Everything was nothing here. Peter Smith had created this world, a world ravaged by madness. All who dwelt in it were not who they could be.

COURSE OF ACTION

'We cannot keep you here for long,' the ancient droning voice slurred. 'You are being called back, drawn back to the life you must lead.'

Peter, torn from his bicycle and the country lane a second ago, found himself in what could only be described as a dark hole. There were others in this hole, all hooded and huddled around him, their features invisible in this dim light and hidden by the shield of cloth over them.

'What do you want?'

'Everything is nothing. No order, no lies,' the voice continued. 'Deny your anchor, scape the goats. Everything is nothing. No boundaries, no battles. Peter Smith. Our last chance. The final link. The final link between the Great Collective and The Space. You, and only you, can restore that which has passed.'

'How?'

'Things have been altered since last we met. We failed you last time and now things have been disturbed.'

'What things? Is this about my memory loss? Can you restore my memory?'

'Reaping Icon has been unleashed to interfere with you. You, and only you, can defeat him and restore that which has passed. Peter, you must re-open The Space.'

'I simply cannot remember these things.'

'There is only one thing we beg your forgetting mind to

recall, and that is this: do *not* read *I Am Dead*. You cannot return to evil and become part of Reaping Icon's set. He will forever goad you to placate the sensual.' A howl of fury echoed down the hole. 'The undiluted must not remain as such.'

All at once, Peter was dragged from this place and thrown back to where he had been taken from.

UNDOING JIM

I've always felt myself a rather small fish in the sea. When they go on about there being plenty more fish in the sea, I guess I'm one of the plenty. I'm in abundance, me. I'm sort of superfluous in a way. Oh, I do my bit down at the station and plod on, but that's about it. Depressed about things isn't really how I'd describe my mindset, but after returning to Myrtleville with David after the last endeavour, I've felt quite down to be honest. We had to go and interview some people up in North Harnlan - weird place. What a trek, but I suppose we did our bit and two murders were solved. Problem was, the second murder was this guy called Roger Parsonage and he was our suspect. Still, it was all solved and we came back.

So, we come back and I start to feel a bit bad. I've developed this facial spasm, see. I had quite a bad turn up in North Harnlan, almost like some kind of fit. I've been checked over and they can't find anything, but it's embarrassing. I mean, had I had it for a long time, I'd have gotten used to it, as would everyone who knows me, but because it's new it's an awkward kinda thing when it starts up in front of people. I feel like I'm going mad. It's an awful thing to say I know, because we're always taught not to link these sort of neurological disorders or whatever they are to real full-on psychoses. You know, madness and generally being a weirdo. Problem is, I'm beginning to feel like a weirdo. Just earlier, I looked over at Lauren that trainee pathologist and I wanted to wear her clothes. She wasn't even showing any of her own clothes; she was in her scrubs. Again, I'm not saying that men who want to wear women's clothes are crackers. It's just that I haven't ever wanted to before, so it seems very odd that my mind feels like it's messing up somehow.

It's now a case of taking one second at a time, let alone minute, hour or day. Things can quickly change and it doesn't take much to alter something. I feel I've been altered, and definitely not for the better. I've gone bananas but I've got to keep it quiet. I'm a police officer and I need the money. If I started blabbing all this to some shrink, God knows what would happen. No, it would make things worse. The best thing for me to do is to keep a lid on this whole thing and hope it's sort of a passing phase. You hear about men going through phases as they get older. This is just a phase.

My urge to kill someone is terrible. Urges are really hard to fight. This is so terrible. It's a tragedy. Why has this happened to me - to Jim? Am I Jim? I don't even know anymore.

Everything is now clear in my mind. I've chosen my victim. Peter Smith. Actually, I haven't chosen him. He chose himself. He made himself known to me, if you can understand that. Of course you can't understand that. I must kill Peter Smith. KILL HIM. I'm gonna kill Peter Smith. I don't even feel any emotions about it. I don't hate him. I don't even know him. He has been chosen. He has been selected. Reaping Icon has revealed himself to me and has decided to fling us onto a level playing field. This will be delicious.

MEMORIES

An attack of conscience is futile. It is desperation, the enormous brink of a dilemma brewing inside the killer's mind beyond the avenging power of man or woman. The place this story begins to end is a simile of everything where all those who are not foolish fear to tread. And it starts this way, with Peter Smith having a bad dream:

'Peter? Come on Peter, get up for school.'

'Mother, I enjoy your jests but I'm in my forties.'

'I'm going to the shops, Peter poo.'

'Mother, stop. You're not supposed to leave the house. You're not well.'

'Get your father, Peter, I'm feeling a bit woozy.'

'But Father's dead, Mother dear. He has been dead for some years, remember?'

'I remember the summer before you were consumed. No, consummated. No, before we created you. You were the sparkle in your father's eye. Or was that a cataract?'

'Mother, you told me last night that I was a mistake.'

'Go away! Leave me alone, you rotter. I don't know who you are, leave me alone. Please help me, somebody! Help me get away from this yob!'

'Calm down, Mother.'

'I have no son! Except Stuart. Stuart is lovely.'

'Don't make me put a pillow over your face, Mother.'

'I can fly like a bird! Like a butterfly I die.'

'Everything dies.'

'Like you, my boy.'

'Pardon me?'

'Haha! Who's worried now, little boy? Tiny little Peter pudding.'

'Please, Mother, you're scaring me.'

'You wimp, scared of a frail old lady like me!'

'You're not old, Mother.'

'Oh but I am my boy, because I was in my forties when I had you.'

'Yes, yes you're remembering things. Doctor Johnson said your memory would come back in fits and starts.'

'Doctor who?'

'Doctor Johnson.'

'He is dead, like me.'

'You're not dead, Mother, please don't talk like that. You're upsetting me.'

'I'll upset you even more if you don't stop calling me Mother all the time. I'm too young to be your mother. Who are you? Are you my husband?'

'Yes, Mother. Whatever you want me to be.'

'Argh! That's it, I've had it with you. You will die now.'

'What did you say?'

'So are we having mashed or boiled potatoes for tea?'

'Boiled for me and mashed for you.'

'Thank you.'

Peter wakened with a heavy head. Heavy with nothing. He had ended up back in Myrtleville somehow, even though he clearly remembered heading in the other direction. Somehow he felt something had stopped him and sent him back. He even had his bicycle back, but he couldn't recall how it had returned. Suffice to say, Noose had put him up for the night, which turned into longer, and what had followed were some awful days of flashbacks and nightmares. Memories were returning, but also visions. Well, Peter couldn't describe them any other way. He saw things that appeared to take place in the future.

'Hey Peter, how's your mother getting on?' Darren asked, rather flustered and bewildered. He was carrying a bag and had been running. This was a little peculiar for the usually lazy man. Peter knew he was lazy, the dream told him, but he didn't know who he was. He looked a bit like The Anarchist, only older.

'Well, you know, as well as could be expected. She still argues with me and threatens to kill me, but she can be quite bright and cheerful at times,' Peter replied rather jovially.

'Anyway, back to the old wife again.' There was an awkward silence as Darren smirked at Peter. 'I bet you're glad you're not married, aren't you Peter!'

'I get lonely at times, you know, when the witch is brewing up some evil in her bedroom.'

They both laughed.

'I better be off then.'

Darren jogged on.

Darren got home and walked into the kitchen.

'Julie, just look what you've done to Lauren,' he tutted rather apathetically, chucking the bag on the table and casually glancing up and down at the naked woman huddled in the corner. She was shaking and refusing eye contact. Julie swaggered in, also naked, as Darren started taking his clothes off.

'You said I could, Darren,' Julie replied, approaching Lauren and bending over her. Lauren tried her best to turn away but Julie grabbed her hair and bent her head back. She spat in Lauren's face before banging her head against the wall. Darren seemed a little displeased at this, which was rather odd.

'You must be mistaken. I don't recall saying you could start without me. Not at all, at all.'

'Stop repeating yourself.'

'I only do it when you get me worked up, worked up.'

'Work? Work? You haven't done a day's work in months.'

'And why? Because you drove me to the brink of insanity until I was even scared of my own shadow. Oh I'm sick of you Julie, sick of you for all these years of pain and torment.' He was now also fully naked. 'I want a divorce.'

'Good, I want a divorce too.' Julie looked down at his penis and laughed. 'You're a joke, Darren. A tiny little joke.' Darren opened the cutlery drawer and grabbed hold of a knife. 'What are you gonna do, kill me?' she laughed again.

'If you want me to. It will save time with the divorce.'

'You haven't got the balls.'

He grabbed hold of her neck and lifted her into the air, thrusting the knife into her chest. She gasped in agony as he pulled the knife out and tossed her carelessly onto the lino.

'I'll meet you in hell,' she blubbered, her flimsy limbs floundering around.

'I've already been.' He licked the knife clean and put it back in the drawer, bending down over Lauren. She had seen the whole thing, but this didn't matter; she was only half there. He tugged at her arm and pulled her up. 'You're very plain but pretty, aren't you?' She dropped onto a chair by the table as he tore off a piece of kitchen roll and wiped her face.

This vision weighed heavily on Peter's mind. It freaked him out in other words. There was the sense that somebody outside of his mind was playing tricks, delivering these things to in some way send him further into a mental stupor. The one mental clip that continued to play in his mind night after night was thus:

'Oh Peter my boy, get down here and rub my feet,' the witch shouted from downstairs.

'Yes, you spawn of evil, it's about time I put everyone out of their misery,' he whispered under his breath as he slowly slunk down the stairs.

'Peter, come on!'

'Oh Mother,' Peter entered the living room, 'do you want to be reunited with Daddy?'

'What? What do you mean my lovely child?' she asked him in her weak, rodent squeak. A bewildered, gaunt Peter dug his dagger into her chest. 'You rotter! You naughty boy Peter, be a good boy for me,' she carried on, looking down at her bloodied blouse. 'Oh dear, Peter, you've been very silly.'

He stepped back, horrified at his actions though intrigued to watch the results of them. She quietly slipped away, causing little bother and making little noise. There was little she could do. Peter had done a terrible thing, but he wasn't in his right mind. The door bell rang.

'Peter, oh Peter? Are you in?' Darren shouted through the letterbox.

'Just coming.'

'Okay, I'll wait then.'

Peter put the dagger down and opened the door.

'Hello Darren, how are you?'

'Well I'm fine, thank you.' A large bin bag sat at his feet on the doorstep. 'I just came to ask whether or not I could put this bin bag in your bin as ours is full to the brim with rubbish?'

'Why of course, Darren. Dead body, is it?' Peter joked, catching a whiff of uncooked meat from the bag.

'Well as a matter of fact...'

Suddenly Jim walked past, carrying a shopping bag and waving to the two chatting men. 'Hello boys, how are you then?' he called over.

'I'm fine thanks, Jim,' Darren hastily replied, turning back to Peter, who picked the bin bag up and stepped back inside.

'See you later Darren, goodbye.' Peter did not look at Jim and slammed the door shut as Darren stepped forward to enter. The door hit him in the face and he fell to the ground.

Peter could still see outside in his dream. Jim dropped his

shopping bag and ran over to Darren. 'Oh no, oh my goodness, what has Peter done to you, Darren?!'

'Haha, I'm going to steal your shopping!' exclaimed a young lad, who promptly did as he said and ran off with Jim's bag.

'That's it, you little git,' Jim yelled after the boy, picking up a rock and chasing him. He soon caught up and pounced on the boy, pounding his head with the rock.

The only people Peter actually knew for definite from these visions were Lauren and Jim. He could, at a leap, understand why Lauren had appeared. After all, he was beginning to think a lot about her in his waking hours as well. These things can seep through to sleep. But Jim? The police officer at Myrtleville Station? That was most odd. He was inconsequential, surely. Peter had given him literally no thought until he appeared. Perhaps Peter's subconscious was calling out, trying to tell him something from his past. Or possibly his future. These were, of course, future visions. Peter had not been used to dreaming, though he had had the nightmare of discovering Lucy's body when he was in the cell. He simply didn't know, if he was going to be truthful with himself. Everything was nothing for him. He was completely at a loss to comprehend anything.

'Look Peter, now I don't want to get rid of you or anything, so don't take it like that,' Noose started as Peter shuffled into the kitchen. It was morning, the worst time of day for both men, and Noose had his back turned to the burning sun pouring between the blinds. 'but don't you think it's time you went home?'

'To Mother?' Peter asked, flopping down on a chair. His eyes caught a beam of light and he recoiled from it like acid had just been poured in them.

'You remember her now?'

'No. But I dream. I'm dreaming all the time. She's old. I kill her.'

Noose came to sit down. 'Dreams are funny things, Peter,

they mean nothing.' Noose chuckled. 'Doesn't mean you're actually going to kill her.' Peter frowned. 'But still, as I said, you're welcome to stay here as long as you like but, you know. You do have a home, and I'm sure your mum would be thrilled to see you again after all this time.' Noose looked towards the window, growing slowly more accustomed to the morning light. 'You two were quite close once.'

'A little too close, maybe. Is that why I do her in?'

'Peter, Peter, it's a dream. I dreamt I did someone in the other day.' He laughed. 'You'd been on a rampage a while back.'

'A rampage?'

'Oh yes, this had a back story and all sorts. It was in the future, you'd killed a bunch of people and then ten years later you escaped, so I killed two people too. Let me think,' Noose tapped his chin, 'your brother Stuart for some strange reason, then some doctor called Johnson.'

'Doctor Johnson? That was the same name that cropped up in my dream.'

Noose laughed it off, standing up again. 'Oh, plus myself. I put the gun to my head too.'

'Maybe these things do happen, in the future. Maybe we're being warned.'

'Don't be stupid, they're just dreams. Silly dreams.' Noose checked his watch. 'Anyway, I've got to go to work. Hastings is back today.' He put his hand on Peter's shoulder. 'I really do think you need to make contact with your family. It is for the best.' Noose took a piece of paper from his pocket and placed it on the table in front of Peter. Written on it was *Miriam Smith* and her telephone number. Peter picked it up and, glancing towards Noose's phone, smiled. But Peter had no intention of making the call. He was too nervous. After Noose left, Peter got his jacket and, chucking the phone number in the bin, left too. Noose didn't want him there so he wasn't going to stay.

PART FOUR

ONCE, TWICE, THRICE DEMISE

ONE

Ruby was a tall, middle-aged woman with wild red hair. She prided herself on being both a housewife and a breadwinner, seeing as her husband Arthur could be summed up in one word: idle. She was stood at the sink on this early morning still in her dressing gown, thrashing soapsuds over various knives, forks, spoons and plates as a microwave rotated beside her. This was the sort of kitchen that should have been replaced long ago, but perhaps financing a new one was hard. Her sixteen-year-old daughter Katie entered, dragging her feet, and came crashing down onto a chair at the table. She wore the same dressing gown as her mother and the two would have been facially identical too had it not been for the years of hard graft which had slightly creased Ruby's features. Her shoulders, too, were slightly arched. Only slightly, but enough to send out the message that the older of the two females in this room had been there and done it. She was a worker and she worked hard. She turned to face her daughter.

'I see the dead's up,' she remarked of the slumped teenager in the room, worn out by sheer youth and all its trappings.

'Is it just me, or does it smell in here?' Katie asked, her nostrils flaring with disgust and intrigue.

Ruby turned around, smirking, and sniffed the air. 'Well, your father's still in bed.'

'What's for breakfast, Mum?' she asked of the slave horse, rubbing sleep from her eyes.

'It's in the microwave.'

'Smells like cabbage boiled with old socks.'

'You'll shut up and eat it, right?' Ruby demanded of her daughter, waving a knife around. The microwave bell rang and Ruby leapt at it, pulling the door open. She grabbed at a plastic container within, removing a cellophane lid, and slammed it down on the table in front of Katie. *'Bon apptit!'* She chucked the cellophane lid towards the bin but its feather weight was not sufficient to propel it far enough and it just missed, landing on the lino. Katie looked horrified at the grub awaiting her consumption.

'What's this?'

'Spaghetti bolognaise.'

'For breakfast?'

'There's no milk. Would you rather have dry cereal?'

'No, but…' She picked up a fork and gingerly picked at the food. Placing a minute portion of it in her mouth, she duly spat it out. 'It's not even cooked, it's half frozen.'

'Quit your whinging. It's all or nothing with you, innit.'

Arthur hobbled in. A bald, tubby man, he looked to be somewhat younger than Ruby. He was not. A life of working his wife had left him with an easy face, though his love of beer had left him with a hideous gut. He kicked a chair out from under the table with his slippered foot and dropped down onto it.

'Breakfast, woman, breakfast!' he yelled, slamming his fist down on the table. He burped as Ruby walked sweetly over to him.

'Here we are my love,' she sang in a sickly serenade, sliding the spaghetti bolognaise over to him and overly fluttering her eyelashes.

'What's this shit?' Arthur asked, lifting it up to his hairy nostrils.

'Your breakfast.'

He took a bite. His face brightened up. 'Delicious.'

Ruby and Katie looked at each other and raised the same eyebrow, before the former turned back to the sink and the latter sank her head in her hands. Peter entered, in matching pyjamas to Arthur's, and opened the fridge and cupboard to go about preparing his breakfast. He was ignored by the others, as though they could not see or sense his presence. Soon he placed a bowl of cereal on the table. Katie eyed it, displeased.

'Is that milk?' she grunted at Peter.

He sat down in front of the bowl with a newspaper and began flicking through it as he raised a spoonful of cornflakes to his lips.

'It's white and it's wet, what else can it be?'

Arthur chuckled at this and was about to retort, but Ruby gave him a domineering glare and a pointed finger.

'Where'd you get it from?' Katie pushed.

'Mysteries, eh,' was Peter's reply as he edged the bowl away from Katie's almost frothing jaws.

'Mum said we had none, Mum, you said we had none... Where did that come from?'

'A cow!' Ruby responded. Katie folded her arms and sat back in a sulk. The door bell rang.

'Alex!' Katie cried, 'I'm not even dressed,' she leapt up in a panic, darting about the room, 'you'll have to tell him I'm dead, tell him I'm dead.'

'You were dead last week,' Ruby pointed out, 'you can't still be dead.'

'Once you're dead you're dead, no qualms about it,' Arthur remarked, trying to get a look-in at Peter's paper.

Ruby opened the door to a teenage boy, the tall and dark-haired Alex, who hadn't been at all affected by acne and didn't even seem to have started any facial hair growth either. He was dressed in the purple school blazer and tie of Myrtleville Secondary School - the best and only secondary school in the local area.

'Hi, everything alright?' he asked, poking his head past the imposing frame of Ruby.

Katie, having not quite managed to get out of the room before being seen, poked her head out from behind the door leading into the hallway.

'Hi Alex! No, everything's fine. I just need to brush my hair.' She vanished, a heavy thud on every step reverberating throughout the entire house as she ran up the stairs.

Ruby stood aside. 'Come in and wait.'

'Thank you, Mrs Edwards.'

'Everybody calls me Ruby.' She grimaced at the poor lad. 'Katie won't be a sec, gotta put some clean knickers on.' She closed the door behind the boy as he passed her, rather puzzled. He sat down next to Arthur.

'Take a seat, why don't you!' Arthur exclaimed, pushing what remained of his breakfast into the middle of the table. He sat back in his chair and stared intently at Alex.

'Mr Edwards,' Alex acknowledged. Arthur undid a button on his pyjama top, his stomach now visible. Alex looked at it cautiously. He ignored Peter, and Peter ignored him. After many seconds of excruciating unease, Katie finally rushed back in, now dressed in the same school uniform as Alex.

'Alex!' She smiled nervously, lingering somewhat at a distance from him. He too blushed slightly, his eyes only momentarily glancing at the ginger teenager.

'I thought you were gonna brush your hair?' he blabbed. Katie, paranoid, looked in desperation at her reflection in one of the glass wall cabinets.

'Why, is it… does it…' She fiddled with her mass of hair.

Ruby opened the door. 'There's nothing wrong with your hair, now naff off, the pair of you.'

Alex jumped up and darted through the door as Katie followed.

The blossoming lovebirds made their way to the bus stop, quickly catching a glimpse of the other when they thought they would not be caught. All at once, Katie felt she had something to say to Alex, and was about to blurt it out.

'Alex, I, erm…'

But all of a sudden Emma appeared behind them, pushing them apart and dancing in front. She was a tall, slim brunette who would no doubt have been hailed as the prettiest of the pair had she and Katie been in a competition. But Katie did have that Celtic look about her; that fresh dreamy quality. She ought to have had freckles too, but didn't quite. Maybe she did.

'Hey guys!' Emma announced to the pair that she was here.

'Hey Emma,' Katie replied, somewhat annoyed.

'Hey Emma!' Alex replied, somewhat delighted. A little too delighted, Katie thought.

She eyed Emma up, then looked back at Alex. His eyes were fixed on the new arrival. The brunette. The one who, at sixteen, was ever so slightly coming of age physically.

'So Alex, I…' Katie tried to continue.

'All ready for the exam, Emma?' Alex asked the other one, ignoring Katie.

'Of course. What about you, Katie?'

Katie looked up the road, checking her watch. 'Yeah, whatever.'

'It's GCSEs, Katie, you gotta be prepared,' Emma pushed.

'I know enough.'

She pushed past Emma and came to a halt at the bus stop. She sat down and folded her arms.

'You better not fail, Katie. Sixth form wouldn't be the same without you,' Emma went on. Katie frowned as Emma and Alex looked back at her with wide grins.

In the school canteen, Emma busied herself nibbling on a piece of toast. Never one to enjoy being watched as she ate, she straightened her back and refused eye contact when Michelle walked up to her. As well as her own insecurities, she feared Michelle the most of all of the school bitches. She was usually seen as the hottest girl in school by the lads, with her striking blonde hair and big boobs, but Emma and the rest of the other attractive girls felt manipulated by her. She was also not that hot, with a bit of a pig nose and her slimy attitude that made her less appealing. However, when a sixteen-year-old boy wants to get his first leg over, he's not that worried about a pig nose or bitchy behaviour. He just sees the blonde hair and big tits and wants in.

'So Emma, where's Katie?' Michelle asked her.

'I don't know,' was Emma's unusual response. She'd have normally said "dunno". 'And I don't care.'

'Excellent.' Emma now looked at the girl. 'Oh nothing, nothing to worry about.' She tapped Emma on the shoulder.

Meanwhile, Katie was at the other end of the canteen, spying on the two girls from behind a large pot plant.

'Look at them chatting away as if butter wouldn't melt,' she whispered to herself.

Suddenly the stout, near-pension age Mr Hancock appeared behind her.

'Katie Edwards, what on God's Earth do you think you're playing at?'

But Katie continued, unfazed by his presence. 'I'm just peeping at a girl over there, Mr Hancock.'

'I hope you don't make a habit of peeping at teenage girls from behind large tropical foliage, young lady.'

She turned and smiled at the man. 'No more than you do, Mr Hancock.'

As if from nowhere, Michelle slid beside him.

'Oh she does, Sir.'

'Right young lady,' he addressed Katie, 'my office, right

now.' He ushered her towards the exit as she struggled to dodge his immense size.

'Leave me alone, I'm fine here.'

'That takes care of Katie,' Michelle said to herself, walking back over to Emma. 'Come on Emma, let's go and have some fun with my lighter.'

'But are you sure Katie's gonna be okay?'

Michelle held her lighter up to Emma's face and sparked it. 'I didn't think you cared?'

'Oh, oh no, Michelle... No, I don't care,' Emma responded, looking at the flame in fear.

Alex entered the canteen just as Katie was escorted away. He looked somewhat perplexed, spotting Emma and Michelle.

'Hey, what was all that with...' He saw that Emma was worried. 'What's up?'

Emma looked briefly at Michelle before focussing back on Alex. 'Katie's in trouble again.'

'Aye, he's a dickhead, that Hancock.'

Michelle stepped up to him. 'Fierce words coming from you, Alex.'

'It's a free country, I can say what I like.'

'Sure, I never said you couldn't.' She pushed him aside, pulling Emma along with her. 'Anyway, come on Emma. We have revising to do.'

Somebody was filming Ruby on a camcorder as she hung her washing out on the line.

'BOOM! BOOM! BOOM!,' a voice roared from behind the camcorder. It was her neighbour Timothy, a vast young man who had nothing better to do than this. 'For thousands of years we thought the dinosaurs extinct. Now, see for yourself the wonders of Ruby, the last living prehistoric animal. Nessy's sister? NO! This is Jurassic Pork!'

Ruby finished hanging the washing out and promptly

walked back inside, unaware that her image had been captured for evermore on tape. Inside, she dropped the washing basket down on the washing machine.

'I'm off to work now,' she called through to the living room. Receiving no response, she marched through. There, on the sofa, lay Arthur and Peter with their eyes sealed shut, cartoons blaring on the TV. 'I said,' she shouted, 'I'm off to work now!' Arthur grunted, his eyes remaining sealed. 'Lazy buggers. That lawn won't mow itself.' She stormed out, slamming the front door behind her. Peter opened one eye, looking around the room, before opening the other. Seeing Arthur asleep, he got up and crept past him. The front door opened again and Ruby was back. 'Bloody car keys,' Peter could hear her mumbling to herself. She grabbed them from the kitchen and went out again, not seeing that Peter had stirred. He continued on his way, heading for the stairs.

Timothy's camcorder spotted Peter at the top of the landing. Peter looked around, and down the stairs, before reaching up and pulling down the attic hatch. He proceeded to pull down a ladder attached to the hatch.

'Hello!' Timothy buoyed, 'What's all this about? Lanky lodger stores rotting remains of his landlord in the family attic!'

Peter, checking the ladder was secure, started to walk up it. However, he froze, coming back down it and walking over to the landing window. He looked directly out of it, into Timothy's camcorder, drawing the curtains. Timothy panned the camcorder to the left, into the house attached to Ruby and Arthur's. In the kitchen window, an elderly lady, Gerty, stared back at Timothy through her binoculars.

Katie paced up and down Mr Hancock's office as he sat behind his desk.

'Please, Katie, sit down.'

'You can't tell me what to do.'

'I can and I will, now sit down.' She relented, sitting down. But she was still fidgety, uneasy, shifting about in the chair as Mr Hancock opened a file on his desk and sorted through some papers in it. 'Now, I'm a little concerned with your erratic behaviour of late. All the teachers are. You're a bright student, Katie, yet you're not focussed on the exams.'

'I am.'

He leant in towards her. 'Your mock results suggest otherwise, I'm afraid.'

'They're not the real thing, are they? Why waste energy on them?' She folded her arms.

'Look, if there is something occupying your mind, we have counsellors...'

'Counsellors? I'm not a psycho!' She scratched her arm and looked from side to side.

'Problems at home? With friends, perhaps?' he fished.

She jumped up, bursting into tears. 'You just don't listen, do you? None of you listen. No one realises...'

'Realises what, Katie?'

She ran out of the room.

Emma and Michelle were stood in a corner of the school yard. Emma tried to get away from her.

'This stays between you and me,' Michelle spat, her pig nose right in Emma's face. She stood in her way and pushed her back into the corner.

'Let me past.'

'You tell anyone and I swear, I'll-'

Emma stepped up to Michelle. 'You'll what?'

'If this gets out we'll both be for it, you hear me?'

Emma slipped past her. 'Yeah, whatever.'

'This is serious,' Michelle hissed, pulling Emma back.

'Yes I know.'

Katie approached the two, her face still red from the tears.

'Hi,' she greeted them, trying to smile and not sniff.

'What's the matter with you?' Emma asked her friend.

'Nothing.' She turned away and wiped her eyes.

A police car sped into the car park just ahead of the yard and slammed its breaks on. Jim and David got out and ran across the yard past Katie, Emma and Michelle.

'Oh God, they know. Do you think they know?' Emma cried.

'Shut up!' Michelle growled, prodding Emma between the breasts.

'Know what?' Katie queried.

Noose's car was the next to pull up and he and Sergeant Stephen Noble stepped out. They spotted Jim and David ahead and headed after them, Noose strolling and Noble jogging in front.

'Keep your trap shut,' Michelle urged Katie, leering at her, before grabbing hold of Emma. 'Come on, we're off.' They left, leaving Katie to be greeted by Alex. She tried to hide her face from his but he saw it.

'Katie, are you okay?'

'What do you care?'

And she ran off.

'I do,' he uttered under his breath, but she hadn't heard. It was not his intention for her to hear. He was far too nervous.

Noose and Noble entered a corridor in the gymnasium leading to the changing rooms. The gymnasium had been haphazardly converted into an exam hall, complete with crumb-covered floor sheeting and graffiti-galore desks. Jim and David were stood talking to a group of teachers.

'Where's Lauren, for God's sake?' Noose roared, more annoyed at being called out at this early hour than concerned about the corpse lying on the floor. The corpse, a man in his thirties, was dressed in overalls. A hard hat lay next to his smashed head. 'Get this place cordoned off, for crying out loud. It's like a circus in here.'

Mr Hancock pushed his way through the other teachers and came face to face with Noose. 'I hear there's been a-' He spotted the body on the floor. 'Oh dear.' Intrigued, he tried to get past Noose for a closer look. However, Noose held him back.

'Oh dear indeed.'

'What a mess,' Mr Hancock went on, studying the fresh corpse in awe.

'He's been hit on the head,' Noble pointed out to Noose.

'I can see that,' Mr Hancock cut in, still struggling to get nearer.

'Familiar with violent crime, are we?' Noose asked the old teacher, turning to look at him square in the face.

'Mr Hancock,' he announced, holding his hand out to Noose. Noose did not shake it. 'I teach maths. Head of department.'

'I hate maths,' Noose replied.

'Oh, I see. Shame, because numbers are everything.'

Lauren entered, carrying her fishing tackle. She dropped her box down on a stack of gym benches and kneeled over the corpse.

'Dear, dear. Poor chap,' Lauren sighed, looking up at Noble. He turned away.

'Come on, come on,' Noose pushed at Mr Hancock, 'clear off out of it.'

Outside the exam hall, on the school yard, Noose walked out with Mr Hancock. The head teacher, Henry Matheson, paced briskly up to the pair. He was rather dashing and charismatic, clearly rather clever as he had risen to such a post rather early in life. He was mid-30s at a push, yet held his own. His hair had already begun to turn grey, but the salt-and-pepper look suited him. Some of the students had also gathered around, whispering and generally out for a bit of intrigue. Alex was pride of place, stood right at the side of the exam hall entrance behind the adults.

'Ah, Henry!' Mr Hancock said as he saw Matheson approach.

'What?' Noose asked.

'Henry,' Mr Hancock continued, greeting Matheson with a sycophantic arm on his shoulder. 'This is...' he turned to Noose, 'Inspector?'

'Inspector Henry Noose.'

'Henry Matheson.'

The two shook hands, much to Mr Hancock's disappointment. Noose and Matheson smiled knowingly at each other. They were two Henrys, and two men in a position of trust and power. They had a lot in common.

'You are the head master, yes?' Noose asked for confirmation, already sensing by the way Matheson held himself that he was important around here.

'Principal, yes.'

'Principal? Bit American, isn't it?'

Matheson scratched the side of his face and tilted his head down, looking up at Noose. 'Rather. Terms are even called semesters now.'

'What a shame,' Noose responded, seeing the world he came into as a boy slowly, and very silently, slipping away from him.

'Quite. Now, we have ourselves a rather awkward situation here, don't we?' He rubbed his hands together.

'We do.'

'The thing is, we have an exam about to take place.'

'It's cancelled.'

The ear-wigging students all cheered.

'But... we can't,' Mr Hancock butted in. 'It's the maths exam.'

'A man is lying dead in there. Murdered,' Noose pointed out to the unreasonable Mr Hancock. The students gasped. Alex was shocked, frozen to the spot at the door. 'And quite possibly by one of you,' Noose continued, pointing at the students.

'Now please, you can't go around accusing the students,'

Matheson retorted, pulling Noose aside for a private word. 'Although, between us two, I suspect that some of them are capable of much worse.'

'Worse than murder?'

Alex walked away, deep in thought. What had happened here, and why was Katie acting so oddly? He just couldn't fathom it out.

Noble went back to Lauren as she was organising a series of forensic tools on the gym benches.

'We need to talk.'

'You choose your moments, don't you?' she replied, looking sideways at Noble and then back at the corpse.

'You haven't replied to my calls, you ignore me at the station. How can we talk when you're acting like that?'

'When I act like that? What about how *you* act?'

'Letting an escaped murder suspect have a shower in your flat then giving him my clothes is nothing, huh?' He bit his lip, shaking his head.

'Will you just…'

Noose entered. She turned away from Noble, back to her work.

'Everything fine and dandy?' Noose asked.

'Of course,' Lauren replied, not looking back at the pair. 'Oh, Inspector, your victim is Graeme Bradbury. Wallet tells all.' She held out a driving licence, still facing the corpse. 'Hit on the head with a blunt object.'

'Any sign of the weapon?'

'No, but I'd say it was one of his tools. The killer must have taken it.'

Matheson and Mr Hancock appeared at the door.

'Can we help?' the older of the two asked eagerly. Noose was about to fume, but calmed himself down.

'Yes, actually.' He took the driving licence from Lauren and held it up to their faces.

'Ah yes,' Matheson responded, 'he's working, or should I say worked, on some renovation work. Who would kill him?'

'You tell me.'

Mr Hancock turned and walked away. 'Mystery to me,' he mumbled.

'Now, do we have any CCTV in operation around here?' Noble asked.

'Yes. Very primitive though. Outside, not in,' Matheson explained.

'It's a start,' Noose chipped in.

The police were busy hurrying to and fro as Katie spotted Alex and turned to head off in the opposite direction. He caught up with her.

'Katie, wait - I've got something to tell you.'

'What is it now?' she snapped.

'Someone's been murdered in the gym.'

'What?' She couldn't believe it. Whatever she had thought was going on was not as bad as that. 'Oh my God, Emma and Michelle...'

'What about them?'

'I've gotta go.'

She ran off, leaving Alex more confused than ever. If that was possible.

Noose and Noble stood beside each other on the doorstep of the Bradbury family home. It was a pleasant house really, though nothing special - a semi-detached in a housing estate, the sort that cropped up everywhere in the 50s and 60s. As small children played on an unkempt grassy patch across from the house and Noble reached for the doorbell yet again, a young attractive woman opened it. Noble spotted this beauty and suddenly livened up. Before acknowledging the two loitering men on her doorstep, she yelled over to the children.

'Hey, get here now, you little shits.' A boy of eight or nine stuck his middle finger up to his mother and ran off. 'Well I'll… I give up.'

Noble held out his police card. 'Detective Sergeant Stephen Noble and Detective Inspector Henry Noose.'

The woman ran her fingers through her bob and sighed. 'What's happened now?'

'Are you Mrs Nicola Bradbury?' Noble asked.

'Call me Nicky.' She smiled, one leg bent as she leant her shoulder on the door. She now started to study the two men. She was not displeased.

'Can we come in please, Mrs Bradbury?' Noose asked. She stood aside and they slipped in past her, glancing at each other with a register of doom on their faces.

Inside, they dodged the plethora of toys and general anarchy that lay strewn around the living room.

'What's all this about? Has Graeme been up to something?'

'Well put it this way, he won't be up to anything now,' Noose retorted unsympathetically. Noble glared at him disapprovingly, trying to ease Nicola onto the sofa with an arm around her shoulder.

'What?' she demanded, struggling from Noble and slipping across the room.

'You should sit down, Nicky,' Noble encouraged, eager to soften the impending blow. An emotional blow akin to the physical blow her husband had just suffered, perhaps.

'Just tell me.'

'Graeme's dead,' Noose announced coldly.

'I'm sorry,' Noble sighed. Genuinely sorry? Who knows. Here now was another single, attractive woman, should Lauren not work out for him. Yes, this Nicola appeared to have children, but that could be dealt with.

She turned her back on them and looked out of the window at the children playing across the way. 'How, why?'

Noose settled down in an armchair and looked around the room. 'Murdered, in Myrtleville Secondary School. A blow to the head.'

Nicola seemed somewhat surprised, turning quickly to face the pair. 'The school? But he's supposed to be doing work for Simon today, I'm sure of it.' She began to clam up, the true nature of all this beginning to dawn on her.

'Simon?' Noose asked.

'Oh God, oh no... the children... Graeme's mother... me,' she sobbed. Noble put his arm around her but she pushed him off.

'Who is Simon?' Noose pushed.

'Graeme is contracted to Berre Construction. Simon Berre.'

'Do you know of anyone who would have wished to harm your husband in this manner?' Noble asked tactfully. Instantly she stopped sobbing and turned her back on them once more.

'No, why? I don't understand it.'

'Nor do we, Mrs Bradbury,' Noose replied.

The front door flew open and two boys, one of them the middle finger lad, ran in. They bounced a football into the room which promptly caught Noose on the head. They spotted Noose and Noble and sniggered.

Arthur and Peter were once again on the sofa, seemingly asleep, with the TV playing aimlessly on in the background. Ruby walked in and spotted the sorry sight.

'Well, I never!'

She snatched the remote off the sofa and switched the TV off. Peter suddenly sprung into life.

'Hey, I was watching that.'

'Who pays the TV licence?' Ruby pointed out to the cheeky lodger. He merely rolled his eyes before closing them again. Ruby was livid. 'I've just been working. What have you two gits been doing all morning?'

'You call cleaning for old people work?' Arthur replied

without opening an eye. 'Now turn that TV back on.'

Ruby slammed the TV remote down on Arthur's head which brought him to life with a cry of pain and anguish. 'Get up off your fat arse and do some work. Those gutters won't clean themselves.'

'That is my TV. I paid for it,' was Arthur's resilient response.

'Ha! Rubbish! You've never paid for a thing in your life. Everything in this room has fallen off the back of a lorry.' Katie slid in and, throwing her school bag down, slumped into an armchair. 'Oh here we go!' Ruby attacked. Katie did not rise to the commotion. 'Come on, why the long face?'

'It's 'cause she's a horse,' Arthur laughed, nudging Peter to laugh too. Peter, not quite understanding the joke, forced out a chuckle to ease Arthur's prods. Ruby spun around and pointed at them.

'I'm warning you two, you'll be out on your ears.' She turned back to Katie. 'Come on, speak up. Ain't your exam on?'

'Someone was murdered in the exam room.'

Arthur sat up straight, all trace of humour drained from his face. Ruby too lowered her leering shoulders and came to sit down next to Arthur. But she only sat on the edge, leaning close to Katie to continue the interrogation. Peter, however, seemed uninterested, more concerned about an itchy eyebrow.

'A murder?' Ruby asked, doubting such a thing possible.

'And I-' Katie started, but jumped up.

'You what?'

She ran out of the room and up the stairs. Arthur turned to Peter.

'A murder in the school!' he exclaimed.

'Shocking, isn't it,' Peter rolled lazily back, indifferent, leaning over Arthur to take the TV remote from Ruby's now loose grip. He pointed it at the TV, turning it back on and settling down to watch.

TWO

The builder's yard of Simon Berre Construction Ltd was pretty standard. Packs of fresh bricks, bags of cement, mountains of sand and various machinery lay haphazardly around, leaving any potential visitors to weave their way in and out of this health and safety nightmare to gain access to the office building within. Noose and Noble were attempting to do just that, leaving Noose's car nearby on the road as they entered on foot in search of the fabled proprietor Simon Berre.

'We're like bloody yo-yos darting about the place,' Noose pointed out to break the silence between the two.

'A yo-yo goes up and down, not about the place... Sir,' Noble replied, prompting a squint from Noose as he put the back of his hand on Noble's chest.

Inside the office, a blonde woman in a suit lead the men down a white corridor.

'Worked here long?' Noose asked, fancying his chances.

'Since inception,' she responded mechanically.

'Can't have been going long then, this company. You're what, early 30s?'

Noose creased his face as he smiled at her. They reached a door.

'I'm 41.'

She opened the door. Sat at a bland desk near the window was Simon Berre, a man with too much gel in his hair for his age. He was close in age to his wife, the woman who had just opened the door, who ushered Noose and Noble inside the room.

'Shut your face,' Simon shouted down the phone, 'I own 51% of that pond. There isn't a chance in hell you're gonna remove it without my express permission.' The person on the other end hung up and Simon slammed the phone down.

'My husband, officers,' Ruth Berre announced, slamming the door shut as she quickly departed. Now she was gone Simon looked up, smiling.

'Please, sit down,' he said, still smiling. Noble eagerly sat down but Noose remained on his feet, looking up at a clock on the wall.

'Simon Berre, we are Detective Sergeant Stephen Noble and Detective Inspector Henry Noose of Myrtleville Police.'

Simon sat back in his chair, his hands lightly gripping the arms of his chair.

'How do you do?'

'Tick tock,' Noose uttered, staring at the clock. 'How long have we got?'

'What?'

The phone started ringing and Noose now looked down at Simon. 'Death, Mr Berre, is a constant shadow.'

'I suppose it is,' Simon replied, ignoring the ringing.

'Trouble?'

'What?'

Noose picked the phone up. 'Hello?' It went dead.

'Oh right, the phone. Yeah, my mother,' Simon told him. Noose dialled 1471 and jotted down the number that had just called on a piece of paper. 'Look, what's all this about?'

'Somebody's dead,' Noble explained.

'What?'

'That's the third time you've said "what" now, Mr Berre,' Noose slyly pointed out.

Simon got on his feet. 'Who the hell's dead?'

'A man contracted to your company. Graeme Bradbury.'

The door suddenly opened and Ruth stepped in. Clearly she had been listening.

'Oh dear, Graeme,' Simon yawned, walking over to the window. Noose followed, standing right by his side.

'Are you very hands-on with your workers, Mr Berre?' Noose asked, sliding his fingers along the dusty grey Venetian blinds before opening them slightly to look out.

'Not as such, no.'

'Not as such,' Noose repeated, tapping his lip and looking over at Ruth.

'A terrible shame, Sergeant,' Simon addressed Noose with a wry smile.

'I'm an inspector.'

'But of course you are,' Simon whispered.

'Where were you this morning between 8.30am and 9.30am?' Noose demanded angrily.

'Here, of course. Working.'

He glanced over to Ruth, returning to sit at his desk.

'I can vouch for that,' Ruth came in, looking at Simon.

'Very well.' Noose stuck his tongue in his bottom lip. 'We have work to do. Have a nice day, Mr Berre. I hope nothing happens to spoil it.'

With this, they left.

Out in the yard, as Noose and Noble made their way back to the car, a middle-aged man wearing an apron and clutching a mop walked briskly by. He kept up with the pair, coughing to get their attention.

'Can we help you?' Noble asked the man.

'I couldn't help overhearing just then, when you were talking to Mr Berre. I'm the cleaner.'

'Go on,' Noose, intrigued, stopped and encouraged the man. But he kept on walking, a bag of nerves, beckoning the two with his hand. He slipped behind some bricks, Noose and Noble following.

'Well, he said… This *will* remain confidential, won't it? I don't want to lose my job.'

'What is this about?' Noose, his patience all gone, demanded.

'Well, I couldn't help overhearing just now when you asked Mr Berre where he had been between 8.30am and 9.30am…' Again the cleaner paused, looking around nervously, desperate for encouragement from the men.

'Yes, yes?' Noose beseeched.

'Well the thing is, he lied. He only arrived at the office five minutes before you did.'

Noose smiled. 'Thank you.' He shook the cleaner man's hand, turning to Noble. 'Rather interesting, don't you think, Stephen?'

Meanwhile, Simon was at his office window. He caught sight of the cleaner man re-emerging from behind the bricks as Noose and Noble got in the car.

'The cleaner has blabbed,' Simon calmly pointed out. Ruth appeared behind him.

'I've given you an alibi, that's all that matters.'

'Is it?' She turned to leave but he turned and put his arms around her. 'I'm so lucky to have you,' he went on at her. She smiled and they kissed just as the phone rang again. He picked it up and, covering the mouthpiece, looked up at his wife again. 'Business.' She left the room. 'Yes, I'll just get him for you,' Simon continued on the phone. He paused for a moment, covering the phone mouthpiece again as he looked through the window. He lifted the phone to his head again and spoke into it with a deeper voice. 'Hello, this is Edward… fine, thank you. Have you got the report?'

Mr Hancock was sitting at his desk, wondering what small talk to make with Noose and Noble. Luckily he was saved by Matheson, who skulked in with a heavy head.

'No luck, I'm afraid,' he said to the men.

'Typical. Bloody CCTV out of action,' Noose responded, shaking his head.

'This whole thing is like one of those dodgy clichéd murder mystery TV shows,' Noble added, a little nervous for some reason. Noose noticed Noble's unease, a little curiously.

'I'm sorry about that, but our school is very underfunded. We simply haven't got the cash to do all this maintenance.'

'Yet you had the cash to hire Graeme Bradbury to do some renovation work?' Noose questioned. At this, Matheson looked somewhat uneasy. 'What exactly was this renovation work?'

'The old gym roof and windows,' Mr Hancock came in, 'they were in a terrible state.' He looked up at Matheson and nodded.

'Why are you having this work done on the morning of an exam?' Noble wondered.

'Erm…' Matheson stumbled.

'Interesting.' Noose yawned. Matheson looked at Mr Hancock for support, who sat up and cleared his throat.

'How things pan out, I suppose,' Mr Hancock chipped in.

'Have you two heard of a Simon Berre?' Noble continued.

'Him?' Mr Hancock laughed, relieved for some reason. 'Oh yes. Why, is he involved in all of this?'

'Everybody is a suspect,' Noose retaliated, looking particularly at Mr Hancock.

'Well yes.' Matheson too now cleared his throat. 'His daughter comes to this school. Michelle Berre. In fact, she's one of the students who should have been sitting an exam this morning.'

Noose tapped his temple and looked sideways at Noble. As they departed the school shortly afterwards, Noose turned to Noble.

'Are you okay, Stephen?' he asked his perspiring deputy.

'Yes, Sir, fine. Why?'

'Oh, nothing. It's just you seemed a little uneasy in there.'

'Schools, isn't it. I don't like schools.' His mind drifted elsewhere to his time in school, and his memory of what Mr Peters had done. He walked on ahead of Noose, desperate to push these things to the back of his mind once more.

It was time to harass Simon Berre at his home, and this was precisely what Noose and Noble were intending to do as they approached the lovely detached abode with double garage in this quiet hamlet.

'We're darting about the place like a cat chasing a mouse,' Noble explained to his superior.

'My mother always used to say: if you don't have anything interesting to say, don't say anything at all.'

Noose slammed his car door shut and headed up the drive.

'An alternative could be: think before you speak,' Noble retorted, following behind.

Noose knocked on the door, and shortly after Michelle opened it and leant on the doorframe.

'Hello, we're from the police. Are you Michelle?' Noose asked her.

'Uh-huh.'

'We're here about... Oh, you do it Stephen.'

'We're here,' Noble took over, sighing, 'to ask you about your father's whereabouts this morning. We understand you were set to sit an exam at 9.30. Did you see him at the school at any time before this?'

'No.'

'Well, how did you get to school?'

'I walked.'

'Four miles?'

'I'm fit.' She focussed on Noose's protruding stomach. 'Alright, he dropped me off.'

'At what time?'

'Dunno, just gone eight.'

'A bit early, wasn't it?'

'He had stuff to do.'

Simon's big car screeched to a halt next to Noose's little one and he leapt out and charged up to the gathering.

'So what now,' he spat, 'harassing my daughter? What next, stalking my wife's goldfish?'

'We're merely asking her some straightforward questions as a process of elimination,' Noble tried to reason.

'You think Michelle killed Graeme?' Simon continued with the show, pointing in Noble's face.

Noose stepped in front of Simon's finger and smiled. 'No. We think you did, Mr Berre.'

Simon threw his arms in the air and dropped them against his sides, turning around.

'Oh come on, I told you. I've been in my office all morning.'

'Not according to a member of your staff, and your daughter,' Noose disclosed. Michelle looked away.

'I see.'

'Quite compelling, wouldn't you say?' Noose stepped around Simon to be in his sight once more. 'Why did you lie to us? You took your daughter to school around the time Graeme was murdered.'

Simon starting clapping slowly. 'Very good, Inspector. I saw Graeme, didn't I.'

'Why?'

'Over a job. He wasn't committed to it.'

'What about phoning him?'

'Had it switched off, didn't he.'

Noose clicked his fingers sarcastically over this eureka moment. 'He did!'

'Of course he did. Think I'm lying?'

'Of course I do.'

'Yeah, well I'm not. Had his phone switched off so I confronted him in person about the Myrtle Mews job.'

'How did you know he was at the school?' Noble questioned.

'Michelle had spotted him working there previously.'

'What is this Myrtle Mews job?' Noose asked.

'Berre Construction have been contracted to make a new road. Look, is this little show over now, bobby?' Simon pushed Noose aside and walked towards Michelle.

'Your little show is definitely coming to an end, builder,' Noose shot back.

Simon slammed his door shut as Noose and Noble made their way back to the car. Michelle went into the living room and sat on the sofa as Simon charged in.

'What the hell were you doing talking to them?' he stormed, looking through the window. Noose turned, catching him looking, and waved. 'Answer me!' Simon screamed.

'Why don't you just shut your fat mouth, you lying bastard,' she screamed back, jumping up and heading out of the room. He grabbed hold of her, but she turned and kneed him in the groin before fulfilling her original wish of exiting. He dropped to his knees in agony.

Katie was lying on her bed watching TV when Ruby knocked on the bedroom door and came in.

'Come on, what was all that about downstairs?' she asked her daughter, who had been crying.

'Nothing, go away,' Katie whined, turning on her bed.

'Hey, have more respect for your mother.'

'Have more respect for me!' She turned the sound up on the TV but Ruby promptly turned it off at the wall.

'Now you listen to me, if you know something about that murder...'

'It's just something I heard.'

Ruby sat next to her daughter on the bed and took hold of her hand. 'What did you hear?' Katie sat up and Ruby squeezed her hand tighter, smiling warmly.

'It was Emma and Michelle. Michelle was threatening her not to tell anyone about what they'd just done.'

Ruby leapt up, the warm smile turning into a cold frown. 'Right, I'm calling the cops.'

'But Mum!'

Ruby rushed out as Katie made after her.

Downstairs, Ruby rushed into the living room where Arthur and Peter were busy munching on popcorn as they watched TV.

'I'm calling the cops,' she announced as Katie galloped in after her. Arthur and Peter simultaneously spat out their mouthfuls of popcorn.

'What?!' Arthur cried, 'You bloody well are not! This house is full of-'

'Full of what, Arthur?' Ruby cut in, grabbing the phone. 'Knock-off gear?'

'Well,' Arthur looked around the room. 'Yeah!'

'Tough titties. Katie's pals were the ones who bumped off that geezer at the school.'

'Mum!' Katie wept as Ruby thrashed out 999.

'A bit of a coincidence that, isn't it?' Noose remarked as he stood on Ruby's doorstep.

'How Simon mentions about his company doing work in Myrtle Mews, then we're called here by somebody professing to know something about the death of Graeme Bradbury?' Noble asked.

Peter opened the door and greeted them with a smile. 'Why hello, you two. Please, come in!'

Noose turned to Noble. 'What was that you said about all this being like one of those dodgy clichéd murder mysteries on TV?'

Ruby, Arthur, Katie, Peter, Noose and Noble were all sitting around the kitchen table as Noose addressed a tearful and nervous Katie.

'So you heard your friends talking about something?'

'Yes, Emma and Michelle,' she sniffed, 'about something they'd done needing to be kept a secret.'

'Michelle. How apt.'

'What do you mean?' Ruby interjected. 'Is she involved in this or something?'

'You could say that. The victim was contracted to her father's building company, Berre Construction.'

Ruby stared back blankly as Arthur looked up to the heavens and gave out a gasp.

'Surely you've heard of them?' Noble explained. 'They're starting some work in this street soon.'

'They're what? First I've heard of it.' Ruby shook her head. Arthur put his head down and stood up, ready to skulk away. 'You're not going anywhere. What do you know about this?' Arthur took his chair, pushing it against one of the kitchen units and standing on it. He reached on top of one of the wall cabinets and brought down a pile of letters, chucking them on the table. Ruby picked one of the letters up as Arthur dragged his chair back to the table and gingerly sat back down, glancing sideways at Peter.

'An eviction notice? What?! How long have you known about this?' she demanded of her husband, scanning the letter with increasing dismay.

'Too long.'

'I don't believe this, we own the house.'

'They're demolishing the house and the entire street. Making way for some kind of new road.'

'They can't do that!' was Katie's astonished reaction.

'And you didn't think of letting me see the letters?!' Ruby barked, slamming the letter she had been reading in Arthur's face.

'Peter and I were gonna try and sort it out...'

'Peter!' She turned to him. 'You knew as well?'

'Sort of,' he whimpered, his neck shrinking as he lowered his head in shame.

Noose picked up one of the letters and glanced through it.

'I don't believe this,' she kept on, shaking her head. She got up and leant against the sink, sniffing as tears welled up. Arthur got up too, putting his arm around her.

'We've been looking for proof that says they can't demolish the houses. It's only a matter of time.'

'By the look of this you don't have much time. In fact, you have a matter of hours,' Noose pointed out, holding the letter up.

Ruby pushed Arthur away and grabbed the letter off Noose. 'What?! You idiot, Arthur.'

A knock came at the front door.

'I'll go,' Peter called out, quickly exiting.

He opened the door to Timothy.

'Oooh, hello! I saw the police and thought I'd pop round to see if everything was okay,' he laughed, trying to look past Peter into the house.

'How do you know they were police?'

'Oh, you can tell.'

'Yeah, 'cause you've been spying and lip reading. If you continue to spy on people, I'm gonna take some drastic action. Got it?' Peter threatened him.

'Moi, spy on people?' He put his hand on his heart. 'How ridiculous!'

Peter slammed the door in his face, but that wasn't enough. His face appeared close up to one of the panes of frosted glass as he peered in.

Peter made his way back into the kitchen.

'What did that weirdo want?' Ruby continued at volume.

'Timothy? He's been watching us through the kitchen window.'

Peter walked over to the window and looked up at Timothy's bedroom window.

'I hope you told him to sling his hook.'

'Trouble in suburbia?' Noble asked, looking at Peter with a forced grin.

'He spies on people - films them too, I reckon,' Arthur explained.

'Sounds a bit odd,' Noose responded, joining Noble by looking at Peter. 'Anyway, thank you for your assistance, Katie. We'll be getting back to you shortly.' He and Noble stood up.

'Yeah, you better had. I don't want to wake up and find a horse's head in my bed,' Ruby went on.

'No but I have to, *every* morning,' Arthur sniggered, looking at the other men in the room for support. They shied away, refusing eye contact.

Ruby clacked him across the head.

'Common assault, that is!' Arthur tried.

Noose and Noble made their way into the hallway, away from this domestic, as Peter followed to let them out.

'So, how's things?' Noose asked his forgetful friend.

'Not bad. Been staying here a bit, you know. Doing some jobs around the place and helping out.'

'Is he buggery!' Ruby shouted from the kitchen. 'Needs a rocket up his arse, that one.'

Peter quickly opened the door and ushered Noose and Noble out.

'How's, er, how's Lauren, Sergeant?' Peter asked nervously.

Noble turned to look around the Myrtle Mews cul-de-sac uneasily. 'She's fine.' He briskly marched down the drive to Noose's waiting car.

Noose and Peter stood for a moment in silence.

'Bye, Peter,' Noose uttered, joining his Sergeant.

'Smug git,' Noble grunted as Peter closed the door and Noose unlocked the car. '*How's Lauren, Sergeant.* I should have…'

'You should have what? He's not interested in women anymore, anyway.' Noose got in the car. 'There was only one woman for him, and she's gone.'

'That Lucy Davies?' Noble asked, getting in the passenger side. 'Well anyway, he's not getting mine.'

'Women aren't objects, Stephen. If anything, men are the objects. Playthings of voluptuous higher beings sent from Venus to sexually enslave us.'

Noble calmed himself and focused his mind once more.

'Anyway, what are your thoughts on this thing with Michelle and this Emma character?' he asked his superior.

'I'm not sure yet… I've been thinking also, we never found a phone on Graeme. No way of finding out if Simon was actually trying to call him.'

It had gone dark and Peter pulled up outside Simon Berre's office building, dismounting his bicycle. He adjusted his hood to ensure his face was sufficiently covered before propping the bicycle up against the building and looked around cautiously to see if he had been spotted by any midnight guards. Silence. Crowbar in hand, he checked the lock on the door. To his surprise, the door was unlocked and ajar so he now gripped the crowbar as a weapon in case he should come across any unwanted company. He looked around one more time before calmly stepping inside.

Inside Simon's office Peter searched through a filing cabinet and came across a file named 'MYRTLE MEWS ROAD'. A quick glance inside confirmed that this was indeed the file he was after. He slipped it into his jacket. He now sat down at Simon's desk and looked at it. There were drawers on the left-hand side of the desk and Peter opened the top one. Inside sat a gun with a silencer. Peter quickly closed the drawer and stood up, remembering to close the filing cabinet as well before making his way to the door. What he did not notice was the CCTV camera filming his every more from above.

As Peter rode away on his bicycle, a shaded figure stepped out of the office building and watched him go.

It was still dark and Ruby and Arthur's next door neighbour Gerty was fast asleep, as you'd expect. One of her five nightly trips to the toilet was not due for at least another half hour and she was snoring like a baby. Above her head sat her attic, which currently lay in darkness. However, a brick began to move in the wall separating her attic from Ruby and Arthur's. It was pulled out and a torch shone through the hole. Peter's eyes suddenly appeared, looking through the hole where the brick once sat. More loose bricks were quickly removed until there was a large enough hole in the wall for Peter to squeeze through. He did so, gently crawling into Gerty's attic with a torch strapped to his head.

Her attic was full of boxes. Peter searched for a while before coming across an old box file. He settled down, opening it to study its contents. In it lay a folder with 'Hinklebottom Construction' printed in the corner. Peter opened the file, but his torch began to fade. He pulled the contents out, but his torch faded even more. He looked towards the attic skylight behind him. The blue moonlight was faint tonight, but it was better than nothing. He moved towards the skylight, now standing straight. His eyes tried to focus on the contents of the folder, but something else caught his eye. Opening the skylight and peering downwards, Peter looked into Timothy's bedroom window. The curtains were wide open and on the bed lay Timothy, on his back, covered in blood. He was dead.

THREE

The following morning, a police cordon surrounded Timothy's house. Ruby and Katie were stood in their garden, watching the proceedings. Arthur stepped out of the back door holding a fold-up garden chair. He unfolded it and sat down on it, folding his arms and keeping watch on the unfolding action. Emma, who lived across the street, was stood by her back door. She and Katie caught sight of each other, but Katie turned away and went inside.

Peter hovered just behind the police cordon as Lauren approached him from Timothy's house. She slipped under the cordon and greeted Peter with a smile.

'It's messy in there,' she told him. 'What are you doing involved in another murder?'

'They seem to follow me around,' he responded, looking down at his feet and smiling.

'Or you follow them around.' She forced another smile and walked on, to the forensic van on the road.

Noose and Noble came out of Timothy's front door and walked towards Peter. He turned to walk away but Noble was soon on him. He brushed past him and turned back to give him a glare as he walked to Lauren.

'Why were you in the attic?' Noose asked Peter. He turned to face the inspector.

'Long story.' Peter tapped his nose playfully.

'Do tell.'

'Well... Oh, have you come across Timothy's camcorder?'

'Not yet, why?'

'Well, he films people. Perhaps he filmed his murderer?' Peter pointed out.

'Filmed his murderer? A bit fanciful, isn't it?'

'No, you know, he got caught filming something he shouldn't have,' Peter explained. Noose scratched his chin and began to walk on, but Peter held him back. 'And if he was filming from his bedroom, that might mean the murderer lives in either the Edwards' house - or is their neighbour Gerty Hinklebottom!'

'If my information is correct, Gertrude Hinklebottom is an elderly lady... Not another OAP crackpot, please!'

'The key to this is his camcorder,' Peter went on.

'If it's missing, perhaps. So why were you in the attic?'

'Ah, now there's a story...'

Meanwhile, Ruby squinted at Noble who was chatting away to Jim by the forensics van.

'The world's gone to pot. None of us are safe. Who's next?!' she called over to them.

'You hopefully,' Noble mumbled under his breath. Jim laughed, looking over at Peter. Suddenly he felt his heart pounding as he clocked his target. But there were too many people about; he didn't want to risk messing it up. He would have to wait to kill Peter Smith. He continued with his work.

Lauren, also hearing Noble's remark, gave him a disappointed look as Noose's car phone rang. Noble stepped over to it and bent through the open window to answer it.

'These things must be done,' Peter said to Noose as their conversation came to a close across the street.

'You're not above the law.'

'The law is an ass.'

'Interesting development,' Noble called over to Noose, who came over, Peter following behind.

'What's happened now?'

Noble spotted Peter loitering behind Noose and turned to try and block him.

'Graeme Bradbury's widow phoned the station, says she has a confession to make,' Noble whispered, but Peter had heard him. He walked away, back to Ruby and Arthur's house, as Emma crossed his path. She came to sit down on their wall and sighed. Peter sat next to her, folding his arms and leaning back.

'Aye!' he broke the silence, grinning. She looked back at him in annoyance as Noose approached them.

'Are you Emma Jones, by any chance?' he asked the girl.

'Yeah.'

'Good, because I want a word with you… later.' He turned back to his car. 'Oh, and stick around, Peter,' he called, 'I'll be back for you, too.' He and Noble got in the car and drove off.

Peter pretended to bite his nails and chatter his teeth at Emma, who rolled her eyes and ran back to her house across the road. Peter saw Lauren and realised she was now away from Noble. He got up and approached her.

'Same killer as Graeme Bradbury?' he asked.

'Timothy was shot. Graeme was hit on the head. Apart from the connection of Simon Berre, I'd say they were unrelated. Although that's just my initial thought,' was her professional response.

'Maybe. Seems too much of a coincidence to me. Shot? Hmm…'

'Well, we'll just have to see, won't we? It was almost impossible to get any forensic clues at the school. And at this one too - we don't even have the weapon used.'

In the Bradbury house living room, Graeme's widow Nicola was on the brink of tears. The house was now deathly quiet compared to the racket of the previous day.

'Where are your boys, Nicky?' Noble asked the attractive widow.

'Upstairs. Yeah, quiet I know. They're just blanking me out.'

'Their way of dealing with the loss, I guess.' Noble placed his hand on hers. She looked up into his moist eyes, comforted.

'You have a confession to make, do you not?' Noose cut in.

'That's right.' She stood up and walked over to the staircase. She looked up the stairs, checking to see if her sons were listening, before coming to sit back down next to Noble. Noose sat across the room in the armchair.

'My husband, Graeme… He…'

'He what?'

'He was a blackmailer.'

Noose sat up. 'Go on.'

'He thought I didn't know, but I did.'

'Why didn't you do anything about it?' Noble asked her.

'You didn't know him.' She now took hold of Noble's hand as he looked over at Noose.

'Who was he blackmailing?' Noose pushed on.

'I don't know.'

'It could lead us to his killer.'

'I don't know.'

'This gets ever more complex,' Noose remarked in the car. 'I'll wager that Timothy was somehow involved in all this. A missing camcorder, blackmailing - that Bradbury woman could even be involved herself.'

'Involved in Timothy's murder? But why tell us about the blackmailing?'

'I don't know. And all that crap about saying Graeme didn't know… Course he did.'

'You don't know.' Noble didn't want to see anything negative about his new friend Nicola Bradbury.

'Not yet.'

Suddenly, a child jumped up at Noose's window and stuck

her tongue out at him. He recoiled as the little girl jogged off in howls of laughter.

'And who was Graeme blackmailing?'

'Simon Berre, of course. Without a doubt.'

The door of Simon Berre's office building opened to Noose and Noble. Ruth sighed.

'You!'

'I say, Mrs Berre - Ruth Berre - aren't we to be welcomed in a kinder fashion than that?' Noose rolled, straightening his tie comically.

'What do you want?' she asked harshly.

'A life… A feeling of self-worth?' Noose pondered, looking up to the sky and yawning.

'You'd better come in.'

She stood aside to let them in and led them to Simon's office. He was sat at his desk, looking somewhat distraught.

'You look flustered, Simon,' Noose remarked as he walked over to the window and fidgeted with the blinds.

'The perils of running your own business, Inspector.'

'Or the guilt of killing someone.'

Simon stood up. 'If this war against me continues much longer…'

Noble put his hand on Simon's shoulder and eased him back into his chair.

'I know Graeme was blackmailing you,' Noose continued, turning to face Simon, who slammed his fist on his desk.

'Rubbish!'

'Blackmailing?' Ruth asked. Noose turned to face her.

'Yes, Mrs Berre, blackmailing,' Noose patronised.

'Clearly yet another attempt to pin this on me,' Simon laughed.

'These murders, Simon. There's been another.'

Simon stood up again. 'What? Who?'

'A resident of Myrtle Mews. Quite a coincidence, don't you think?' At this inference from Noose, Simon came from behind his desk and stepped closer to him. Noble stood close by. 'You look worried Simon, but why? Surely now with your blackmailer dead, you can rest easy?'

Simon grabbed hold of Noose's shirt but Noble grabbed hold of Simon's arm and twisted it behind his back.

'Get out of my office and off my property,' he spat, struggling away from Noble.

'Your wife's property, Mr Berre,' Noose smirked, looking back at Ruth. 'Yes, we've done our research. You live off your wife's money. No shame in that, of course. My wife took me to the cleaners.'

They turned to leave, Noose looking back at Simon and Ruth with a knowing glint in his eyes. As soon as they'd gone, the phone rang. Simon picked it up, looking out of the window at Noose and Noble stepping out into the yard.

'Berre Construction, Simon Berre speaking.'

'You still owe me,' a muffled voice spoke back.

'What?!'

'I haven't gone away.'

'You're dead.'

'I am not dead. Bradbury is dead. Now I'm in control. You want what you're after, you pay me. Understand?'

'Go on,' Simon replied, restrained, the anger burning inside him.

Peter was bending behind the sofa when Katie entered the living room. Startled, he quickly stood up straight and smiled at her.

'What are you doing?' she asked the lodger.

'I could ask you the same question.'

'I was asking you.'

He sat down on the sofa and flicked through the channels

on the TV. 'Watching the telly,' he replied. She sat down next to him. 'Anyway, why aren't you in school today?'

'Err, there *has* been a murder, in case you've forgotten.'

'Two murders. Let us not forget the unfortunate slaying of the peeping tom.'

'You were telling Timothy off yesterday - I could hear you when you opened the door. You made threats,' she pointed out, looking at him suspiciously.

'And?'

'Well, you could have done it.'

At this Peter threw the TV remote down. 'Well, I didn't.'

'Discovering his body by looking through a skylight? Hmm,' she continued.

'Why don't you go and snog Alex? Give the poor lad a thrill.'

Katie stormed out.

Peter entered his attic bedroom and pulled the ladder up, closing the hatch. He sat on the bed and flicked through the Hinklebottom Construction box file. The various papers inside had turned slightly yellow from age and the damp atmosphere in the attic. He came across a contract, dated 20ᵗʰ February nineteen years ago, signed by Edward Coates. Next, Peter removed an envelope from his jacket pocket and took a piece of paper out from inside it. It was a warrant for the demolition of Myrtle Mews, dated recently and signed by Edward Coates. However, the signatures did not match. Another piece of paper from Peter's jacket pocket revealed a print-out of a photograph of a gravestone - that of Edward Coates. He had been dead for years, yet somehow apparently signed the contract. Peter had struck gold.

Emma opened her door to Noose and Noble.

'Yes?' she nervously asked the two men stood expectantly in front of her.

'We need to speak to you, Emma,' Noose told her.

She stepped out and closed the door behind her. 'Yes?'

'We believe you and Michelle Berre were acting suspiciously yesterday morning, around the time of the murder at your school.'

'No.' She looked away.

'We have an independent witness.'

'Katie?'

'You need to tell us and tell us quickly, Emma. Why were you acting suspiciously? At the moment you're making yourself appear very guilty of something.'

'I know nothing, okay?' Her eyes began to redden.

'You're lying,' Noose pushed.

'How do you know?'

'Women have lied to me before.'

'I'm only a teenage girl.'

Peter, watching from across the street, stepped back inside the back door into Ruby and Arthur's kitchen and chucked the papers down on the table in front of the homeowners.

'Conclusive proof that Simon Berre cannot legally demolish this street,' he announced smugly. 'The demolition was approved by a dead man. Edward Coates has been dead for years.'

'Who was he?' Ruby asked, astonished, fumbling over the papers.

'A council official. According to the warrant to demolish the street, it sits on a dangerous set of mines and could collapse at any minute. Utter rubbish.'

'Bloody hell,' Arthur laughed.

'If all the residents agreed, the houses could be demolished. Simon Berre has forged all your signatures to give to the council.'

Peter sorted through the papers on the table and handed one to Ruby.

'That's not my signature!'

'Indeed,' Peter chuckled. 'And he also gave the council a false report from a deceased builder, your neighbour Gerty's husband Raymond, who has been dead for five years. Edward Coates came into play when Simon needed to convince Gerty to get on board. She didn't know about Coates' death but trusted him when he used to contract her husband's business.'

'But why not just forge her signature as well?' Ruby asked.

'Gerty's been pretending her husband's alive, taking calls from the council and the like. Even claiming his pension, believe it or not.'

'What? This all seems mad. Why would she do that if she thought this Edward Coates had approved the whole thing anyway?'

'Well, it appears Coates and Raymond were something of a rogue set-up. She was likely in on the game in their heyday, too. She was guaranteed a nice payout from Simon. She owns more than one house so she wasn't worried about Myrtle Mews being knocked down,' Peter explained. Ruby sat there, her face almost purple by now. 'I suspect Simon even went as far as posing as Coates over the phone with Gerty.'

'So she's as much a crook as Simon Berre?' Ruby asked.

'Pretty much, yeah.'

Ruby laughed through gritted teeth as Peter opened the fridge and helped himself to a can of pop. Ruby leapt up and galloped out of the door.

'Shiiiiiiit,' Arthur droned, getting up and darting after her. Peter casually followed after them. She marched down Gerty's drive and banged on the door. 'Maybe this isn't such a good idea, Ruby,' Arthur bleated as Ruby thrashed again at the door.

'Pipe down,' she bawled back at her husband. 'Get out here, you old hag,' she shouted through the letterbox. Noose and Noble, hearing the commotion from Emma's house across the road, ran over. Gerty opened the door and Ruby grabbed hold of her by the scruff of the neck. Shoving the contract down

Gerty's throat, she continued her rage, 'How can a dead man sign his own name?'

'Good morning, Mrs Hinklebottom!' Peter chortled, raising his can.

Jim and David joined Noose and Noble and the four attempted to pull Ruby from Gerty. Eventually they succeeded, after a struggle, and held her back as she frothed at the mouth at the sight of the old woman in her doorway.

'Oh my!' Gerty cried, 'What lewd behaviour. You could have choked me.' She spat the last of the contract out. 'I should smack your botty.'

'I'll do more than choke you in a minute, you batty old bint,' Ruby snarled. 'Officers, arrest that woman.'

Katie was sat staring at the TV, expressionless.

'Katie? Katie?' Emma's voice called out from the kitchen. 'You in?' She appeared at the living room door and saw Katie sat on the sofa.

'Do you make a habit of walking into people's houses uninvited?'

'You're not just anyone, though. You're my friend.'

'Crap.'

'I can't tell you about what happened, Michelle would kill me.'

'Maybe she's already killed. Two people are dead and you won't even tell *your friend* about something.'

'I just want this whole murder thing to blow over first, I swear.' She came down to sit next to Katie, who shifted to the other end of the sofa away from her.

'Murders don't just blow over, you know. And stay away from Alex, too.'

Emma stood up. 'You can't stop me seeing him.'

'You're not *seeing* him though, are you. I'm, I want…' she burst into tears. Emma moved in to try and hug her but she was pushed away. 'Just get out, get out.'

Ruby was now being restrained by Jim and David as Noble refereed between her and Gerty as they traded insults.

'Listen, let's all calm down here,' Noble urged.

'Calm down? Our houses are about to get illegally demolished and you're asking me to calm down?' Ruby shouted back.

'Okay, okay, let's all discuss this like civilised people,' Noble kept on.

'Civilised?' Gerty chuckled, 'That hot-head can't even *spell* civilised.'

Ruby got one of her arms free and made a swing for Gerty's face, but Noble stepped in front and got clobbered instead.

Meanwhile, Noose and Peter were stood back watching.

'How are things between Noble and Lauren?' Peter asked.

'Well, the engagement is still off, which is nothing new. They haven't spoken properly since, you know. Acting like kids. He can be quite stubborn when he wants to be. An odd character, in many ways. It's almost like he's two different people.' Noose glanced down at Peter as he looked over at Noble getting another whack from Ruby that was intended for Gerty. 'How's the memory, anyway, and how was your mother?'

Peter checked his watch. 'I've gotta go, things to do!'

'Don't go far. I may need your help in this signature fraud thing.'

'Sure.'

Simon approached the alleyway on foot. He looked around before walking down it. A shadowy figure stepped out from behind an industrial bin.

'You have the videotape?' Simon asked the shadow.

The shadow stepped out into the light. It was Peter. 'A videotape! Interesting. Good to know.'

'I want it.'

'Why, what's on it?'

'You filmed it, you tell me. Did you like watching it, sicko?'

A van pulled up next to the alleyway and the side door slid open to make way for two hefty men to jump out. One held some rope as the other clutched onto a metal bar. They walked past Simon and approached Peter, who stepped back and gulped.

Peter dangled from a chain attached to the ceiling in a storage room just off Simon's office. The two hefty men watched smugly as Simon circled Peter with a knuckle duster on his hand.

'I told you,' Peter went on, 'I don't have the videotape.'

'Then why were you in the alleyway?'

'I wanted to find out if you were in fact being blackmailed, and what you were after.'

'Ah, I see. So you did make the call?'

'Yes.'

Simon grabbed hold of Peter's jaw and pulled his face closer to his own. 'The problem is, I revealed too much in that conversation, and you already seem to be too involved yourself. Graeme Bradbury *was* blackmailing me. And it *was* about a videotape.' Peter tried to pull his face away, but Simon squeezed tighter. 'You do know what that means?'

'That you're gonna have to silence me?'

'What an astute young man you are.' He pushed Peter's head away, punching him in the stomach with the knuckle duster. Peter cried out in agony and swung about on the chain.

'It's a shame, I *could* help you,' Peter muttered through his coughs.

Simon, about to signal to the hefty men, turned back to face Peter.

'How can a piece of shit like you help a marvellous powerful man like me?'

'Myrtle Mews.'

'What about it?'

'I know it's all illegal, but I could destroy the evidence.'

Simon stepped back to Peter and grabbed his face once more. 'Are you trying to blackmail me?'

Peter paused a second for breath, and comedic timing. 'Yes.'

'How do you know it's illegal?'

'I took the files from your office last night.'

Simon thumped him in the stomach again. This time Peter coughed up blood.

'How did you get in?'

'The door was unlocked.'

Simon turned to address the hefties. 'Check the CCTV from last night. Keep rewinding until you find this clown. If you find nothing, he dies.' One of the hefties exited.

'Just check your filing cabinet, the Myrtle Mews file is missing.'

Simon signalled to the other hefty, who exited as well. He turned back to Peter and grimaced. 'Who are you, anyway? Why are you involving yourself in all this?'

'I don't know,' Peter replied, managing to raise an eyebrow and smile.

'You're a nobody - I speck of dirt on the ground. I could kill you right now and no-one would miss you.' He clicked his fingers.

'Like you killed Graeme and Timothy?'

'Who is this Timothy?'

'He was the one who filmed you, by my guess.'

'I haven't killed anyone.'

'Then why start with me?'

'You will live just long enough to tell me where the Myrtle Mews file is, if indeed you have it, then you will die at the hands of my two helpers.' Simon turned his back on Peter to look in the direction that the hefties had just exited. Peter seized his chance and, swinging on the chain, kicked Simon hard in the back. He fell to the floor, but quickly turned and got back on his feet. Peter swung again, but Simon grabbed hold of his legs. Peter headbutted Simon and sent him tumbling back. He pulled hard on the chain, trying to break free, but it was just too solid. 'You little bastard,' Simon shot back, his nose bloodied, as he thumped Peter yet again in the stomach. Peter's head dropped down and he was left dangling by his wrists, out cold. The hefties ran back in. 'Don't worry, I dealt with it. Was he on the CCTV?' The hefties nodded. 'Get him down, let's see if we can't teach him a lesson or two about thieving.'

Simon stepped over and pulled a white sheet off a table with a bandsaw on it. His men undid the chains holding Peter up. He fell to the floor. Unknown to the men, Peter was not unconscious and secretly gripped onto a brick he had fallen on. As one of the men bent to pick Peter up he sprang into life and smashed him across the head with the brick. Stunned, he recoiled, falling backwards, unconscious. The other hefty grabbed hold of Peter and pulled him to his feet, swinging him around and throwing him across the room into some boxes. Simon stepped over to the man who was out cold and slapped him across either side of his face. Nothing. The conscious hefty approached Peter, who threw one of the broken boxes into the man's face, but he easily knocked it out of the way. Peter struggled out of the way as the hefty lunged forward. He pushed him into the boxes and the man stumbled over them. Spotting a hammer on one of the work benches, Peter grabbed it and threw it at the hefty. It hit him in the arm and he shouted in pain as he clutched the injury. Now even more enraged, he charged after Peter, who stood still until the last moment and then moved out of the way. The hefty ran straight into a work bench, pulling down a shelf full of tools on top of himself. He struggled to get up, weakened, pulling down even more tools.

Peter held onto his chest, in obvious agony after being punched. He was coughing up blood. He now eyed Simon up as they circled around the bandsaw. Simon grabbed a screwdriver and quickly darted around the bandsaw at Peter.

He moved out of the way and sent Simon charging into the wall. The screwdriver was stuck in the wall and, as Simon tried to pull it out, Peter made for the door. Seeing his prisoner escaping, Simon left the screwdriver and chased after him.

In Simon's office, Peter pushed the filing cabinet over against the door just as Simon stuck his hand out. The door slammed shut on his hand and Peter stumbled to freedom.

The injured man, clutching his chest in absolute agony, struggled towards his lodgings. He opened the back door and fumbled into the kitchen, where Ruby was washing up. Seeing her, he collapsed onto the floor.

'For crying out loud, I've just mopped that floor,' Ruby exclaimed.

Peter leant against one of the cold metal slabs usually reserved for the dead in Lauren's lab.

'Take your top off,' she instructed him methodically. He did so, lifting himself up onto the slab. 'Lie flat.' Again, he did so, gazing up into her eyes. She pressed on his chest. He cried out. 'You should go to the hospital for an X-ray. He's done some damage there.'

'If you reckon there's nothing broken, that's fine by me.'

'You could have internal bleeding or anything. You coughed up blood.'

'I'll live.'

'I can't force you, I suppose.'

Their eyes met and she put her hand flat on his chest. Suddenly Noble entered and stopped dead when he spotted what was going on.

'I thought I'd find you here,' Noble calmly spoke to Peter. 'Noose wants to take a statement.'

Peter struggled up and, after Lauren helped him put his top back on, hobbled out of the room. She turned to Noble.

'Stephen, I...'

But he ignored her, following Peter out of the room.

Noose's office was even duller than usual, even though it was fairly sunny outside. The weather had been good of late. It tended to rain at night in Myrtleville, though they did get the odd afternoon shower. This afternoon, however, the ground was very dry - as was the air in Noose's office. Noose was sat at his desk, drinking coffee from a paper cup and watching TV. Noble entered and stood aside for Peter to enter, who made straight for a chair and eased himself onto it with considerable difficulty. Noble did not stay, his moist eyes glazed over more than usual. He closed the door, sealing the two inside.

'Wonder what's up with him,' Noose pondered.

'Just caught me with my top off with Lauren.'

'I see. On another note, Peter, you've just received a rather nasty beating.'

'That I have.'

'Yes, from Simon Berre.' Noose stood up. Peter, in considerable pain, gave Noose the thumbs up. 'Good, now I have a statement I can arrest him.'

'You still think he's the murderer too?' Peter asked with a struggle.

'Sure of it. All we need is evidence that he shot Timothy.'

'Well I did find a gun in his office.'

'You what?'

'When I was snooping around last night. There's one in the top drawer of his desk. I thought he'd likely use it to kill me - after he'd threatened to do so.'

'Why didn't you tell me this before?' Noose yelled, rushing to the door. 'Come on, come on. We have a murderer to arrest.'

Peter, struggling to his feet, clutched his chest. 'And a serious assaulter.'

'Yeah, yeah.'

Noble was sat in a dark cubicle in the police station library, looking at a large projection ahead. Pages from newspapers flashed past on the screen. He looked on in growing frustration. Suddenly, something caught his eye. The headline read, 'Three Murdered In Secret Club 'Sacrifice''. Noble's eyes widened and he took notes.

Noose's car pulled into Simon Berre's builder's yard, Jim and David close behind in a police car. Noose, Peter, Jim and David made their way towards the office building as David looked at Peter and shook his head a little. His mind was off elsewhere, to a time Peter could not, or did not want to, remember. Jim, a switch clicking in his own mind, smiled to himself as he slotted Peter and David together. He was hatching his plan and it had just entered a new phase.

Simon was standing against the wall with Jim and David positioned either side of him as Noose came out of the room that had held Peter during the assault. Peter, stood in the centre of the room, grinned victoriously at Simon. Lauren entered.

'Ah, Lauren,' Noose called her over as he walked to Simon's desk. 'In the top drawer.'

Wearing gloves and with a plastic bag ready, Lauren opened the top drawer and picked up the gun within. She smelt it.

'Hmm.' She placed the gun in the bag and sealed it.

'Thoughts?' Noose asked.

'Not yet. Better take his clothes, too.' She pointed out Simon's jacket, draped over the back of the chair.

'You've been a bad boy, haven't you?' Noose addressed Simon, who eyed the inspector with contempt. 'If nothing else, we have proof that you beat Peter.'

Simon looked at Peter and sniggered. 'Peter? I didn't touch him.'

Some forensic scientists entered. Noose stepped aside and ushered them into the storage room. Inside, they put their cases down and looked around. Peter poked his head in and pointed out the bolt in the ceiling.

'That's where they chained me up,' he explained proudly.

Simon was being led off to the police car by Jim and David as Ruth grabbed hold of Jim's arm and tried to pull him off her husband. But Jim was strong and managed to resist long enough to get Simon into the car and shut the door.

'Will you get off me, please?' he asked her nicely.

'This is a violation of his human rights. You're pinning these murders on him.'

Noose had caught up. 'Kindly desist or you will be arrested too, Mrs Berre.'

She backed away reluctantly. 'He's innocent, and when you realise that, we'll be suing you for incompetence.'

Noose walked to his car, rolling his eyes, as Peter slowly ambled after him.

Later on, Noose paid Lauren a visit in the lab. She was busy working at a desk with a microscope.

'What do we have?'

'This *was* the gun that killed Timothy,' Lauren revealed.

'We've got him,' Noose reeled with glee.

'Simon's fingerprints are the only ones on the gun.'

'Anything on his clothes?'

Lauren stood up and walked over to a stand where Simon's jacket was hanging in a plastic bag. 'Traces of gunshot residue on the front, here,' she pointed out, 'and in a pocket.'

Noose rubbed his hands together. 'Excellent. Does his DNA match anything found at either scene?'

'No.'

'Well, the gun is a start. Great stuff, thanks Lauren.'

She returned to her stool and continued at the microscope.

'It's a pleasure.'

'Oh, you haven't seen Stephen, have you?'

'Sadly, no,' she replied with a sarcastic grin.

Simon paced back and forth in the interview room. Jim and David both stood blocking the door.

'When can I go?' Simon demanded.

'You won't be going anywhere, Mr Berre. Not for a very long time,' Jim told him.

Simon marched up to Jim. 'You filth are all as thick as you look.' Suddenly Jim's breathing seemed to alter; it slowed down even though he quickly lashed out at Simon and threw him against the wall. 'Take your hands off me, pig,' Simon spat. David pulled Jim off, who relaxed at David's touch. 'That's right, keep your boyfriend under control.'

Jim turned and looked at David with a smile, which startled him. He was acting very peculiar indeed.

The door opened and Noose walked in. 'Please, Simon, take a seat.'

'No. One of your officers has just assaulted me.'

'Take a seat,' Noose carried on. Simon did sit down, after Noose, and folded his arms. Noble came in, sitting next to Noose. 'Ah, Sergeant. Where've you been hiding?' Noose asked him.

'Doing a little digging,' he responded. Noose didn't quite understand, and now wasn't the time to probe further, so he turned back to Simon.

'Simon, Simon. We have evidence that you killed Timothy.'

Simon leant in, puzzled. 'What evidence?'

'The gun we found in your office was the one used to shoot Timothy, and we found gunshot residue on your jacket.'

'Anyone could have taken the gun and jacket. Peter broke in last night - it was him.'

'Broke in? There's no sign of forced entry.'

'The door was unlocked, according to him.'

'Why would you leave the door unlocked, Simon?'

'I don't know.'

'Do you know, Sergeant?' Noose asked Noble. He turned to Jim and David stood at the door. 'What about you two?' He turned back to face Simon.

'Check the CCTV tape. That'll show you who took the gun,' Simon shot back, refusing to accept the blame.

'Very well.' Noose turned to Jim and David again. 'Have the CCTV tape brought to my office.'

'Sir,' Jim replied.

'Speaking of tapes, Simon, we hear from your victim Peter that you were after a tape from him.'

'No comment.'

'Let me take it further, Simon. Peter posed as a blackmailer to discover what was going on. He discovered that you were being blackmailed by Graeme Bradbury, confirmed by Graeme's widow Nicola.'

Simon sat up straight, intrigued. 'What's she told you?'

'Enough. What's on the tape?'

'No comment.'

'Where is it now?' Noose continued.

'Whoever killed Graeme has it.'

'So you admit there *is* a tape and that Graeme was blackmailing you with it?'

'No comment.'

'This gets ever more intriguing, doesn't it, Sergeant?' Noose smirked at Noble.

'It's fascinating, Inspector.'

'Look, Simon, you're already under arrest for assaulting Peter, and we are building a very strong case against you for murder.' Noose made it clear.

'I want my lawyer.'

Noose sat at his desk, fidgeting with the built-in VCR on his antique TV. He shoved the CCTV tape into it and pressed play. A darkened image of Simon's office filled the screen, with a hooded figure just exiting the room. Noose rewound a little until he could make out that the figure was Peter, who could be seen snooping in the filing cabinet. He was shown opening the top drawer and closing it again, with the gun still inside. Noose continued to watch for a little while until a knock sounded at the door. He stopped the tape and turned the TV off. 'Come in,' he called out. A pale-faced Peter opened the door, struggling in.

'Think I'd better be getting home... Back to Ruby and Arthur's.'

'Want a lift?'

Noose and Peter pulled up outside Ruby and Arthur's house. Peter undid his seatbelt and opened the door

'You should go to the hospital. I'll run you there.'

'No, I'm fine.'

'Very well.'

Peter hauled himself to his feet. 'Thanks for the lift.'

'You look after yourself, and stay out of police business from now on.'

Peter smiled, shutting the door. He tapped on the car roof as Noose pulled away.

FOUR

Peter now had a good excuse to be sprawled on the sofa watching TV. Ruby wasn't quite as angry at him now. Arthur too was sprawled on the armchair, fast asleep, as Katie crept in.

'Let me sit down,' she whispered, pushing Peter's feet out of the way.

'No rest for the wicked,' he joked, struggling to sit up. She stared at him. 'What's eating you?'

She looked over at Arthur to make sure he definitely was asleep. 'I, I know you're quite crafty.'

'Thank you.' He seemed quite pleased at this observation, letting slip a smile.

'Well, I know you can find stuff out. I want to know something.'

Peter turned to face the TV, feigning indifference. 'Alex *does* fancy you, you know. He prefers you to Emma.'

'Not that… What? He does? What makes you say that?' She blushed.

'Ah ha, as you said, I'm very crafty.' He tapped his nose.

'I'm not on about Alex, I'm on about Emma and Michelle.'

'But you do fancy him as well, don't you?' Peter kept on.

'What's it to you?'

'Just making chit chat. So, what's all this about Emma and Michelle, then?'

'Well, what's their big secret? What were they doing when that builder was murdered?'

'Why don't you just ask them?'

'I've tried. Look, will you help me or not?'

'Yeah, of course I will. Look, it's getting late. I've got nothing planned tomorrow, we'll see what we can do.'

'Cheers Peter.' She placed her hand on his. 'You're not that useless after all.'

'I'm as useless as a one-legged man at a bum-kicking party,' he joked. She tried not to, but ended up smiling before leaving the room. But it wasn't long before she called him from the hallway.

'Hey Peter, there's a letter here for you.'

She brought the letter to him. It was addressed simply to 'Peter, Myrtle Mews.' There was no stamp.

'Did you see who posted it?' Peter asked her.

'No.'

He opened it. Inside was a letter which read, 'THE VIDEOTAPE WILL COST YOU FIVE THOUSAND POUNDS. MEET ME IN MYRTLEVIEW PARK AT MIDNIGHT TONIGHT AND COME ALONE.'

Noose and Noble had arrived and studied the letter.

'We'll check with the neighbours, see if they saw who posted it,' Noose explained. 'We'll put up the money and send you there too.'

By now, Myrtleview park was dark, the trees weeding out any remaining light from the light pollution outside. Noose, disguised in a tweed coat with his face partly covered by a cap, strolled around the field with a dog. Peter, carrying a plastic bag full of money, walked across the field towards some trees. A torchlight shone at him so he moved towards it. Soon he found himself surrounded by trees as a branch touched his shoulder. A figure appeared in front, an electronic voice masking their own.

'Put the money on the branch,' the voice instructed him.

He did as commanded, hooking the bag onto the end of the branch. It was pulled away and disappeared into the darkness.

'What about the tape?' Peter called out.

A brown envelope landed by his feet. As he fumbled to pick it up, another branch pushed him to the ground and the figure scurried away. Noose's dog started barking and ran into the trees. Noose followed, the quickest he had moved since he shagged Williams last. He shone his torch ahead as the dog leapt onto somebody.

'Stay right where you are,' Noose called out.

'It's me,' Peter called back. 'They got away.'

Back at Noose's office, the two men settled down to watch the tape from the brown envelope. The door opened and Noble walked in.

'We bundled that,' Noble gasped. 'Apparently the infrared binoculars Jim was using were broken.' He joined the other two in front of the TV as Noose ejected the CCTV tape and popped the new tape into the slot.

'We all ready for tonight's movie?' Noose asked.

The image on the screen was initially blank. Then, Timothy's voice came on.

'For thousands of years, men and women have had sex. Not quite like this, though...'

A shaky handheld image from a camcorder showed a bedroom window. The picture zoomed in on two people in the throws of passion. The two people were Simon Berre and Nicola Bradbury.

'That's Graeme's wife,' Noble pointed out, half shocked and half excited.

'And Simon,' Noose, squinting, realised.

'You're a naughty boy, Mr Berre,' Timothy's voice sounded.

'Let me out!' Simon yelled, banging on the cell door. 'You can't keep me here like this.'

The serving hatch in the cell door opened and Jim appeared. 'Shut up,' he told him, before slamming the hatch shut.

'I'm innocent. Somebody stole my gun and jacket and put them back afterwards. I've been framed. Rewind the CCTV tape.'

Jim opened the hatch again. 'Better make yourself comfortable.'

'Where's my lawyer? I asked for her hours ago.'

'Can't make it down until the morning, sadly. Shame really.'

Jim shut the hatch for good.

'Let me out!' Simon repeated.

'What you reading?' Peter asked Ruby.

'A murder mystery,' she responded from her armchair, casually flicking to the next page.

'Oh aye?'

'Yeah, with a difference.'

'Oh, I read that,' Arthur chipped in from his armchair, eyeing the cover of the book.

'You've never read a book in your life,' Ruby retorted.

'Don't be soft, of course I have. Wasn't that Penny a bitch?'

Ruby looked surprised. Maybe her husband *had* read it. 'God yeah.'

'Can you two keep it down please,' Katie grunted from the sofa, her eyes fixed on the TV.

'They're not real,' Peter noted of the characters in the book, sat next to Katie on the sofa.

'No, but there *are* people like that,' Ruby replied, trying valiantly to read on.

'Yeah, you can relate to them,' Arthur added.

Ruby turned to the blurb on the back. 'Penny may be a bitch,' she read out, 'but we can all relate to her.' She squared her eyes at a sheepish Arthur. 'You haven't damn well read it, you lying git, you've only read the back.'

'Ah well, people like her do exist. Good book that. Women are bitches,' Arthur sniggered.

'Hmm. A murder mystery with a difference,' Peter pondered.

'Well, you sympathise with the murderer,' Ruby tried to rationalise.

'Sympathise?'

'That's how it's written. The reader sort of… The reader isn't supposed to feel scared of the killer; more understand why they did it.'

'Sick,' Katie responded.

'Yeah,' Arthur stirred, 'the end of civilisation, that is.'

'You what?' Ruby snapped.

Arthur sat up, smug. 'That book signifies the end of human civilisation. We're fucked, all fucked.'

'It's just a fantasy - make-believe,' Ruby went on.

'Hang on, so we're all supposed to relate to all that make-believe crap?' Arthur laughed.

'Then again,' Peter came in, 'is there any point to life outside the confines of fantasy anyway?'

'Why is fantasy a confine?' Ruby argued.

'That book *is* civilisation,' Arthur laughed. 'It is the sum of all that we've achieved. It is the final thought of man! Man can go no further!' Arthur mocked.

Ruby stood up. 'No, but woman can,' she said, and slammed the book down on Arthur's head.

It was time for Jim and David to call it a night, and it was David's turn to give Jim a lift home. In the car outside Jim's house, he put his hand on David's leg.

'What are you doing?' David asked him.

'What I want to,' Jim replied, leaning in to kiss his colleague. David pushed him off.

'Hey, mate, you don't swing that way. You're into women.'

'Maybe I am, or was. Now I'm into you, David.' He leant in again but David squirmed away. 'Come on, you're gay, let's do this.'

'Yes, I'm gay, but we're mates, and colleagues, and I don't just go with anyone.'

'You went with Peter Smith, didn't you?'

'I what?'

'I know there's history, come on. Wanna do with me what you did with him?'

David laughed. 'You have no idea what Peter and I did.'

'Then tell me,' Jim continued, running his hand up David's leg. David slapped it off.

'You think because I'm gay I want to shag you? Come on Jim, what's wrong with you? You haven't been right since we went to North Harlan. Talk to me.'

Jim turned away from David and lowered his head as his eyes rolled back into his head. He began to convulse, trembling and twitching. He turned back to David, who lay slumped in the seat, blood running from his ears. Jim lifted his arm up and checked for a pulse, but he was dead.

The morning light shone through the sky light onto Peter. He lay on his back in bed, his mouth, chin and neck soaked in blood. Katie knocked at the attic hatch.

'You getting up?' she called. With no reply, she opened the hatch and climbed up the ladder into the attic. Poking her head up inside, she caught sight of the gruesome scene. 'Mum!' she shouted down the ladder. 'Call an ambulance!'

Noose stood on Nicola Bradbury's doorstep.

'This should be amusing,' he told himself. She opened the door. 'Ah, hello *Nicky*, mind if I have a word?'

In her living room, she sat down expectantly.

'What do you want this time, Inspector?'

'Are the children about?' he asked.

'It's like that, is it?'

'Like what?'

She stood up. 'Staying with Graeme's mother.' She stepped closer to Noose. 'Come without your sergeant today, haven't you?' She pouted her lips.

'He's on other business.' Noose looked at the TV and spotted a VCR under it. 'Ah, good, good.'

'What are you doing?'

'Take a seat, Nicky,' he told her. She did so. He slotted the tape into the VCR and turned the TV on. Soon the screen was filled with the image of her and Simon at it. 'Was this why your husband was killed - because he was blackmailing Simon Berre?'

'Yes, fine, Simon and I were having an affair,' she admitted.

'Now, the police went to great lengths to retrieve this tape. Somebody took this from Graeme before he died… Or did he hand it to someone? A friend, an accomplice?'

Nicola stood up again. Noose came to stand in front of her. 'I don't know. He had no friends, Inspector.'

'What's the story behind all this, Mrs Bradbury? Your husband has been murdered, we know you were having an affair with Simon. Just tell me the truth.'

'Fine. Simon and I had been having an affair for a while. He came to the house once and we just - just hit it off.'

'Bit of a charmer, our Simon?'

'Hmm. He was nicer than Graeme, at any rate. We started having an affair and then one day a package arrived, addressed to Graeme. It was that damn video. We sat down and watched it together. I almost jumped out of my skin.' She moved closer to Noose. 'He went quiet, then all of a sudden just beat me. The children were asleep upstairs thank God. After he'd finished with me, he went to see Simon. Simon was keen his wife didn't find out and offered to keep Graeme quiet. Graeme kept asking for more and more money... I guess it got too much for Simon in the end.'

'Too much?'

'Oh, I don't mean... Simon, kill someone? No. I don't know.'

'How do I know you're not lying?' Noose asked her as she stepped even closer again.

'Why would I lie?'

'You did before. You should have told me.'

'I was afraid that Simon would do something.'

Nicola studied Noose's face, calmly running her fingers through his hair.

'What are you doing, Mrs Bradbury?'

'Please, Inspector, don't call me that. I'm not Bradbury anymore. I must cast that off. Graeme has gone now.' She gripped Noose's head and pulled it to hers, kissing him on the lips.

'This isn't right, Mrs Bradbury.'

'I like men in power.' She kissed again. He did not pull away.

'Your fling has just murdered your husband and you're making a pass at the investigating officer.'

She lowered one hand towards Noose's trousers, but he pushed her away. 'This cannot happen.'

'But you want it to. And I want it to.'

Noose froze, looking at her wet lips. He did find her very attractive, but this simply could not happen. Or could it? What was stopping him?

Peter lay in a hospital bed, hooked up to various machines and drips, completely drained. Ruby, Arthur and Katie all stood at the foot of the bed looking worriedly on at him.

'Can I help you?' he murmured.

'You should be dead,' Ruby pointed out.

'Internal bleeding they say, from the beating,' Arthur explained.

Peter yawned, looking around the room. He was surrounded by a curtain. Suddenly he had some kind of vision, a feeling that he had experienced something similar before. Or maybe in the future. He could not tell, but he instinctively knew that last time, for some reason, he could not move at all. He could not feel his body. This time he could, and he crossed his legs.

'Sorry Katie, I don't think I'll be helping you today,' Peter sighed.

'I'm gonna ask Alex,' she grinned. Peter smiled back, glad that something good may come of it. Blossoming romance seemed something important to him. He wished for romance himself, in this new life he was now leading. A new life strewn with near-death experiences at every turn, yes, but at least he was still alive. And so was Lauren. Here, too, by his bed were three loving people who, despite their faults, were family to him now. He had been accepted by them. They cared not for the past he could not remember, and though Ruby could give them all a hard time, she only did it because she wanted the best out of them. She did not want them to go to waste. Peter realised that, should he get up from this bed alive, he would waste not a second more of his life watching TV.

Noose and Noble barged past Michelle into Simon's house and found Ruth sat eating breakfast.

'What are you doing? What's going on?' Michelle called out as Noble showed her his warrant card.

'Ruth Berre,' Noose announced, 'you are under arrest for the murder of Graeme Bradbury. You do not have to say anything, but anything you do say may be taken down and later used as evidence against you in a court of law...'

Michelle screamed, punching and kicking at Noose and Noble as they led her mother out.

Whilst Ruth was waiting in the interview room, Noose and Noble entered Superintendent Hastings' office.

'You wanted to see us, Sir?' Noose asked for confirmation.

'Yes,' he said gravely, taking a deep breath. 'We've lost one of our men.'

'We've - we've what?' Noble, stunned, fumbled.

'David, last night.'

'Oh no, no,' Noose shook his head, dropping onto a chair, his head in his hands.

'But, how, why? Murdered?'

'No, no,' Hastings explained. 'He was dropping Jim off last night and,' Hastings welled up, a single tear rolling down his cheek. 'I'm sorry, I do get attached to the boys. He was growing into a fine officer.' Hastings pulled himself together. 'He had some kind of haemorrhage or aneurysm. He passed away peacefully before Jim's eyes in the car.'

'Poor David,' Noose sobbed.

'Poor Jim,' Noble sighed.

Noose and Noble, collecting themselves in the corridor outside, gave each other a nod before entering the interview room. Ruth was sat at the table with her arms folded.

'Sorry to keep you waiting, Mrs Berre. Now, let's see... I have the lunch menu here.' Noose handed it to her. 'Choose what you want and I'll have it brought down to you, pronto.'

She slammed the menu down and shouted, 'I've been arrested. I want to talk to my lawyer.'

'The same lawyer as Mr Berre? Don't worry, she'll be arriving for lunch.' Noose picked the menu up. 'She's having the welsh rarebit.' He handed the menu back to her and smiled.

The students, including Katie, Emma and Alex, were sitting at their exam desks. Mr Hancock and Principal Matheson were standing at the front of the hall.

'Now,' Matheson addressed the yawning teenagers, 'just because there has been a murder here recently does not mean you can all fail your exams.' The students groaned as he turned to Mr Hancock and commented, 'Although, some of them likely will anyway.'

'We are still going to be strict about exam conditions. Now, luckily for you, today's exam has had to be cancelled due to unforeseen circumstances *beyond* the murder of a jobbing joiner,' Mr Hancock explained.

Emma looked briefly over to Katie.

'Today's exam will be re-arranged and a revised date will be sent to you. Thank you, and see you tomorrow for the best of the bunch: chemistry,' Matheson finished.

More groaning. The students began filing out as Katie made her way towards Alex.

'Hi Alex. Sorry for being snappy with you lately.'

'Hey, don't worry about it. Women's trouble, eh?' he asked, winking awkwardly. Katie stared at him, either confused or angered. Emma appeared from behind and broke the atmosphere.

'Hi guys,' she greeted them joyfully. Katie turned and hurried on ahead.

Just outside, Katie was lying in wait for Alex and Emma to emerge. When they did, Alex spotted the ginger teenager loitering somewhat awkwardly behind the opened fire door of the gym, saying his goodbyes to Emma and joining her. Katie, thinking he was taking too long, grabbed hold of his arm and pulled him behind the door.

'What's going on?' he asked the one he had eyes for, but was too nervous to admit as such.

'There's something going on between Emma and Michelle,' Katie whispered, keeping on the lookout for potential eavesdroppers, 'and you're gonna help me find out what. Michelle's dad's been arrested for murdering my neighbour.'

'This is getting creepy.'

'You gonna help me?'

'Yeah.'

She let go of his arm and let her hand fall to her side. Suddenly, the two mutually took hold of each other's hand and, not wanting to make too much of an issue out of it, pretended it wasn't happening. A police officer, the young Kennedy, walked past.

'Here we are, let's follow him,' Katie urged, pulling Alex along for the ride.

Mr Hancock was sitting at his desk across from Kennedy.

'Is Principal Matheson about, Mr Hancock?'

'He'll be here shortly. I'll fill you in.'

'Please do.'

'We have found a pack of exam papers open.'

'Ah. That's quite serious, I take it?'

'It is. We've had to cancel an exam this morning. We don't know when the pack has been opened, because we leave them in storage until the morning of the actual exam.'

'Do you suspect one or more of the pupils?'

'It could be. They're kept in a room just off from the corridor where Graeme Bradbury was murdered.'

'I'm sorry, I'm not familiar with the recent events around here. I'm standing in for another officer. Has the room not been searched?'

'Yes, but they wouldn't open the packs. Would they?' Mr Hancock narrowed his eyes at the young officer. 'Kennedy? Didn't you used to come to this school?'

'I did, yes.'

'Ah yes, I remember you.'

'I remember you too.'

'You slacked in geography.'

'And I excelled in everything else.'

'Did you indeed?'

'That was always your problem.'

'My problem?'

'You were quick with the criticism and slow with the praise. Look at me now.' Kennedy grinned. 'Your nickname was Hand Cock.'

'Still is,' Mr Hancock sighed.

Just outside, Katie and Alex had been listening up against the door. They both looked at each other.

'That's what they did. It must be them,' Katie whispered.

'Why keep it such a secret? Michelle must have really done a number on her.'

'She's a nasty piece of work, that Michelle.' Katie looked down at Alex's lips. 'Thanks for helping.'

The two gazed into each other's eyes once more, slowly moving in and kissing on the lips. Alex pulled back gently and smiled, before moving in again for a longer snog. Suddenly, Matheson appeared behind them and they jumped apart.

'Osculating in a school corridor? Come on, run along and do that somewhere a little more appropriate, please. There's a bike shed outside,' he commanded, not displeased at the pair. Embarrassed, they ran off.

The two lovebirds skipped into the hospital ward that housed the infamous Peter Smith. Alex was clutching onto a bag of grapes and, spotting a sign that said 'NIL BY MOUTH' above Peter's head, he raised an eyebrow and became a little disheartened. Needless to say, they both sat down next to Peter's bed and looked at his sleeping face.

'You awake, Peter?' Katie whispered.

'Lucy,' he mumbled, turning his head to face her.

'No, it's Katie.'

'Who's Lucy?' Alex asked, but Peter suddenly opened his eyes wide and, spotting the grapes, snatched them off Alex and quickly turned his back on the pair. 'Well, I brought them for you.'

'I don't like grapes,' Peter whimpered back. This must have upset Alex somewhat as a sulk came over him.

'Look, we think we know what Emma and Michelle have been up to,' Katie explained. Peter rolled over once more to face her. 'We overheard Mr Hancock talking to some copper about an exam paper being read or something.'

Peter, noticing Katie and Alex were holding hands, grinned. 'You two going out?'

Simultaneously, they dropped each other's hands.

'We're gonna go and force a confession out of Emma now.'

'Can you be forceful, Alex?' Peter questioned the sop with a sarcastic smirk.

Noose entered and Katie and Alex promptly stood up.

'Ah, are you busy?' he asked.

'We're just leaving,' Katie responded. 'Oh,' she rummaged around in her bag and brought out a battered old book. 'I brought this for you to read.' She placed the book on Peter's bedside cabinet. 'Well, it came for you in the post, actually. Dunno where it's from. Haven't read it yet.'

'Thanks.' He smiled, turning casually to glance at the title of the book. *I Am Dead*. Katie and Alex filed out as Noose came to sit down. Peter smiled distantly through him. 'That was Lucy,' he uttered.

'No,' Noose responded sadly, picking Peter's hospital notes up to see just how many painkillers he was being doped up on. 'Anyway, how are you? If you're lucid enough to answer.'

'Very well, thank you,' he shot back, lucid enough.

'Good. We've arrested Ruth Berre now.'

'Why?'

'An old police trick.'

'Getting sued for false arrest?'

'We're making the first move, flushing the blackmailer out. It could even be Ruth herself.'

'It could be. Have you rewound the CCTV tape yet?'

'I forgot all about that with this new tape.' Noose stood up as Peter picked up the book. But, yawning, he dropped it on the bed.

Katie banged on Emma's door as Alex stood meekly beside her. Emma opened the door.

'We know what you've done.'

'You do?'

'You read the exam paper, didn't you? That's why today's exam was cancelled.'

'Michelle forced me.'

'Why didn't you just tell me, Emma? We're supposed to be friends.'

'Oh Katie,' Emma cried, throwing her arms around her friend. They hugged. 'I'm sorry. Michelle really scares me, I thought she'd do something horrible if I told you.'

'Well, we all know now,' Alex pointed out, 'and Michelle ain't gonna do anything once we've told the teachers.'

'We can't do that!' Emma screeched in panic.

'We can, and we will,' Katie boomed with the confidence of her mother.

Noose was busy rewinding the CCTV tape at his desk when he came across the moment a hooded figure walked into the room and took Simon's gun and jacket. Noose paused the image, studying it and rewinding again. Pressing play, Noose saw the person leaning for a moment on the doorframe leading into the storage room, before turning back and going towards the desk.

'Who has a key to get in?' Noose mumbled to himself.

Noose walked into the interview room and smiled at Ruth.

'At last,' she snarled. 'How much longer must I sit here?'

'Chosen your lunch yet?'

'I've been waiting here hours. Why?'

Noose walked over to the barred window and raised his head to look out. 'I've had things to do, such as watching the CCTV tape of your husband's office on the night Timothy was murdered. Someone wearing a hood *did* take the gun and jacket. Now, that could easily be Simon. He was the one who insisted I rewind the tape, after all. Then again, it could quite easily be you taking the gun and jacket - couldn't it, Mrs Berre?'

'First Simon's the killer, now I am!' she laughed in disbelief, folding her arms.

He turned to face her. 'Whoever took the gun and jacket had a key to get in.'

'That could be any number of people. That cleaner who was so keen to snitch, for example!'

'Could be, could be. Much more likely to be you though, don't you think?'

'I demand my lawyer.'

'Very well.' He made for the door. 'I did initially arrest you just to provoke the blackmailer, though.'

'What?'

'Yes. You seem to be somewhat of a victim in all this - or at least you appear that way. I suppose the blackmailer could easily have a soft spot for you and dislike the fact that you've been arrested.'

'You've gone too far, you're a nutter.'

'Two people are dead and someone I care a great deal about is half dead in hospital because of your husband, Mrs Berre. He is the nutter, not me.' Noose reached for the door, but before he could open it Jim opened it for him and walked in. He saw Noose and twitched straight away. Holding his spasming eye, he looked down. 'Jim? What on Earth are you doing in today? Good grief, man.' He stepped outside, away from Ruth, pulling Jim with him into the corridor.

'I, I had to. I had to come in,' Jim stuttered.

'But Jim, oh God Jim. I'm so sorry about David. I know you two were really close friends.'

Jim's twitching stopped and he looked at Noose. 'Really close? What are you saying?'

'Oh no, Jim,' Noose fumbled. 'Not like that. Goodness, no. No, I mean you two are - were - friends as well as colleagues. We all are. We, we stick together, sort of thing.'

Kennedy walked past in the corridor, looking back at Jim with a blank stare. Suddenly Jim collapsed, convulsing all over as some bizarre image flashed in his mind. He was older, in a huge perspex tank and straightjacket, as that officer, Kennedy, older too, stood outside, looking in. And then, another man appeared just beyond Kennedy and called him. Called Jim.

'Jim, are you alright?' Noose called out close by, though Jim only heard him in the distance. All at once, Jim felt himself coming to again and he got to his feet, pushing Noose aside as he strolled down the corridor after Kennedy.

Someone was watching from a distance down the school corridor as Katie and Alex kissed by the lockers. Emma, who was stood near them, was startled when Mr Hancock appeared behind her. Their watcher kept on looking.

'We are taking the matter very seriously, Emma, and have sent someone around to Michelle's house to confront her. I'm doing my best to ensure that you don't get withdrawn from all of the exams,' he explained to her.

'Thank you, Mr Hancock. Michelle was bullying me.'

'Yes, I realise that. Let's just keep our fingers crossed, shall we?'

Emma smiled as he walked on. Alex gave Katie another kiss before dashing off to the toilet. The watcher followed him, intent on causing more carnage.

Alex stood at a urinal. The piss flowed, bringing about a rather relieved expression on the young lad's face. When he was done he shook his penis about, some urine splashing on his trousers, before slipping it back in and zipping up his flies. As he turned around, his relief turned into horror as a metal pipe came crashing down across his face. He fell to the floor as his attacker dropped an envelope on his chest and raised the pipe once more, ready to finish the empty-bladdered teen. But, Mr Hancock suddenly entered and the hooded attacker fled through the window.

'Bloody hell!' Mr Hancock yelled, making no attempt to run after the escaping perpetrator.

Katie ran in. 'What's going on?' Seeing Alex strewn on the dried urine-soaked floor, she dropped to her knees beside him in floods of tears. 'Alex! Oh no, please don't be dead.'

Mr Hancock picked the envelope up off Alex's chest and opened it. 'The police are wrong yet again,' he read from the letter within, 'and will pay for their mistakes with another life. Simon Berre has murdered two people. Release his wife or more will die needlessly.'

FIVE

Peter strained to see through the thin crack between the curtains drawn around him. In the bed opposite lay Alex, unconscious, and Peter could just about keep an eye on him. Lying here had given Peter time to think about himself. His memory was still vague, though he was increasingly plagued by all the recurring dreams. Nonetheless, he soldiered on, taking each day as it came. He gave more thought to Neville and the book *I Am Dead* that he had spoken of. He felt sure this Neville had sent the book to him in Myrtle Mews, but he could not bring himself to read it. He could not even bring himself to open the book, let alone read it. Something held him back, some distant recess of his memory which knew he should not read it. Perhaps it would bring back his memory, perhaps not. But Peter did not want his memory back. He felt sure his past was bad, negative, and should remain forgotten. He had the chance to start anew, and he would.

Noose was again busily studying the CCTV tape. He kept rewinding and pausing on the hooded figure leaning on the doorframe. He threw himself back into his chair in anguish, spinning around as he tried to bring some memory back to the fore. And then he had it. He played the tape once more, watching as the figure leant on the doorframe. He leapt into the air and darted out of the room.

Katie and Emma were eating fruit salad in the hospital café. Very healthy.

'I hope Alex is okay,' Katie sighed, pushing the fruit about the plastic box with her fork. 'We've kissed, you know.'

'Yeah I saw you in the corridor at school… Finally!'

'Hey?'

'Oh come on, it's been obvious to everyone that it was only a matter of time.'

'Really?'

'Yeah.'

Katie laughed a little, then became more subdued. 'But I wonder who attacked him, and why.'

'They probably saw him up the street and thought they'd choose him to attack. It's awful. The blackmailer could even be Michelle,' Emma suggested.

'Oh?'

'Well after we looked at the exam paper, I went back onto the yard and she went into the exam hall. She was gone about five minutes. She could easily have stolen the tape off the dead body.'

'Bit of a coincidence that it was her dad who'd killed the man, though,' Katie pointed out, suddenly having a rather sinister realisation. Her heart sank and she looked at Emma. 'You don't think?'

Suddenly Noose ran past and they rushed after him.

Through the slit in the curtain, Peter spotted a figure entering, slipping a metal rod in between the handles of the doors to stop anyone else getting in. Then there was a noise - a bedside cabinet pushed against the door. Adrenaline kicked in and he got out of bed and dived under it to hide just in time for the figure to rip his curtains apart and peer in to find an empty bed. Alex, however, could not slip out of bed and hide. The figure moved to his bed, pulling a pillow from under his head and placing it over his face.

Noose, Katie and Emma reached the door and banged on the windows, unable to get in. Hearing the noise, the figure turned to face them. It was Michelle. She stared blankly at them, seemingly not even registering who they were, before continuing to smother Alex. Katie frantically thrashed at the window, screaming for her Alex who lay helpless merely feet away.

'Fetch something to smash this window with,' Noose called out at a group of perplexed nurses.

'That glass is reinforced with metal wire,' one of the nurses exclaimed, 'it'll take something.'

'Just do it!' Noose yelled.

Peter came up behind Michelle and pulled her off, but only for a second. She easily twisted out of his weak grip and kicked him in the stomach. He recoiled in agony, stumbling over the bedside cabinet blocking the door.

'Michelle, Michelle,' Emma cried out, 'look at me.'

'Don't tell me what to do. Don't *ever* tell me what to do,' she called back, renewing her efforts to kill Alex. 'Alex can identify me, you see. He saw me just before I hit him across the face.'

'What's the good of killing him now? We can all identify you,' Noose shot back.

'Then I'll kill all of you!'

'Just like you killed Graeme and Timothy,' Noose pointed out.

'You're lying.'

'No, Michelle. It was you who took your dad's gun and jacket. I recognised the way you leant against the doorframe on the CCTV image. You did the same thing when I first came to your house. All of a sudden it made perfect sense; the blackmailer was also the killer.'

'And you also left me for five minutes on the morning Graeme was murdered,' Emma added, horrified. 'You did it, didn't you?'

'I killed them, okay. Just like I'm now gonna kill Alex and the weirdo man on the floor.' She turned to look down where

Peter had fallen, but he was not there. Instantaneously, a chair came crashing down on her head from behind. She dropped to the floor. Peter placed the chair down and flopped onto it.

The cell door opened and Noose and Noble appeared at it as Simon got up from the concrete bed.

'You're free to go,' Noose told him.

'About time.' He pushed past Noose, who grabbed hold of him and pulled him back.

'You still beat Peter Smith up. He's critical in hospital. If he dies, you go down for murder. At the moment it's only attempted murder.'

'Attempted murder? I barely laid a finger on him,' Simon laughed. Noose pulled his fist back, ready to punch the slimy devil, but Noble held him back. 'That's right, Sergeant, keep your inspector on a tighter leash.'

Simon turned to spot Ruth standing in the corridor.

'I know,' she uttered calmly.

'How? Who told you?'

'You're a monster.'

Simon swung around and threw Noose against the wall. 'You told her I slept with Nicola? You bastard!' Noble pulled him off.

'Thought you could keep your seedy little life from me?' she asked Simon, stepping closer as Noble wrestled him to the floor.

Michelle was led past in handcuffs. Seeing her parents, she stopped and pulled from Kennedy to step into the cell. 'You're free to go now, Mum,' she spoke. 'You should be free of him too.' She glared at her father, suddenly kicking him in the face before Noble could lift him up. Kennedy pulled her away as Simon cowered on the floor.

'You turned our own daughter into a murderer,' Ruth wept.

'Why would she do it?' Simon asked in despair to anyone who was listening.

'Because of you!'

'I didn't want to hurt you,' Simon whimpered at his wife, 'that's why I covered the affair up.'

'And that resulted in our daughter murdering two people and trying to kill a third.'

'But Ruth,' was all Simon could say.

'You married me for the money. Berre Construction no longer requires your services.'

'But that's my company.'

'No Simon, it's mine. You're fired. Go to hell.' She stormed out as Michelle was led away.

Michelle was sitting sullen-faced in the interview room. Noose and Noble were sat across from her.

'So, Michelle, what have you been up to?' Noose asked her. Silence.

'Tell us your side of what happened,' Noble added. 'Tell us why you murdered Graeme and Timothy.'

'I wanted to read the exam papers,' she reeled off without flinching, 'I am guilty of that. I took my friend Emma along, too. Whilst we were there, I saw Graeme walk past. I knew my dad had been trying to contact him. My dad saw his van in the school car park when he dropped me off in the morning for the exam. I told Emma to go and wait for me back on the yard. She left, and I went into the exam hall. I could hear Graeme and my dad talking about something, Graeme seemed to be threatening him. When I got into the corridor, Dad had gone and Graeme was putting some money into his wallet. I approached him and asked what was going on. He started looking at me, up and down, then said he'd give me twenty quid if I'd suck his cock. I picked up one of his tools and he said I was feisty and if I ever wanted to mess around, he was up for it. I was going to leave, but he took out a big envelope and told me to tell my dad he still had a copy of the video and would keep on asking for more money.' She paused, taking a deep breath, relieved that it was all finally coming out.

'What happened next?'

'I asked him what was on the video and he told me. Then he said Dad wasn't getting enough from Mum and that his wife Nicola was too hot to handle for any man. He turned and I hit him on the head.'

'What did you do with the tool you hit him with?'

'I put it in my school bag. I took the money from his wallet, too, and the envelope. The video was the one I got five grand for.'

'Where is the tool now?'

'I put it in the boot of Dad's car. You didn't even search for it.'

'What about Timothy?'

'It sickened me how someone had filmed them having sex. What a pervert. I'd heard ages ago from Emma and Katie about a weirdo up their street who filmed people. I went to his house and he admitted it was him. He said he had more tapes of Dad if I wanted to buy them. I knew he had to die.'

'But why?'

'It's just not right doing that. Plus I'd killed one, I wanted to kill again. Just how it is.' She smiled. 'This time I'd frame Dad, so I stole his gun and jacket and set him up.'

'And Alex?'

'When you arrested my mum, I flipped. You shouldn't have done that. Alex's death would have been your fault.'

'Dear oh dear.'

Noose sat silent for a moment, taking it all in. It seemed to wash over Noble a bit more.

'Why sell the tape to Peter?' he asked her as Noose pondered the whole thing.

'It was time people knew what my dad had done, and it reinforced his motive as a killer. It almost paid off.'

'Ah well,' Noose sighed.

Lauren was packing her things away for the day in the lab. Noble pushed the door open and slowly walked up to her.

'What have you got to say for yourself now?' she asked him outright, sick of his games. He had more, he kissed her. She indulged, the old flame rekindled, but he pulled away.

'Don't worry about Peter,' he uttered, grimacing.

'Don't worry?'

'I love you Lauren.'

With this he briskly exited the way he had entered, and as quickly, leaving her even more confused than before. Now she didn't know what she wanted.

'You and dying don't seem to go together, Peter,' Arthur chuckled as he, Ruby, and Emma gathered around his bed. Sat next to his bed was Alex, a big bruise across his face, with Katie sat on his knee.

'Too true my friend, too true,' Peter replied glibly.

'Come on then Ruby,' he took his wife in hand, 'let's go for a drink.'

'You mean you're actually gonna buy me one?' she retorted. He laughed, pulling her on. However, soon it was her doing the pulling as she insisted on being in charge. They left, giving a wave as they went. Alex put his arm around Katie.

'Looks like I've missed an exciting few goings-on,' Peter continued, looking at the lovebirds. Emma rolled her eyes.

'See what I have to put up with?' Emma yawned as Katie and Alex kissed.

Noble appeared at the door, prompting the teenagers to get up. Alex, feeling very sorry for himself, struggled away as Katie pampered him. He kept his eyes off Noble, looking rather embarrassed, and the three said their goodbyes and departed. When they were out of sight, Noble pulled the curtains closed around the bed and stepped closer to Peter.

'You've gone too far with Lauren, my friend.'

'I beg your pardon?'

'You listen to me, chum,' Noble continued, getting even closer. 'Lauren is mine, not yours. I know about the museum club murders that Inspector Trout was on about the other week. You stay away from Lauren and I won't tell your cosy new mum and dad Ruby and Arthur about who you really are.'

'Are you blackmailing me?'

'You heard what I said.'

'And what is this crucial information?'

'Don't pull that memory loss bull with me, you and I both know what I mean. Remember, Peter, stay away from Lauren and all will be happy.'

After his recovery, Peter took to walking. The bicycle was handy, yes, but walking was much easier on the achy bones. Still, he was young and seemed to recover quite quickly from all these attacks he had sustained since he had become a new, forgetting man. One of his regular haunts during these walks was the country lane that he had suddenly found himself on that fateful day some time before. He would often now come here, half wanting his memory to suddenly restore itself and half happy that he couldn't remember himself. It was almost immaterial to him now, since his stable existence as a lodger in Myrtle Mews. That's all he wanted.

He took *I Am Dead* from his pocket and, checking either end of the lane to ensure that he was not being watched, casually tossed it into the ditch. He strolled on, quite happy and content to live in obscurity. He was a nobody, he thought, and wanted to live the way he had been doing since he found himself in this lane. Without the constant barrage of attempts on his life, of course. As he made his way down the lane, a car suddenly sped behind him and knocked him over. He came crashing to the ground, unconscious. The car screeched to a halt and Jim jumped out with a can of petrol and a box of matches. He dragged Peter into a nearby field and poured the petrol over his unconscious body. He felt someone or something breathing behind him. He turned and came face to face with a bull. Surprised, he splashed the rest of the petrol over himself before dropping the empty can. The bull's nostrils flared as he sniffed Jim's face, grunting.

'Go away,' Jim commanded the bull, getting a match out of the box. As he tried to strike it, the bull butted him and sent him tumbling backwards over Peter. He got back on his feet. Enraged, the bull came again at Jim and knocked him down, trampling him. He struggled to his feet one last time and made a dash for the fence, but the bull charged after him and knocked him down. Jim, battered and bruised under the bull, struggled with the matches and managed to strike one. The fire sizzled the skin off his face as the bull pulverised him. A farmer came galloping up with an air rifle and shot the bull, pulling Peter from the spreading flames. However, the damage had been done to Jim and he had had it, and it was his own silly, silly fault. Both Tony and Jim had tried to put an end to Peter. Both had failed. But two of the chosen four were yet to try. Stephen or Darren, either alone or together, would be next. The only problem was none of them even knew why they wanted to kill Peter Smith. They were all simply following Reaping Icon's request.

EPILOGUE

'But, Elder Icon, there is much I do not understand,' one of the children said. The wise woman was taken aback. One of the children questioning that which they had been told? This had never happened before during her time as Elder Icon. But she remembered a time before she had risen to the position. A time when she was a mere child herself. There had been one of her contemporaries who had spoken up - questioned that which they had been told - and awful things had befallen him. She was sorry for this child, now sat in front of her, questioning the recounting of how Reaping Icon had set that space by which to goad Peter Smith to placate the sensual.

'You must not question,' she told him, desperate that her mind convince her she was not emotionally attached to the child in question.

'I do not question,' she went on, standing, 'I only say that I do not understand.'

'What do you not understand?' Elder Icon asked reluctantly.

'We are taught to follow the word of Peter Smith, and yet our beloved Reaping Icon taunts him so in the text and wishes to take away his power. Why?' The child spoke so clearly and expressed herself so well. There was disquiet, and the other children started to whisper to each other with concern.

'Please, there is much more you have all yet to hear. We must continue.' Elder Icon looked outside. It was dark. 'But now you must disperse for the evening. Go, and think upon how best you may worship that which I have told you.'

'There is much more,' the child continued. 'Why would Jim not try to kill Peter as he killed David - with his mind?'

'Child!' Elder Icon raised her voice. The children fell silent, holding their breath. 'You must all bow down before the tight space between us.'

The children sighed, but left. The girl who had questioned what she had been told did not run across the brook with the other children, but remained just outside Elder Icon's home until silence fell. She crept up to a window and peeped in to see the wise woman staring out of the opposite window, shaking in terror.

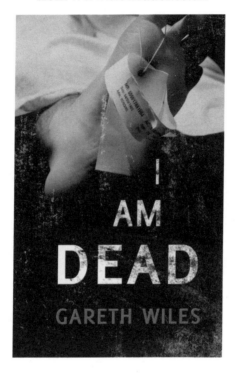

Peter Smith is dead. No getting away from that. Or is there?

Being dead is the least of his worries when he finds himself prosecuted in an ethereal court on dubious charges – and the prosecutor is his brother, Stuart. When Peter is sent to the waiting room, he re-lives his final day on Earth. We see his ambiguous relationship with his mother, who he lived alone with, and his brother Stuart and his wife Diane, who bring news of pregnancy. Peter is devastated at the news and leaves the house – only to be killed instantly.